For my late wife, and the
legacy that we shared

Kitso & Pansa
- *Spirit Dawning* -

By E. Fox

~*PROLOGUE*~

"Very good, Kitso! Try to steady your arm... and keep both your eyes open!"

I am Kitso, a member of the Vulpani Tribe. That is to say, beings with features resembling that of creatures some call foxes. I am unsure why others relate us to these animals—it isn't as though they walk about on two legs, or even speak any sort of recognizable tongue. Though, I do admit that our fur does bear a striking similarity.

We are known for our cunning wit and keen foraging skills. We take the least of what we are given, and make the very most of it that we can. We learn to survive on little, and thrive on much. In the wilderness, it is important to observe your surroundings, keeping your eyes and ears open to every sight and sound you may notice, and picking up on signs and signals for that which you don't.

At six years, I learned to use a bow and arrow. I vividly recall everything that was taught to me, and continue to hone this art of both hunting and combat.

"Don't slouch when making a first impression. It can be quite rude to someone who is observant."

By the age of ten, I was taught about social relations and the importance of one's stance on an introduction.

It's no surprise that meeting someone for the first time can be occasionally daunting, especially if meeting with the ambassador representing another tribe. You would, however, find yourself at a loss if you fail to understand how important impressions are to us Vulpani—an integral part of our social behavior, it's imperative to engage with others both near and far with the utmost concern.

"Inevitably, you're going to be traveling alone some day. I won't be able to help you beyond that."

Long before I became completely of age at twenty-four, I very much made myself aware of the tribulations that we endure once we attain said age. I always found it strange that we spend the entirety of our lives up to that point with those who bear us and those who raise us, and then find ourselves making our own way for upwards of eight months. Of course, with the right skills, one could make a friend or three in the midst of their trial, making it far easier to manage, and possibly return sooner.

You see, within the Vulpani, we don't stay at home when we begin to walk and communicate, and we don't learn the essentials of survival from our parents. Although we do remain under parentage for basics, such as sleeping or eating, nearly everything else is bestowed upon us by another of the tribe who specializes in the skills and knowledge needed to thrive in the outside world. It is from there that we decide whether we wish to dwell amongst this tribe we are familiar with in order to train those risen up under ourselves.

The alternative is to prepare yourself with all you've learned, and set out to form a new tribe with a mate. I really haven't considered myself material for such relations, but I wasn't about to remain within the confines I've come to know all my life. I sought new experiences, and I would not find them but out there. It is when we return from our time of trial that we are expected to conclude the final decision, and I knew what I wanted to do.

I had been assigned my teacher when I was four, ripe for learning fundamentals. It was she that taught me to hunt and to defend myself—my development as an individual part of a whole her responsibility. She learned me what I could not myself, and ensured that no experience to teach was lost.

I garnered all I could from her, and went so far as to ask many questions—as many as I could possibly conceive over these years. Because of this, she was convinced that I very much inclined to travel and see what I could in my lifetime. To glean from the land more than just fruit and vegetable—it was knowledge and understanding that I sought. My mentor has always believed in this yearning for adventure, and for that, I will always regard her for life.

❖ ❖ ❖

"Well, that should just about do it. Hey, don't touch that! Ugh, I *just* washed that."

My name is Pansa, a part of the Panteo Clan, and apparently I'm a parent of more than twenty children.

Oh, don't get me wrong. I've never had any of my own, and I'm not sure I ever want to. Actually, I am totally convinced that I'm not even capable of bearing them...

It isn't as though I would deny the life of someone brought into the world. I just... I don't know.

Our clan is very proud of heading a great life, full of accomplishments, but not without struggle. We work considerably hard for what we have, and never give up on the goals we have set before us. Tell us we can't build a home, and we'll fashion a palace. If you say we can't cross a stream, we'll build a bridge to cross a river. You dare call our clan worthless, and we will make sure there is nothing left standing but our clan. Our ferocity isn't to be trifled with, but should you call us friend, we will be your greatest ally.

We Panteo sport beautiful, deep black fur with few, but unique, markings. I have no particular markings to speak of, but I don't care. I always found myself to be different, and I want to stay that way. We look like large cats, only less scrawny. Even us women rival some of the men in build. My father suggests my green eyes give me a look of complacency—I am anything but most of the time. I should be, what with everything I've done, but I am still left unsatisfied with how it all turned out.

Anyway, I was mostly forced into learning the "joys" of motherhood by the age of eight. I wish I were kidding, but sadly my mother had passed away before I even really got to know her. She left behind not only myself, but also my father, brother and sister, and every one of them looked up to me for some odd reason I could never figure out.

It is because you are strong of heart that they look up to you.

These words resonate within me regularly, though I have never actually heard them before. I don't know where the thought came from, but it's all I have to empower me to care for my own.

Not long after all this occurred, I wound up mothering everyone that has ever needed someone to care for them. Even local children saw me as a prominent mother figure. You might consider it fate, or destiny, but I only see it as an unfortunate circumstance that has led me to forgo everything I had ever dreamed of. I didn't ask to be cooped up with family matters, and I never wanted to be bound to obligations beyond my ability. Though, I somehow managed, and I guess I have no regrets—it has only made me stronger.

I came home late one evening after caring for all these children—it's been many months since my last breakdown over these five years, but I couldn't tear myself away. They had nobody to look up to, and nothing to live for but their own existence. Though, as time went on, I could feel my very being wither away. Many weeks of few scraps to eat, early mornings and very long nights of no sleep. I kept denying myself for their sake, and in the end, I felt as though I had denied them.

My father couldn't bear to watch his own fur and blood destroy itself, so he took it upon himself to see that I was tended to for once. When I arrived home that night, he offered me a fresh portion of ground parupeteng flower to alleviate some of the pains I had suffered.

Unbeknownst to me, he had also mixed in something else—what of, I'll never know. All I could remember from then on was leaving behind my clan. I was tasked with the single most vital thing in my life, and I had failed.

Chapter 1

My life has finally drawn to this point of realization—the time when I can head out on my own for a time, utilizing every ability I have honed to succeed.

"I am proud of you, Kitso, for reaching this point," remarks my instructor with a smile upon her face. "I imagine Vixona and Renado are as well."

I reply with precocious manner. "Thank you, Vulpena. I cannot wait to see how I fare on my own for eight months."

"Just remember that you needn't go it entirely alone. Should you cross paths with another traveler, be mindful about the opportunity to make a friend. Those notes on first impressions don't only extend to prestigious meetings, you know."

"Yes, I know that," I say, looking out into the surrounding woods. I frown at myself, and glance up at her. "I'm sorry. Thank you for reminding me."

Vulpena ruffles a tuft of fur on my head, reminding me of younger days. "You always were quite the charmer, weren't you?" She laughs. "That remarkable attitude of yours is bound to find yourself a wonderful mate, Kitso. Whoever she may be, just love her for who she is."

I smile, and look back toward the beginning of my future. "Well, I believe I am ready to head out now.

Please forward my love to mother, and tell her I harbor no ill regard for my father's will." With that, I take my leave, never glancing behind me.

Placid tranquility—that is how some would describe their first outing at their coming of age. Quiet trees, a few birds whistling about, and the occasional brook made for quite the relaxing time. One thing you learn very quickly is how vital that first day is. Your own choices in those first hours of the day will define the very nature of your trial. Every hour you spend admiring the fresh, new landscape is an hour that otherwise would be spent seeking your temporary home away from home. Should you forget—even for only a moment—that first and foremost goal of yours, you will realize how extremely dangerous those peaceful woods become, for we are not alone.

Many decades have been detailed with tragic incidents of Vulpani who took their trial a bit too lightly. Seen by the overly-ambitious as an opportunity to get a pre-emptive start on their new life, forgetting that it's meant to tone you for survival, and also teach you patience and perseverance. These two points alone set apart their outcomes: those who choose to resettle into their tribe, and those who travel to begin their own.

My father, Renado, was a master at survival. He was one of very few who returned in under seven months, having achieved all he could on his trial. Vulpena was his mentor, and by the time I was bore to the world, she had insisted on raising his son. Our council was divided on the matter, saying that it might hinder my ability to develop a unique sense of growth due to potential bias. My parents were left with the final say, to which they consented with a rebuttal, insinuating that her training my father was the reason they wanted her to reside in our family's growth. If I was to be anything like my father, she knew how to handle it. Vulpena eventually became my godmother, though we never spoke openly of it. Such a matter was treated with little else than disdain. I never fully understood why.

So my journey began with me seeking out some workable territory that I could call my own for now. I passed by a large stream, with lots of fresh crisp water flowing swiftly betwixt the trees. I knew better than to reside by the water, for despite the warm weather we experience, the rushing rapids can lend for a brisk draft in the middle of the night. Not to mention the hindrance of passing creatures seeking a drink, disturbing your sleep.

Further outward, I came upon a small valley wrought with foliage. Although it'd keep me out of the wind, again the trouble of water following a downpour could spell trouble.

I pressed onward, the sun bearing high amidst the canopy, peering through the dense brush with rays of light. It seemed much darker than one would expect, but I was keen on keeping track of my time spent wandering, comfortable with my progress. I took a small break to sit on a nearby rock, lowering my satchel from my shoulder, to renew myself with a small portion of berries and stewed moss. It reminded me of many a meal my kin and I had together. My older brother would snag a few extra berries after the meal to take with him on our mini excursions of play. Sometimes our younger sister would tag along, but she typically preferred to stay with mother, spending her time hearing stories.

It isn't often I think of my siblings—my brother is only half-related to me, but I always will consider him a full brother, as he is the only one I have. He left to travel at a mere age of twenty-three, a year shy of his age of trial, and four from my own. It is up to us whether or not we await that time. If we're completely sure of ourselves, then there is nothing the council does to cease it. I didn't ask why, and wasn't told. My sister was determined to leave, just as father had. She remained content to wait until her trial, only two years after I was to return from mine.

Sated with new energy, I packed up and continued. The sun's light hadn't moved much, but I must still manage my time well. I stay passively focused during rest, as it saves much trouble in meandering.

Not much longer after I had eaten, I neared a small meadow within the gradually thinning forest. I hesitated to take in my surroundings, and noticed a hushed crack. I held my breath, glancing around in a few directions, before spotting a doe with her fawn closely nearby. I slowly knelt down to display my docile nature, and silently watched them saunter off before moving. Upon closer inspection, I found I was very pleased with this meadow.

It had a few fairly large trees on the other side of it—perfect for a lean-to during my first night. One of these trees sported a decent hollow in its bole, an excellent place to store my belongings and perhaps some firewood. Off to my left was a craggy precipice, embedded in the base of a hill, which would make for a nice lookout during the afternoon. Lastly, several yards off to my right was a pond with an inlet. I was sure I could gather some clean water throughout my time here, and perhaps some fish. The meadow itself was stunning to look at. It seemed to accept just the right amount of light during mid-day, and the soft, warm grass featured many small flowers of a variety of colors. It was undoubtedly healthy soil, of which I could borrow to till a few good plants from around this area.

I laid my satchel aside, withdrew a couple tools from it, and began to harvest some fresh timber. Some was to be my structure, some for burning. I took great care to gather only what wasn't steadfast in growing, as I began to think about my plans for a more intricate fortification tomorrow. I was familiar with finding rest in a small area, but I was wiser than that. I would need plenty of workable space to survive this time away.

Stowing away the dry wood, I began to assemble a formidable outline of my lean-to, intertwining the limbs with one another, and tied them off with woven roots and plant fibers. Vulpena found it fascinating that I could weave with such ease. It was one skill that I taught myself without any instruction. She told me that it was a very valuable skill to have, that it would save me a lot of time to form extra bundles whenever I had the chance. I keep at least three clews of it on my person at all times.

With the first part finished, I wandered around to look for some loose brush and fallen pine branches. They would help to keep any rain off me while I sleep. I stuffed any holes I found with foliage and moss to keep insulated, and finally set a sizable piece of tree bark against the opening. I nodded to myself, content with the work I had made. Though it would only last me for a night, I knew that this craftsmanship would provide me a decent night's sleep. The coming day, I would build off of it, and this structure of mine would be used as extra storage for food and other things.

I put away the work tools, and withdrew my fishing rod. I designed it to be collapsible for ease of transportation, and compact for storing. I dug about for a few worms, hooked them, and headed over to the pond. There was a part of land that extended into the water a few feet—surely that'd give me an advantage for fish who prefer to stay nearer to the center.

I cast out, and sat patiently. If there is one task that minds you of your ability to wait, it is fishing. Sitting and waiting for something to happen isn't difficult for me. Although fishing isn't one of my better skills, I managed a couple of them now and again. I recast, and continued to await the first fish. As I began to wave the rod around, I felt a gentle tug. Drawing the line in, it gave way, and I realized the worm was gone. With a small sigh, I hooked another, and gave it one more go. A few moments later, I felt a bite. Using caution, I let the fish pull for a minute, and brought it up. "Got you," I exclaimed with a grin. It was indeed a fish, albeit smaller than I expected.

As the sun decided to finish its journey downward, I decided too that it was about time to call the day's end for myself. I would have to make do with my catch and the remainder of my food from earlier. It would do no good to get to bed on a partial stomach full—I needed to store the calories for tomorrow, as that would be when I truly begin.

Making it back to the site, I put away the gear I had on me, and took a trowel in hand. I formed a ditch until I hit rougher dirt, and surrounded it with small stones I had pocketed after fishing. I exchanged the trowel for a bucket and a few waterskins, filled the bucket with sand from the edge of the pond, and the skins with clean water off the inlet. After filling the ditch partway, I kept the rest of the sand for any urgent use, and strung up my drinking water under my lean-to. I wouldn't want to spill it in my sleep, as it'd make for a most unpleasant awakening.

I started a small fire, stuck the fish on a branch, and set it by to cook slowly. I like my meat tender, and usually prefer it cooked lightly. I would find some game meat when I wake to provide me a heartier beginning. In fact, I will probably spend the first half of the day hunting, and work the rest of the day away building a better site.

My dinner was had, and I laid down by the warmth to gaze at the peering stars that had begun to form. I could make out patches of sky betwixt the holes of the canopy above—it seemed as a loose mosaic of deep umber and gold, with a gradient becoming navy and specks of light to the west. It was like a giant canvas made just for admiring.

As I felt my body settle into a daze, I took a small clay bowl, gently doused the flames with a sprinkle of sand, and gathered the embers into my vessel. This would keep me a little warmer as I sleep.

I stored away what I could into the tree, and brought the bowl with me under brush. I unrolled an elk fell, laid upon it, and began to meditate. Not only does meditating help me settle down into sleep, but it also guards me against wandering spirits in these woods. I am no stranger to these entities, and although I haven't become fully aware of how they manifest, everyone knows that many of them don't have your best interest.

Chapter 2

Before I knew it, the dawn of the next day breached. I slept until the nearing noon brought me out of slumber. I would need this extra rest if I were to make the most of this day.

I was not the type of early riser that most everyone is. For some reason, I found myself needing a little more sleep than others. It was of no particular concern to us Vulpani—we tend to function well enough with what we're given. Where other members would burn out by sunset, I often found myself working into the night to complete tasks left for morning. It became obvious how this work was done, and nobody else appeared to mind. In fact, they were grateful for my endurance.

With bow in hand, I shouldered a quiver fashioned from leather, pocketed a hunting knife, and took off for the precipice. I settled upon the crag, and began to take in the scene. I heard a few birds sing farewell to the morning, and greet the afternoon. I felt a small breeze, and noticed that it carried the scent of rabbit. "Excellent. Rabbit for breakfast," I whisper. With such a quick find, I would have some spare time to begin right away on improving my site.

I continued to sit and watch for signs of scurrying, and sure enough, a small, furry head made its way out from the growth rounding the hill. "Hm, there must be a den nearby. Perhaps I should wait to see if it returns."

I sat still, watching its path lead toward my camp to sate its curiosity. I quietly withdrew an arrow, nocked it, and silently watched the bunny return. I took aim, drew a breath, and loosed the arrow. It flew swiftly to its target, and not more than a moment after the arrow left my bow, the rabbit fell still.

I hopped from my makeshift stand, and walked over to the dead rabbit. I brought it back to the fire pit and sat down, offering a silent prayer over it. The rabbit gave its life to sustain mine, and I was grateful for that. After replacing the embers I used to harbor warmth, I restarted the fire. I worked on skinning it, humming to myself. "The freshest game is the best game, and I believe this will be a fine breakfast." I laid the hide out to dry, and cut up the meat. Sticking pieces onto a cooking branch, I set it up as best I could to cook evenly.

While the rabbit was cooking, I took up my tools, including a hatchet this time, and started to collect what I could for a sturdier base. I fashioned a spit for roasting when I find bigger game, and carved a few shafts for new arrows. I had at least a dozen, but it would be asinine to let myself run low. Lost game due to a shortage is lost time, as more is spent hunting, and less working.

I returned to my meal, only to find it missing. "What on earth... where did it go?!" To say I was upset would be an understatement. That food was my source of energy that would have carried me into evening, and it was gone. I glanced about with another arrow nocked. It's quite fortunate that I keep my weapons on me until I am content with my game, as I am sure to find another unfortunate animal very shortly.

I heard total silence, standing armed and ready. Looking around, I didn't notice anything else out of place. Then, I heard a ruffle not more than a dozen paces from myself. I glance toward the sound, and watch. Suddenly, a flash of black darted out, and I let the arrow fly. It stuck in the figure, which let out a roar. I felt a shiver of despair, and realized I had hit a panther. I was not armed to face one, and lacking provision, a bit too esurient to focus completely.

I ran for the hill, jumped up the rocks, nocked another arrow, and turned about to ready another shot. I had not accounted for this one's speed, and found myself on the ground before I even knew it. We tussled for several minutes, and I took a few cuts before I managed my knife from my pocket. I realized the arrow had broken off where I hit the beast, and quickly jabbed it with my fist. The creature roared again, and rolled off me. I jumped up, taking a defensive stance, as the panther shouted at me.

"What is your problem?! Do you just go and shoot everyone you meet, or is it just me?!"

I almost tripped over myself when I heard those words. The beast stood up to sit on the rock face, holding its right arm, blood seeping through its fingers.

With no idea how to respond, I relaxed my stance. I didn't even notice the deep red tunic until now. Apparently, the panther was female.

"Do you even talk, or am I speaking to an imbecile?"

I scrambled around my mind for any words that wouldn't come off as stupid. "You're... bleeding." I was instantly dismayed at my insolence.

"Oh, really? And who do you suppose is at fault?"

I knew that now was certainly not the best time to make an enemy. "I'm sorry. Please let me help you."

She gave me a long, sideways glance. I was not sure what she was considering, but it quickly became obvious that she did not desire to kill me. "You... want to help me? You stuck me with an arrow, you idiot."

"Yes, I know, and I really am sorry. I want to make up for that by tending to it, if you'll let me..." My words hung in the air for what seemed like eternity before I got a reply.

She looked at me sternly. "If you want to help me, you will let me stay with you for a couple days to rest and heal. Then I'll continue my adventure when I am good and ready." She opened a small pouch at her side, pulled out a piece of meat, and handed it to me. "Take this. It's our way of extending trust to you, so don't disappoint me."

I accept her offering, and begin to eat. "Thank you. I lost my breakfast to some animal. I presume you were also hunting?"

"No, I was just passing through, and happened upon your camp." She adjusted her hand covering the wound, and winced. "It was a pretty good breakfast, though."

I was taken aback by her comment. "That was you?!"

"Yes, and I am glad you find my comment flattering." She smiled and got up to walk toward the site.

I was going to say something, but figured it was better to not rescind my progress with this individual. I followed after her to my fire pit, and dug into my satchel for some cloth and a jar of salve. I also grab a waterskin, and go to kneel by her side. She gives me a cautious look, but allows me to see the wound.

"That's pretty nasty-looking," I say, and open the waterskin to wash the blood away. After cleaning, I dip my fingers into the salve, and softly begin to spread it on her arm. She grimaces, but doesn't move. I wrap the cloth around the area, and make it taut.

"Thank you," she said. "What's your name?"

"I am Kitso, a member of the Vulpani Tribe."

She nods. "Well I am Pansa, a part of the Panteo Clan."

"Is your tribe from around here?" I ask.

She frowns at me. "It's not a tribe."

"Oh, sorry. What's the difference?" I begin to mind my manners with a little more integrity.

"The difference is that your tribe is based on a foundation of morality and principles decided as a whole. My clan is more or less formed from others who seek common interest."

"Ah, I see." I take a seat, and poke at the embers.

"You don't get out much, do you?"

I take a moment before speaking again. "No, not really. This would be my first full day away from any of my tribe."

She responds with a sense of disbelief. "Wait... so you've never been away from your family? How young are you?"

"I'm twenty-four. Amongst the Vulpani, we hold tradition that members remain with their family as they grow. When we are old enough to communicate efficiently, we are taken under a mentor—a teacher to learn many valuable skills from, and to hone our innate abilities with. This continues all the way through my age, where the ritual of spending eight months in solitude helps us learn how to survive with what we've learned, and also to provide us time to decide whether we end up returning to stay and raise our descendants, or leave to form a new tribe with a mate."

The panther ponders all I've told her for a while, and seems to warm up to conversation. "That's a very intriguing way of life. My name is Pansa, and the clan I belong to holds my relatives, a couple other small families, and many individuals who are also mostly of our species. We make rare exceptions as to whom we accept, but prefer those who are at least related to our specie. Not that we're hostile or anything to others, but rather we remain generally cautious."

That explains her initial stance with me, I think to myself.

Pansa stands up for a moment, raising a fist to her chest. "We Panteo are very prideful in what we accomplish. We don't let anyone tell us what we can or cannot do, and we do everything we can to gain not only territory, but also respect from any surrounding clans."

"Oh, well that sounds fulfilling, and good for growth. Though, we personally believe that respect is given, and not earned."

Pansa huffs at my statement. "Despite what you believe, we are very happy with the respect we get from others. We don't get anywhere handing it out."

I decided to leave the topic where it stood. Pansa obviously comes from a very strong background, so I would not want to upset her. Actually, come to think of it, she would probably be a great ally.

In the meantime, I'd better just let her be. I don't want to seem desperate for help.

"What sort of adventure are you on?"

Pansa was silent again. She sat back down, drew a breath, and let out a long sigh. "To be honest, I am not really sure. I left my family to find some purpose to my life. Don't think badly of me—I love them all, and would do anything I could for them. I just couldn't find much more that I could do, so I felt that if I left, I could find some answers for their sake." She shook her head. "Look, it's complicated. If anything, I should be asking you what you plan on doing while you're out here for eight months."

I took a sip off the waterskin, and passed it to her, which she accepted. "I always imagined myself traversing the lands, seeing new things, and experiencing what I could out here. Vulpena—my mentor—always found me to harbor an adventurous spirit. I am very patient with most things, but she also knew I couldn't sit still for very long any time we were to set out to learn something new.

"Any time I had the chance, I would go on a little adventure with my brother—we would use our minds to go beyond any place we ever saw, thinking about how great it would be to seek out the hidden treasures of the land."

She handed the waterskin back to me. "Is your brother older or younger?"

"Older," I replied. "He decided to go on his own a year before his time, and so he never returned. I also have a younger sister who is awaiting her time in about three years from now. I expect she will want to leave the tribe as well, but only because our father..."

Pansa must have seen the sadness in my eyes. She didn't ask anything further, but instead she directed the conversation back to me. "It must have been hard, being right in the middle of the three of you. Getting blamed for things you didn't do, and criticized for what you did accomplish."

"Actually, we all got along fairly well. Sure, we had some rivalry, but I should think that's natural for most siblings. You'll always have some things you're greater at, and some things lesser."

Pansa looked down and off to the side. "It would have been nice if my own got along a little better. We quarreled over the smallest matters, like 'who gets to hunt', or 'where did the leftovers go?' Sometimes, I find myself wishing I wasn't tied down to them, but I guess I got my wish..."

I gave her a warm smile. "At least we don't have to go through our own trials alone. For a couple days, anyway."

She looked at me, and got up. She fished out a pale, off-white flower from her pouch, and ate it.

"Oh, what's that? Is it nutritious?"

"It's parupeteng flower. And I only have a few right now, so don't ask for any."

I said nothing. I was aware of this plant, though only by name and look, and did not intend on asking for one.

I glanced upward, and saw the sun was shifting lazily over its apex. "I am going to start working on a better structure, especially now that you are here."

I once again set off to gather materials for my home-to-be. Pansa entertained herself with what I had for a site, so I decided to look farther for better timber, as I knew nobody would be nearing the site with her around.

On the other side of the pond, I found an array of what appeared to be a large pile of branches. It seemed unusually neat, so I took a closer look. A couple of hornets popped out from under it, and knew to not anger them, for where there were a few, there was a horde. I felt better about my decision as I went farther still, for I happened upon a small grove of fallen trees. Excited at my find, I went to work, harvesting the limbs, and tying them off with one of the clews I had.

Returning to the site, bundles in tow, Pansa noticed me, and came over to help.

"It's alright, I have it."

She sneered. "Just because I suffered an unfortunate run in with a local savage, it doesn't make me weak."

I was grateful for the extra set of hands, and let her do as she desired. I knew she would anyway, whether I encouraged her or not.

*   *   *

I laid out a few limbs to size up the plans I had in mind, and Pansa began to set up posts from the blunt, shorter pieces.

"You seem to know what you're doing. Did you have lots of training in building?" I asked her.

"You forget—our clan learns from experience alone. But yes, I suppose you could say I am proficient in building. I had to house a couple dozen children."

"That's quite a lot. Did you bear them all yourself?"

She shot me a deadly look, but receded. "No, I did not. Bearing children is not in my future, as far as I am concerned. A few of them were related to me, but most of them were abandoned by their own. I took it upon myself to see they were cared for."

"That's a good quality to have, even if you do not foresee kits of your own."

She laughed. "That'd be *kittens*. And thanks, I guess."

I have never gotten to meet a panther in person, much less an intelligent one. I have heard stories about them before, but none that were particularly pleasant. Despite what I've been told in the past, I am finding they have a lot in common with us Vulpani. Though, something tells me she would deny any similarity.

We finish up the frame quicker than I anticipated—the sun was still about a third from the horizon. I might get to have some spare time to hunt later as the more nocturnal creatures begin to come out for food of their own.

"Would you like to help me gather some bark and brush for the walls and roof, Pansa?"

"Certainly." She removes a hatchet of her own from beneath her tunic folds.

"Wow, that's beautiful. Did you craft it yourself?"

"No. I traded for it from a merchant about a year ago. I wish I could make something like this." She follows me back to the grove I had found before.

"Do you have many travelers come through your tribe's —I mean—your clan's territory?"

"On occasion, we see one or two. When it becomes warmer, we often see groups of several parade themselves into our area, as though they own it. It frustrates us a little, but they do offer many things for a decent price."

"It sounds interesting. We never see anyone like that. Usually, just a passer-by looking for a night to stay, or a meal to eat. We are happy to help in any way we can."

She crouches down to cut away at one of the fallen trees. "You know, you can't always be giving away things to help strangers, Kitso. Sometimes, you have to get what you can to keep, or you'll have nothing to give."

Though we have different views on hospitality, Pansa doesn't seem to totally disagree with what I say. She makes very good points that have me think about our tribe getting along all these years. Was it okay to give freely so all the time? Were there reasons that one might decide to withhold?

It seems I've more to learn out here than I initially thought. We gather many large brushes, and use the last of the root and fiber to transport them back. When unwrapped, the fibers can be used to secure everything.

Upon arrival, I laid down the bark, and we put them up to form the walls. After they were set, I drove the longest and thickest branch we had into the ground at the center of the structure.

We loosed the limbs of brush, and arranged them to form a pointed roof. I cut the cord into a dozen lengths, and together we went around, securing every limb and lattice in place.

I dug around in my satchel and found some bone fragments, and got ready to drive them into the bark, hammer at the ready.

"Hold on," Pansa said quickly. "I've got something better for you to use."

She gave me a handful of small metal shafts, much like the ones we made arrows out of, but with a blunt tip instead of an arrowhead. "What are these?"

"The one I got them from called them 'nails'. They're like stakes, only smaller."

I nodded appreciation, and worked them into the bark. They were surprisingly easy to manage, and far better for the job. "Thank you. I should learn how to craft these."

She chuckled. "I heard working with metal is difficult, but I bet you could figure it out."

Dusk was settling over the land, and no sooner than the last of the sun hid itself did the creatures of the night come out to play. I heard mice find their way out of their dens. Seemingly ignorant of the world, they began to search for food. I spotted a hawk overhead—it must be getting ready to take advantage of one final meal before it sleeps.

I donned my bow and arrows while Pansa kindled a new fire. "I'll keep this burning while you hunt."

As she tended the pit-fire, I navigated around the hill. "I wonder what animals live on the other side," I spoke aimlessly. I was determined to find at least one more rabbit, or maybe a small boar. I've seen boars plod out this way when they passed by our tribe in the night.

Rounding the convex land, I saw a pair of glittering eyes not far from where I stood for only a second, then heard it scamper off. I wasn't about to pick a fight with another nocturnal beast, nor did I desire to find out whatever the eyes belonged to, so I let it be.

I took in the temperate night air, and trailed the scent of something odd. When I caught up with it, I noticed that it had a small, ringed tail. I've known raccoons to be messy eaters, but they tasted just as well.

I followed until it found something to eat, and quickly sent an arrow after it.

When I came back with prize in hand, Pansa was not at the fire. I sat down to prepare our dinner, when she returned with all of my waterskins, bulged to the brim. "I noticed that our water supply was low, so I filled them up."

"Thank you for doing that. I got us a raccoon." I held it up for her to admire.

"Eh, it's not really my kind of game. Besides, I have some meat I need to finish off before it goes bad."

I was fine with her decision—the more we conserve, the less hunting we would have to do.

I set it to roast, and cleaned the skin. I would later make it into a new waterskin, or maybe a cap to keep warm in the colder nights.

After we ate, I reorganized my belongings, and took note of things I would need to replenish. With satchel organized and tucked away, I stayed by the fire, and began to work on several roots I had dug up with the worms. Trimming and splicing, I fashioned them to create a new bundle, bit by bit.

Pansa drew her legs up, arms folded across them, and watched me intently. "That's fascinating. You don't seem the type who would enjoy such a craft."

I continued to focus on my work. "It's something I find to be very relaxing. It's an innate ability that Vulpena helped me to discover. Weaving also helps my mind to rest so that I may find better sleep come bedtime."

She yawns. "I'm starting to feel the work from today catch up with me. When do you sleep usually?"

"A few hours before the rise of dawn."

"Hm, that's pretty atypical. I'm not sure I could manage that nightly."

"That is just how I've always been," I say, as I make progress on the slowly-forming clew. "Though, it has proven its advantages. When others around me ready themselves for sleep, I find myself picking up on things that can be done, such as crafting or cooking."

Pansa interjected her understanding. "Mm, it sounds like a productive trait. Well, I am going to tuck in now. Enjoy the night—I'll see you in the noon."

"Sleep well."

I finish up what root was left, and set it to my side. I recline while staring upward, talking to myself. "Pansa is certainly helpful and pleasant company. I wonder if she'll possibly reconsider her temporary stay."

I lounge for a little while longer, the fire lambent, until only a few mere licks of flame dance about.

It's probably better to let her decide. She's far too prideful to let the opportunity be mentioned by anyone else.

Chapter 3

I walk into the hut, and find Pansa sleeping soundly. I do what I can to not disturb her, and grab my rod and the worms.

Heading over to the pond, I notice the moon's light shining through the holes in the canopy, shimmering and dancing along the ripples of what fish might be swimming the night away.

I sit down on my usual spot, hook one of the worms, and toss my line nonchalantly into the black and white deep. A short moment later, I feel the line become taut. I give it a small pull, and it pulls back. Determined to keep this catch, I quickly stand up and adjust my grip. I sense the direction of the movement, and try to work with it until the tension begins to lessen.

Just as the line gives, I give it one good pull to my side. My feet slip, and as I fall, the line draws me into the pond. I catch my breath right before I hit the surface, and am suddenly surrounded by cold darkness. I attempt to release my grip, but find I am unable to do so.

As the black waters rush by my face, I try to open my eyes, and see a blinding flash.

I awaken instantly, drenched down my shoulders to the scent of fish wafting into the hut. I sit up, and wipe my eyes to clear the water from them. One of the waterskins had slipped from the overhang—it must have burst open when it hit me. I take a spare cloth from my satchel, and dry myself off. Stretching and yawning, I slowly make my way outside.

By the pit-fire sat two erect branches, supporting five fish altogether. Pansa is garnishing them with sprinkles of salt when she notices me. "Morning, Kitso. Or rather, afternoon." She giggles to herself.

"Afternoon, Pansa." I sit alongside the fire, and stretch my feet out. "When did you catch these?"

"About an hour ago. It got warmer earlier than usual, so I went to see if any fish were sunning about. Sure enough, about a dozen were swimming around. I just put them near the fire not more than ten minutes ago."

"I noticed that you didn't have much gear with you. Did my fishing rod give you any trouble?"

Pansa laughed. "I didn't have to use it. We of the Panteo profess in certain types of hunting." She extends her claws, admiring them in the sunlight.

"Ah, well I will keep practicing with a rod. I may as well continue to hone my skill with fishing."

I help myself to a fish. "These are amazing. I appreciate that you didn't overcook them. They're far better this way."

She also takes one. "I agree completely. I cannot stand over-done meat. Are you going to have another after?"

"No, I should be fine with this."

The remaining fish get tucked into one of her pouches, which she brings into the hut. She comes back out, garb folded over her arm. "I am going to go for a swim."

I try not to notice her unclad stance. "Oh, alright, Enjoy the waters." I turn over a few coals, and sift them with the sand to douse the fire. I retrieve my bow and quiver, and wander out to look for birds.

* * *

I set my tunic upon a nearby rock, looking earnestly at the clear waters before jumping in.

The cool water invigorates my skin as it washes over my fur, brushing away the dirt and sweat from yesterday's labor. Both refreshing and relaxing, I feel as though I could swim all my worries away.

I watch the fish dart away from me a few times before their curiosity gets the better of them. I allow myself to lazily float beneath the surface for a while. They come to investigate this unusual creature in their world before taking off to find something else to discover.

I am not sure what goes through their minds—if anything at all—but they seem content enough with the same surroundings every day of their lives, never the wiser to the worlds beyond their home.

Glad to have the ability to do so, I resurface for fresh air and examine the woods. Though I've seen many areas, this particular one has a certain feel.

It's relieving in a way, and causes me to not stress over what bothers me day to day.

After about fifteen minutes of washing, I leave the pond, and sun for a few moments before putting my tunic back on. My fur tends to get a little ruffled if I don't let it dry completely.

Walking back to our base, I notice Kitso isn't there. Perhaps he went to hunt some more.

I sit by the hut, take a parupeteng flower out, and ingest it. They help to reduce any pain I suffer from, but have an unappealing after-taste. If it weren't the only thing I knew that helped me, I'd prefer to not eat them, but they don't seem to have much in the way of undesirable side-effects. Unless you account for an on-going craving developed from them, of course.

Kitso returns, with a couple of medium-size birds in tow. He sits down across from me, and begins to feather the birds.

"Hey Pansa. How was your swim?"

"It was wonderful. The pond is not too shallow, and the water is crisp and refreshing. I see your hunt was successful today."

He sets a pile of feathers down, and continues to pluck more. "Yeah, the pair were feeding on worms from the wet soil. I managed to stick them both with a single arrow." He smiles. "I am going to use the feathers to fletch some more arrows, and then cut up the meat for bait to attract bigger game."

"Very smart." I nod with a smirk.

As he feathers a few of the shafts, he glances at me. "What are some of your long-term goals? I know you mentioned that you weren't quite sure what you would do after today, but I remember you talking a bit about your family."

I shift a bit, still unsure about everything, and sigh. "I still don't know what I'm gonna do. I was wondering, do you think I could stick around a little while longer? I feel like I took you for granted at first, but I am thankful I happened upon your time out here. I understand if you want to go it alone—it's important to you, and I don't want to be a burden. It's just… since we got to know each other, I feel like I'm watching two chipmunks run around a tree after one another." I look down. "I know, it sounds stupid."

Kitso hesitates, and sets his work aside. He stares at me for what felt like an eternity. "I'm glad you mentioned something first. In honesty, I was hoping you'd reconsider, and stay for a while more. Not only are you helpful and decent company, but I feel like my skills have only gotten sharper with you around."

I feel a release of tension within me, as though I dove into a hot spring to settle beneath the water. "That makes me happy. I'm sure I'll find out what I want to do in time."

"I hope to be of help also. Family should come first."

I express my happiness to him. "Thank you for understanding. It isn't very often others get me."

Kitso returns to his fletching as I go into the hut. I recline on my knees, considering my situation. "Thank you for watching over me, mother. I promise I will do anything to help my loved ones out, as soon as I figure out what it is that can be done."

That moment in time, the desire for that remaining parupeteng flower hadn't even crossed my mind.

After a little while, I wander back out, hatchet in tow. "Hey Kitso, I'm going to go find some useful limbs to fortify our hut some more. I'll be back in a little while."

"Alright Pansa, just be careful." He gives me an assured look. "As if I have to tell you that."

"Heh, thanks. Nice arrows, by the way. The gray and blue feathers give them a distinct look."

As I find my way further out, I notice a shift in the atmosphere. I hesitate momentarily, but continue to move forward. I stop after a few minutes, and sit down on a stump. "I'm sorry."

A dark, hazy figure begins to manifest itself beside me, as if a breeze were pushing the light around.

I've been waiting since last night. You were supposed to arrive then.

I stay silent, unable to find words I want to speak.

The figure slides in front of me, and I draw my gaze upward to the treetops.

You're just confused, that's all. The words it forms, though inaudible, seep into my face like ice.

You need not worry about your friend. He's determined to complete this trial of his, with or without you. It is his will.

I look off to my side. "I know. I'm hoping that he'll just forget about me when I move on. I don't think he took me seriously. He was just... well, being nice."

That's right. He'll return to his tribe either way, and be about his own. He does not intend to leave them, so don't allow him to give you a sense of false bearing.

Just as quickly as the figure had formed, so too it disappeared, leaving behind a few parupeteng plants in its wake. They look as though they've been growing for a few weeks to full maturity. I look over my shoulders, carefully cut the flowers off the thorny stalk, and slip them into my pouch.

I feel like I just stabbed myself with a hot knife.

* * *

I collect the arrows when they're done, and slide them into my quiver. The day is starting to fade, leaving less light to work by. I'll have to carve some arrowheads for them another time. I wonder when Pansa will return, and if she'll be hungry.

Forgoing my intent to use the birds as bait, I set them up to roast. Satisfied with what I've done for the afternoon, I lay down and relax, admiring the sights around me. The woods have been my entire life, and so it's all I've known. A couple of squirrels jump around the branches above, as though they're scouting the upper world.

I hear some leaves rustle—Pansa must be back.

I look over to find her holding an armful of sturdy-looking limbs. "I'm back, Kitso. Sorry it took me so long." She sets them down by our hut, and flops by the fire pit. "They were a bit tough to work off the trees, but I think they'll do."

Sitting up, I gesture to the little roasts. "Hungry? I put them over after I finished with the feathers."

"Thank you for that." She grabs one, taking in the aroma before eating. "It's very good. You may have to cook more," she speaks with a mouth full of bird.

"Not if you don't mind your manners," I retort with a hearty laugh. She sticks her tongue out at me, at which I shrug. "I enjoy cooking now and again. One of my favorite things to make is a stuffed salmon—an assortment of mushrooms and herbs goes in, and it gets grilled to a nice golden brown."

Her eyes widen a bit. "Tell you what—I'll do the fishing, and you do the grilling."

"You've got a deal. I'll forage for some ingredients this evening, and keep my eyes open for a nearby salmon run." I take my bird and place it into my satchel. "I'll have this while I'm out and about."

Pansa swallows, and picks at her teeth. "You might try out west from the hill. I heard a river not far from where I cut the limbs. You'll see where about a hundred paces beyond the last curve."

I nod, and grab a waterskin, bow and quiver slung. "If I'm quick, I bet I'll find more prey while searching."

Walking along the hillside, I follow the trees with the slope, gathering a few mushrooms and plants, until the ground becomes fairly level once more. A short time later, Pansa's pruning job presents itself, and I head west. My ears pick up on the sound of the river.

"That must be it," I say. "I imagine the salmon will be making use of their time as the season draws cooler." I find a handful of mushrooms near an old, dried stump. "Mm, these look... huh?"

Some trimmed plants catch my eye. "Parupeteng plants? They're cut." I figure only one individual must have come through here.

I sigh. "No, I can't assume anything."

A small boar appears not four yards from me. I quietly speak to myself. "This is not your lucky day, little friend." Drawing my bow, arrow set in place, I take aim. The very moment I intend to release, a larger boar wanders over. I mutter with a sigh. "I guess it is, after all. Give your mother my regards." I set the arrow away and head back.

I see Pansa sunning herself when I return. Her fur is slightly damp under her clothes—she must have gone swimming.

She notices me as I wander over. "Hey Kitso, welcome back. The pond is unusually warm this evening—you should go for a dip."

I try not to make eye contact.

"What's wrong? Was there no river? I could have sworn I heard something."

I don't want her to think I'm ignoring her. "No, there was a river. I also saw a little boar, but its mother was about, so I couldn't bring myself to shoot it."

She gives a short sigh. "I'm sorry—we still have some food for tonight, if you're still hungry. I'll go fishing first thing in the morning!"

"Actually, I didn't eat my bird. I kind of lost my appetite."

Pansa offers me a hug. "It's okay. I'm not one to break a promise."

I sit down at the pit-fire, poking at it with a stick. I can feel her concern emanating. "It isn't that... it's just, well, I saw a few trimmed plants by a stump. Parupeteng plants."

Pansa crosses her arms, and settles to one side. "What of it?"

"Well, I... I know you partake of them. I only hope you don't eat them regularly."

"Define *regularly*," She says flatly.

"Um... one every few days or so, I suppose."

She says nothing, walks up to the hut, and rests her hands against the upper frame of the doorway. She lowers her head. "Look, I know you aren't fond of it, but they help me with a lot of my stress and pain. You've probably never consumed any of them yourself, so I don't expect you to understand anything."

I become cautious with my words. "That's true, I haven't ever had one. But I have heard a few things about them."

"Like what?"

"I know that they've been known to shorten one's lifespan, and some others I once knew developed an infection from ingesting them daily."

Pansa huffs with an incredulous manner, her demeanor rough. "No, you don't *know*, you've *heard*. Do you believe everything you hear about?"

I go to respond, but decide not to. "That's what I thought. Look, I don't care what you think of me, but don't think you can tell me what I can or can't do."

"... I'm sorry."

"No you're—no, you know what? I'm done. I don't need your sympathy, or your company. I can do well enough on my own, as I have before I met you, and as I will tomorrow." She storms into the hut without so much as a second glance.

I lay against a half-submerged log, arms at my side, watching the tadpoles explore my fingers. The water is indeed warm tonight, as Pansa had mentioned. Though, I still feel a bit cold from her words.

"I shouldn't have said anything. She will leave tomorrow, and I'll be alone again. I know I cannot expect someone to always be with me, until I take a mate in my travels." The tadpoles don't respond, unsurprisingly.

I slide down a bit, sending up swirls of debris beneath the surface. "Father, I only hope that you are safe wherever you've decided to go. I wonder if you ever had troubles like this. You were charismatic, your ability to negotiate with anyone. What should I say, if anything?"

A gentle breeze picks up, and I thought I heard the words.

Follow the wind.

The sun makes way for the night once again, and I get up from the pond. Drying myself off, I wonder about what Pansa had said, and I only hope her travels bring her happiness. I pull my garb on, and get ready to settle in for an early night.

Chapter 4

After a dreamless sleep, I awaken to find that it's barely dawn, and that Pansa isn't here. She must have left before the sun began its rise. I drift off, but fail to dream.

I come to a little sooner than I wanted, but feel rested enough to begin my day. I empty one of the waterskins to quench my arid throat, but find it no easier to manage than the air I breathe. I still feel terrible about yesterday.

Wandering around the site for a time, I am unsure of what to do with myself. I hadn't realized how lonely it could be out here—I became readily acclimated with her presence to the point of putting all thoughts of isolation aside. I hadn't considered myself the most social being, but it was nice to have someone to talk with.

I shake my head. "Come now, Kitso. You can't very well mull such things over. It's of no use to your survival."

Coming to terms with myself, I fetch my bow and quiver. I end up spending a good portion of time hunting to no avail, and quickly become frustrated. I spot a deer, but as I ready an arrow, it takes off. Before long, I give in, an empty feeling in my stomach to keep the feeling of solitude company.

Unable to break from my own mind, I concede to whittle the afternoon away by working on my camp.

I return, only to find someone sitting at the fire pit, watching smoke curl upward.

"I knew you'd return shortly," she says quietly.

Lost for words, I slowly approach the pit, sitting with the utmost of care.

"You're not going to break a rock by sitting upon it," she comments with a sigh.

"Pansa—"

"Please don't. I... look, I'm the one who should be sorry. I tend to get highly irritable without having them, and believe me, I don't enjoy it. I'm not in denial of the things they may cause—I just don't like thinking about it. If I had an alternative, I'd take it up in the beat of a heart. But I don't, so until then, I'm not going to stop."

I breathe out with a bit of reluctance, but feel greatly relieved. "Thank you."

"For what?"

"For coming back."

She perks up slightly. "Oh, yeah, I almost forgot." Pansa removes a batch of five salmon from the breast of her clothes. "Like I said before, I keep my promises. So here, work your magic."

I accept them, and take out my knife to fillet. "I'm happy that you decided to return. Even though my trial revolves around my ability to test my limits, it's a lot less enjoyable being alone."

"Nobody enjoys being alone, including myself. Not that that's the only reason I came back, mind you. I feel like I'm going to find out what I should do, so long as I dwell here.

Whether or not I do find out, I'll see. Perhaps that time will take me through the cold season."

With the fish prepared and filled with ingredients, I set them to grill over the flame.

"Then I hope you find what you seek whilst here."

"I am sure I will. I'm going to rest for a bit, so let me know when the salmon are done."

By mid-afternoon, we had our lunch. Pansa found it to be extraordinary, and suggested that I consider bartering with the food I make. I told her that there weren't many who would trade something away for food, but she claimed that a lot of goods are swapped further south. Apparently, there is a market solely for the distribution of rations.

Pansa and I decide that the site could use a few more things, such as a larger fire pit, additional storage, a sturdier hut, and a more convenient place to relieve ourselves.

I take my satchel to go find more materials to work on the hut and storage, and she heads over to the pond to dig up some clay I noticed while bathing the night before.

To the north, I come across a rabbit run, and set up a couple snares with my weavings. There's a small gathering of old trees further along—some fallen, and some almost entirely deteriorated. One particular tree was a red oak, covered with an assortment of mosses and mushrooms. There's a trail of ants strewn along it.

I help myself to a bagful of the fruity fungi, along with a few clumps of moss. Then I work out a large portion of the root system, cut several lengths free, and store them into my tunic folds. I pull up a large root, and set it back down.

With hatchet in hand, I hew several branches free from the oak, cording them together with the thicker root, then cut it from the ground. I strip off a giant piece of bark, and settle everything upon it.

As I drag the load back to camp, I find one of the snares with a rabbit. The other one was broken and scattered. Perhaps something came along and swiped my catch.

Back at our site, I show Pansa what I had found, and start to size up the hut to find the best side for storage. The back side shows promise, so I remove the panel of bark, and rework the opening.

Pansa works a few large masses of clay with our water supply, forming it into various things. She makes a small platter, a cruse, and a round column surrounding the fire pit, explaining aloud that it'll help to cook food easier. "It'll also provide the heat necessary to fire these things," she exclaims as she forms a handle for the jar.

After I finish the outline for the storage cubby, I walk over to see her progress. "That's very intuitive. I wonder what else we can make with it."

"Well, I was thinking we could redo the roof with tiles. It'd keep the water off completely, and look nicer."

"I haven't really considered the aesthetic of my hut as a survival aspect."

She snorts. "It isn't always about surviving. If you're going to travel with a mate, she is probably going to think about how you make things, and not just what you make. Females have a keen eye on detail, even if we never say it.

"One of the many things we keep in check is presentation. It makes us feel safe and cared for." She stops suddenly. "Sorry, I'm rambling. Do you need any help with the storage?"

"No worries. That's pretty helpful to know, actually. I've been told I am artistic, but I have been more focused on doing what I can to make my trial easier. And yes, I'd love some help."

We both work on various improvements, showing each other things we've come to learn, and improving from one another's skills. Pansa taught me a new way to bind limbs together, and I displayed an alternate method for preparing meat. She also explained another technique to approach fishing—she called it spearfishing. Although I have never used a spear, she was confident I could learn.

By evening, we were working on several bundles of woven roots. Enjoying a portion of rabbit and mushrooms, we discussed our lives in more detail.

"That's where I got my weaving abilities from. Crafting of all types appear to run in our line, and Vulpena was known for drawing those abilities out best. My mother made this tunic for me when I was only thirteen—she made our clothes larger than necessary, so that we could get more use out of them as we age."

"Your mother sounds like a very passionate lady." Pansa ties off the last clew, and continues eating. "I never really knew my mother, but from what I have heard, everyone appreciated her cooking. Food held a particular comfort for me, which is likely why I savor yours so much."

I look down. "I appreciate that. I myself have always loved food of all sorts. It is mostly due to a high metabolism, which is why I have so much energy to carry me into the night.

"Mother used to jest with me, expressing that if I didn't manage my intake, I'd eat the entire tribe out of home."

My last statement made Pansa snort when she laughed. Her laughter always seems to cheer me up.

Her end of family tales picks up afterward. "My siblings and I have always gone out together on adventures of our own with our friends. The elders always approved, as I found out later that they were able to find great peace and quiet from our absence.

"We had so many great encounters. We once found this old cave not far from where our clan stayed. One of our members cautioned us about it being an old burial tomb, but we were pretty reckless then. Not a whole lot of things could scare us."

"You all must have been very brave."

"I know I was, but the youngest of us children were too afraid to go inside, so we presented them the opportunity to play 'lookout' while we explored."

"Did you find anything in there?" I ask, curious about burial sites.

"Mostly some old enclosures along the walls, and maybe the occasional bone. It looked as though it had been cleared out at one point or another. I did find this, though."

She withdraws an ornament from a small pouch hidden within her garb, and hands it to me. It's a silver statuette resembling a panther—it seems to be praying.

"Wow, that's beautiful."

"It is, isn't it?" She turns it around in her hand, admiring the silvery sheen it casts. "I believe that they were ancestral grounds of our predecessors. I'm hoping to find a scholar familiar with the area, or some sort of archive containing writings."

"I'm not familiar with much history beyond the stories I was told growing up, but one's background always fascinates me. It's fun to consider what our ancestors did with their time living in this world."

Pansa puts the figure away. "That is one of my greatest goals—to find out all that I can. I figure I can go from there to help my kin."

We finish up what we can, and store our belongings within.

"I'm going to refill the waterskins, Pansa." I gather them up and head over to the inlet.

"That sounds like a good idea," she says as I leave.

When I return, I find that she's already fallen asleep—I imagine the day must have taken a lot out of us both. I decide to carve at some bone for my new arrows. I grab my whittling stone and a handful of the larger bones, and sit by the dwindling fire.

Working into the night, I notice a calm breeze begin to pick up. I look upward to gaze at the stars. *It really is a peaceful night out tonight*, I think to myself. *I hope it stays this warm for a while.*

I attach the arrowheads one after another, and leave none incomplete. "Brilliant as always. I am going to find us a good batch of meals tomorrow."

* * *

I come to the next morning, and see Kitso sleeping soundly. I try my best to not awaken him while I grab my bag.

Squinting from the beaming sun, I step out of our shelter and breathe in deeply. "It's an amazing morning," I whisper. "I know just what to do today."

I wander out into the woods to find a good pair of small trees. Happening upon a pair of newly-growing maples, I clap with levity, and cut them from the ground.

Saplings in hand, I go back to our camp, and start to strip the bark, fashioning the pieces into a pair of spears. I notch the tips several inches up to hook prey.

I head into our shelter, and watch Kitso as he sleeps. *He looks very peaceful, smiling like that.*

Gently, I awaken him. "Kitso...," I whisper—no response. I speak a little louder, and softly shake him. "Hey, Kitso."

"Huh... afternoon already...?" He rests on one arm, and rubs his eyes.

"Yes, sleepy head. I've got a surprise for you."

Kitso appears more attentive. "Oh? What is it?"

I giggle. "You'll have to get up and see for yourself."

Kitso takes his time waking up, and heads outside to meet up with me. "Alright, I am up. What do you have for me?"

"I have something for the both of us." I toss him one of the spears, which he almost drops. "They're spears. One for you, and one for me."

He examines it, testing the quality. "It has some remarkable detail, and it's quite balanced. I can tell you've made a number of these before."

"Thanks. Carving wood is one of my favorite hobbies. Now, let's head to the river and teach you some fishing the fun way!"

I take off running, at which Kitso follows suit. "Try to keep up!" I glance over my shoulder briefly. *Wow, he's faster than I thought! Maybe we'll have some fun...*

We run through the trees, bounding over rocks, curving around the hills. A rabbit is startled, darting out of our way. A few birds jump, and fly overhead as we race each other, as though they're sizing up our ability to travel compared to flying.

Arriving at the edge of the river, I lean forward to catch my breath—Kitso is also panting. "I never knew... you were such a fast runner, Kitso."

"I was the fastest... out of all... us kids. Nobody ever outran me."

I take a seat, and draw off my waterskin. "We'll have to race some time."

He looks surprised. "I thought that's what we were doing. You beat me hands down."

"Only because I got a head-start." I stick my tongue out and wink. "Let's have a real race next time."

I peer over the water's edge, Kitso beside me. There are a variety of little fish swimming about.

"Look at them, totally unaware of their coming demise," I say with a grin. "Are you ready then?"

"Yes, I believe I understood everything," he replies.

Spear in hand, I hop out to one of the rocks betwixt the rapids. I steady my footing, and commence fishing. I determine my target, and quickly strike. In a flash, I have one lanced, flopping wildly in a desperate attempt for water. "Got it!" I announce triumphantly. "Now it's your turn."

I jump back to safety, and watch Kitso as he manages the leap. "Very smooth. Now, look for an easy one."

He looks about, trailing the fish with his big, brown eyes, and focuses on one.

He raises his spear... and slips! Before he could catch his footing, he goes tumbling into the river, and I can't help but laugh.

"Oh my... are you alright?!" Despite my attempt at showing concern, the laughter inevitably finds its way back out. "You poor dear—you're sodden!"

Kitso drags himself back on the riverside, and takes off his clothing to clear his face and wring it out. *I hadn't noticed how toned he was.* I feel my face warm up, and draw my hands up to my eyes. Thankfully, he didn't seem to notice me staring.

"Yes, that was hilarious, I'm sure..." He retorts.

"I'm sorry," I begin, every ounce of me attempting to stifle the giggling. "You just looked so helpless when you fell in."

He replaced his clothes and shook his head, sending a light sprinkle about. "I guess I'm not so good at this after all."

I clear my throat. "Hey, don't be too hard on yourself—you've never done this before. It's easy to make a mistake." I look up, and back at him. "I fell in at least twice before I found my knack."

"I find that difficult to imagine."

"Oh, it's true. The first time, I was only four. I went with my father, and he had to pull me out before I got washed away. The other time, I was seven. I went out on my own, determined to get this huge one that was eating all the little fish before they were able to mature. When I did fall, it came after me, but I quickly stuck out my spear in time, and it ended up lancing itself.

"So, I kind of became the hero after all." I frown a bit. "Nobody ever knew what really happened."

Kitso must have picked up on my meaning, because he read me perfectly. "I can see why that would upset you." He confirms my suspicion. "You felt bad because you were praised for a false sense of honor, as though you've been given credit undue."

My eyes widen, but I don't say anything.

"Your clan must really admire you for your sense of honesty and integrity."

"I lead them to believe that I actually *succeeded* in spearing it!"

He thinks for a moment in silence. "But you were successful. It might not have been the way you wanted it to go, but you still managed to get it."

I tried to find the words I felt, but I couldn't. Kitso was right—no matter how you look at it, I set out to do something, and simply did it with what I had.

"That means a lot to me," I tell him.

Eventually, Kitso picks up on it, without any additional accidents. We go back to our base with prizes stuck—seven for me, and three for him. He holds the spear over a shoulder, as though he were showing anyone following him of his proud achievement.

"Not bad at all for a first-time spearfisher."

He smiles at me, and glances at his spear. "I had a pretty good teacher, and a fine spear to learn with."

I ruffle the tuft of fur on his head. "Just take good care of it, alright?"

He stops a moment to look down.

"Did I say something wrong?"

He shakes his head quickly, and continues on. "No, it's just... my instructor used to do that to me all the time. It reminds me how fond I've always been of her."

Kitso continues walking. I watch him for a couple seconds, smiling, and follow along. *You really had a very good upbringing, Kitso. I don't ever want to ruin that for you.*

* * *

Evening sets in just as we approach our base, the air clean and quiet.

He lays his spear against the shelter, and sets some tinder aflame. "Let's make some magic," He grabs the fish, and starts to fillet.

I prop my catch on a nearby limb, and fetch his pouch of herbs and mushrooms, which he thanks me for. I leave him be, going for my usual swim.

Clothes set aside, I wade into the pond, feeling the warm sand beneath my feet. The water is a little cooler than last time, but still temperate.

When I reach my waist, I push out into the depths, and begin to paddle around. I then dive underneath.

I've always loved swimming, the waters surrounding me with total serenity. Deep, warm colors—a silent chamber of peaceful submersion. I forget about every worry in my life, as though I push them further away with every stroke, until they breach the outer limit of my subconscious.

I come up for air, and lazily push my way over to a small sand bar slightly peeking over the surface. Sitting upon the sand, I feel as though I am resting on the water itself.

A breeze comes in, and I draw my knees up toward my chest, shivering slightly.

I recognize this feeling.

Pleasant evening, isn't it?

I don't respond, and rub my arms, looking about.

It isn't nice to ignore those speaking to you.

"But you're not actually speaking."

The haze forms, this time directly in front of me. My arms tense a bit.

Oh, what are words, but an elaborate transition of thought into sound.

The figure becomes a bit more prominent than ever before. I can almost see eyes staring right through my core. *You can still hear me,* it says with unrelenting.

"Yes. What do you want with me tonight?"

Nothing, really. I only wish to see how you're faring, is all. You do remember what I had told you a short time ago, do you not?

I nod my head, barely noticeable.

Good. We wouldn't want you to forget.

"No, we wouldn't..." My voice is nigh inaudible.

Very well. I can see when I am not wanted around. Simply continue as you are, and don't let opportunity pass you by, for I fear your friend may suffer a most unfortunate... doing.

The being fades out. I make my way out of the pond, feeling weak at the knees. I wander over to a nearby thicket, and get sick.

I return to camp, and see Kitso sitting faced away from me, carving at something in his lap. The receding fire casts a warm glow around his silhouette. I take a deep breath, and sit down next to him. He looks focused, but smiles when I sit.

"What have you got there, Kitso?"

He gives the object a few more notches, and holds it up for me to see in the light.

"It's a panther, sleeping on her side, carved from a piece of lime I found by the inlet. I figured you could add it to your new collection of trinkets." He evaluates his work, and adds to the detail.

The way he said "sleeping on her side" almost makes me want to cry. "It's nice." My voice cracks unexpectedly.

He sets it down on the log we're sitting on, and looks up at my face. "What's wrong? ...Your face looks a bit disturbed."

The fact that he can tell my face is unsettled in the near dark makes me want to hide, but I know I cannot. I wipe my eyes. "It's nothing. Really."

"Oh, come now, you cannot expect me to believe that there's nothing wrong."

I try to remain as calm as I can. "I'm just... I'm tired, okay?" I stare at him, despair written plainly on my face, until he concedes.

"Alright, I won't pressure you. Will you at least allow me to hug you?"

Without moving a single muscle, I let him hug me. I reciprocate, not ever wanting to let go. After what seems to be forever, he releases me, and watches me as I head in for the night.

I hear him whistling cheerfully as he carves away, and I silently cry myself to sleep.

Chapter 5

The new day dawns, and it is a very warm afternoon. Pansa was still asleep when I awoke. I decided to let her rest—she seemed she could use it since last night.

I head out to source some decent timber for upgrading our shelter. I felt that Pansa might be happier with a room of her own, so she can come and go without concerning herself with my sleep, and to have some private time for meditation.

When I found what I was looking for, I head back, tying off bits of root on various trees to direct me back. Upon returning, I prepare a small meal for Pansa.

She must have sensed it when it was done, because shortly after, she came out.

"Morning, Pansa! Or rather, afternoon." I plate the food, and hand it over to her. "I figured that you would be hungry after such a good night's sleep. Yesterday was pretty busy for us both."

"Thank you. It smells lovely." She sits on the ground.

I sit down on the log, and begin to furbish my hatchet. "I found another great place to gather some more wood."

"That's nice." She pokes at her food for a moment, and looks up at me. "Are you still going to travel when you complete your trial?"

I reply, focused on my task. "Oh, definitely. Expanding my horizon has only made me desire more. I want to see as much of the world as I can before resettling."

"Your loved ones might miss you."

"True... but they've always been strongly supportive of my decision since my adventuring spirit became more distinct." I hold up my hatchet to examine the blade, and polish it with a cloth. "Actually, if it weren't for my relatives, I'd probably have stayed with them for life. It's interesting how it worked like that."

Pansa begins to eat. "What if you don't find a mate?"

I glance at her. "Now, who wouldn't want a gentleman like me?" I laugh, but Pansa looks a bit somber. "Don't worry, Pansa. Wherever I end up, we'll still be friends. This I promise you."

She seems to cheer up a bit, smiling faintly.

The bright sun peers through the canopy to greet us as we begin our day together. I lead my friend to the new location, hatchet in tow. I explain my plans for our shelter, which enthralls her. Seeing her so happy reminds me of everything I've worked for, and what I aim to accomplish in life.

I start to glean from the little grove, listening to the birds chatter overhead. "They must be talking about us."

"Huh?" Pansa looks confused.

"I mean the birds. They sound like their discussing our efforts, trying to decide what we are planning."

"Oh, yeah. We must be quite the conversation subjects."

"What do you think they're saying?"

Pondering my words, she says something to leave me bemused. "I believe that they're talking about our plans to form a new clan together."

Wandering back, Pansa offered to pull the load of wood, roots and moss, so I began weaving some new fibers. As we traipse on, I continue to mull her words over in my head. *Why would she speak such things? Was she teasing, or was she simply being modest?* All my thoughts become increasingly convoluted with one another, as though I weave my very mind betwixt my fingers. I'm almost certain she was just having fun. Almost.

We arrive at our site, and I help Pansa unload the materials. She suggests adding an additional door off from her room, so she can come and go at her leisure, without the worry of disturbing me.

I cut the timber, notch the limbs at the ends, and set them in place. Pansa reinforces them at the base with some mud and shale. The walls and roof are done in the same fashion as the main part, save for a little window.

We step back to examine our craftsmanship. It looks absolutely marvelous.

"Thank you for doing this for me, Kitso. It means a lot." She gives me a long hug, which I embrace.

That moment confirmed what I have valued all my life: Helping others is what makes my life worth living, and I intend on helping everyone that I can. I am personally led to believe that Pansa is of the same mind when it comes to everyone else.

* * *

I let go of Kitso, and head into my room to spruce up the inside. I settle a plank of bark on one of the walls with a couple branches, take out my trinket, and place it neatly in the center. It looks a little lonely, but it's sure to get some company soon.

"Kitso," I call out. He comes in, and I point to the shelf. "What do you think?"

He removes the lime carving from a pouch, and sets it beside the one I found. "I think she looks much happier with company," he states with a chuckle.

"Do you think she'll find any more friends?"

He sets a hand under his chin, as if in deep thought, and smiles. "If not by nature, then I'll see to it myself." He nods, and goes about his business.

I watch him leave, and then look back at the shelf.

When I go back outside, I see Kitso weaving. "Have you ever learned to weave anything else?"

"Like what?" he asks me.

"Well, I've seen some other things made—baskets, artwork, or even clothing—with a loom."

"What's a loom?"

I giggle. "I suppose that answers that."

"Heh, I guess I cannot say that I've woven anything other than roots and plant fibers for survival purposes.

If we happen upon the chance, I would love to learn how to weave many different things."

I forget that most everything he has come to learn was out of the necessity for survival. Much of what I know was derived from caring for my clan.

I ask him if he would show me how to prepare fish as he does. He says that if I catch some more tonight, then he will happily show me. I decide to fish at the pond, this time with my claws—I must keep my senses sharp for the coming season.

I return with two for dinner tonight, and he hands me his knife.

"Are you alright with me using this?" I scan over it in my hand—it's incredible.

"I am more than alright. It was my grandfather's."

I jerked promptly, staring with wide eyes.

"No, really, it's okay. I'd trust you with more than a mere knife."

Kitso guides my every movement with illustrating hands, correcting me whenever I stray, and praising me as I do well. Watching him work with food always seemed so simple, but I never imagined just how much detail he focuses on when preparing it.

Whenever I had made a meal for my family, I tended to just throw something together. So long as they were fed, I had one less thing to worry about. Cooking here with Kitso has taught me all the intricacies of actually appreciating the fine details of care that can go into a dish to bring out the best qualities.

I've seen many meals prepared from all sorts of locations, and I have come to know of various techniques and methods, but there was something very peculiar about the way he tended to dinner. It was as though his very heart extended not only to the food, but through it, tailored to whoever savors it.

We settle by the fire pit that night, sharing a couple stories about life in general, and our aspirations—what we want to see, where we want to go, and how we came to decide these goals. It is evident to me that Kitso presents a great deal of enthusiasm for my direction.

I have spent a lot of time around others growing up, but they've always looked up to me for something they couldn't attain for themselves.

Kitso doesn't expect anything of me, other than being myself. The time he invests in me is totally selfless, and for the first time in my life, I feel truly cared for.

I head out to the river, wandering by the moon and starlight, and recall striding through the trees—it was such an exhilarating moment in time where I felt free. Instead of running from my problems, I was racing into a new experience. My time with Kitso has provided me an entirely fresh perspective on life, and I wanted to chase that to the end!

* * *

I sit atop a protrusion extended from up river—it hangs out over a bend, as though a hand is guiding the river's path. It rushes along freely, but not without direction and cause.

I am meditating, thinking about what has come of my adventure thus far, and considering what I want from it. If you were to ask me what I expected to find when I left my family for answers, I would have told you that I was unsure, and without direction or goal in mind. I'd have tried to generate an elaborate explanation —a facade to conceal my cluelessness, and my fear.

Now I feel like I can be true to myself, and I'm not afraid to admit that I didn't have any idea as to what I was doing or where I was going. I have a sense of guidance and control. I no longer fear the unknown, but embrace it.

The moon is set over the horizon, casting a brilliant reflection off the rapids—they dance about with the moon's light, reaching for her, longing to hold her, never being able to do so. Yet, they try with every passing night, never letting the opportunity pass by.

Standing up, I breathe the cool, night air, feeling reinvigorated, despite my approaching need for sleep. I catch a sudden updraft from the river, sending a slight mist about me, and a chill goes up my back. I shake off the cold feeling, and step away from the water.

The moon is undeniably beautiful.

"It is. She reminds me of myself."

You seem to be exuding a most pleasant demeanor tonight, Pansa.

"Thank you. I am feeling wonderful. Nothing could get me down."

Mist sprays upward, becoming denser, and breaches the ledge with a splash. Black smoke unfurls from the scattered water—blackness rivaling the night itself.

You're becoming reckless, losing sight of your objective.

"Actually, I feel as though I'm coming to terms with my real objective."

A crack in the atmosphere startles me with what sounds like glass shattering, as though lightning had struck by me, almost causing me to lose my footing. *Don't be a fool, Pansa! You'd not have survived those years without my help. I have guided you into your fate, and you have no other way.*

I stand motionless, hands at my side tense. As I begin heading back to camp, the smoke drifts in my stead, reforming itself in my path. I close my eyes, exhale, and glance down. A large parupeteng plant springs up, and blooms with a deep intensity. It faces me, inviting me to take from it. My hands clench into tight fists, my breathing hastening.

I'll always be here for you—

"*No!*" Enraged, I slam my foot into the ground, crushing the plant. My foot stings from the barbs, but the pain is distant in my anger. "I am *not* under your command anymore!"

You're wrong about him. He does not care for you!

"No, that's where *you're* wrong. He does care about me, and does what he can to help me, unlike you!"

I take off in a maddening sprint, pushing my way through the forest, twigs brushing my face as I fly by. They mark up my face, but I don't care. My foot sends needles up my leg with every step, but I had to get away from it—from the torment that follows me where I go.

I make my way back to our camp, and collapse on my hands and knees, entirely out of breath. I gasp for air, but seem to be unable to breathe. My vision grows darker at the edges of my sight... and a hand rests on my shoulder.

I lash out, striking Kitso across the face, and he stumbles onto the ground. He lies still for a moment, and there's a trace of blood on my hand. I slump my torso into the ground, crying, and beat the ground with a fist. Again, his hand rests upon my shoulder, and this time I fall silent, tears dropping into the dirt.

He says nothing, but remains there by my side, unmoving. He then begins to softly stroke my hair, and hums an unfamiliar tune. I want to stop crying, but am unable to do so.

"*Why?!*" I shout, incoherent to myself. "Why don't you run away from me...?!"

Kitso stops humming, but continues to run his hand through my hair.

"I don't understand." I weep almost inaudibly. "I just don't understand…"

He removes his hand, and sits on the ground. I can sense that he considers my words with severity. "You aren't meant to understand everything. I don't know what happened to you out there, but it's apparent to me that it has caused you a great deal of pain. I cannot promise to make it go away, but I can promise you one thing: that I'll always be here for you."

My heart skips a beat—I had to remind myself that it was Kitso speaking. I exhale, my face still on the ground, and then he says something almost expected.

"… You're bleeding."

If I wasn't in so much anguish, I probably would have laughed.

I am resting up against a tree a couple yards from the fire, opposite our shelter. Kitso adds more kindling, and starts turning the coals about.

Slowly, I work on a parupeteng flower. I know that it must hurt him to watch me like this.

"I'm sorry you had to see me like that. I just deal with… these terrors. It's like they take control of me, making me say and do things that I don't want to. I retain complete consciousness, but feel as though I'm watching my actions through a tiny window."

"I understa—"

"Please don't. Don't act like you understand what I deal with."

"I mean—" He shakes his head. "No, that's not what I meant. Look, I understand that you're dealing with an incredibly hard situation, and even though I could not possibly comprehend exactly what you are going through, I do know that if you had the choice, you would be done with it all.

"You don't allow these things to happen on your own accord. They don't even enter your head until you're faced with stress. And I know beyond any doubt that you really love your family and will do anything for them, but they too must have caused inundant amounts of pressure in your life."

I hide my face in my hands, my fingers pressing into my forehead. *How can you know these things, Kitso? How could he possibly know…?*

"I don't know if you believe the things I say, but I do notice these things, however insignificant they might seem to you."

Neither of us say anything for quite some time.

He finally speaks again. "It really is amazing."

"What do you mean?"

"The will-fire."

"Alright, I am genuinely confused."

He almost smiles, absorbed into his own thoughts. "Your will-fire. It's what I call that driving force that enables someone to do something, despite the odds against them. A totally uninhibited, burning passion to set forth to accomplish anything, no matter the magnitude, and no matter the costs."

I get up from where I sit, amble nearer to him on the other side of the fire, and sit back down on the ground.

"How can you tarry around somebody like me? Someone who is reckless and out of control, and even out of touch with reality."

He takes more time before answering. "It is because I see the real you, scared to put herself forward, and when presented the chance, hides behind herself. Yet, there she remains, wanting to be seen, even if not heard. To be recognized would mean the world to her."

I quite literally cannot find any words. He sees my total reality, when I can't even see beyond myself. Then I find them—the words. I take every desperate measure within to find something else, *anything* else to say.

But alas, they present themselves, bold and clear.

"Please don't think me weird for saying this... but... I think I love you."

* * *

Her words reverberate in my head, endlessly echoing. I am unsure why, but I feel as though I have always shared the same sentiment for her. Was I confusing my compassion for infatuation, or was I only denying myself connection with her in such a way?

She went to bed shortly after saying it. I remained weaving at the fire, trying to clear my mind. It is unlike any member of the Vulpani to share in such relations with those outside our specie, but did that make it wrong otherwise? Though unheard of, I cannot reason as to why it was this way.

Of course, there was the fact that we couldn't have children of our own...

I rest my hands in my lap, thinking silently. *Why am I even considering this matter? If I'm to travel, I will have to take up a mate for myself to begin a new tribe.* "I can't expect myself to accomplish that with another specie!"

I quickly place a hand over my mouth—I hadn't even realized that my thoughts made their way into actual words. I glance over at our shelter, and hear little else but the crackling flames and an owl. I rest my head into my palms. "What is wrong with me?" I whisper. "Do I, or do I not also feel this way for her?"

That remarkable attitude of yours is bound to find yourself a wonderful mate, Kitso.

Vulpena spoke those words when I was younger. What else was it that she said? I know there was something...

Whoever she may be, just love her for who she is.

The words could not have been made any more simple. I recognize her for who she is, and I readily acknowledge that with my actions.

... So why could I not love her also?

Chapter 6

I rose to the light of another day, filled with warmth—a pleasant afternoon breeze drifted through the crevices in the walls. I imagine they will need to be patched up before the atmosphere becomes brisk with cold.

I sense something roasting... no, grilling from outside.

As I peer out the door, Pansa greets me with a simper, and turns back to breakfast. "Somebody slept well," she says, as if speaking to the fish over the heat. "I wonder if he's hungry."

"Hi, Pansa. I see that you've put the skills I've shown you to great use."

I settle on the log next to her, and she hands me my portion. "Yep, and I even gathered my own mushrooms and herbs for them. I wanted it all to be as fresh as possible."

"That is very considerate of you." I breath in the aroma, and find it quite pleasing.

"I hope you enjoy it, love." She helps herself to more.

I place the piece I was about to ingest back down, and look at her. She looks into my eyes, a gentle gaze presenting itself. "What? I didn't recall hearing you deny anything last night, unless I'm mistaken, in which case, I'm sorry."

I look down, and laugh. "No, I suppose I didn't."

"But... I also don't remember you saying anything either."

She maintains her gaze, her eyes large and beautiful. I try to push myself to speak, but find it easier to let the words work themselves out. "I love you, too."

Pansa embraces me. I hold her, and rest my mouth in her soft, warm fur. Her ear twitches each time I exhale.

"Don't ever leave me, Kitso."

"I won't, Pansa. I promise, I won't."

Finishing our breakfast, we pack our tools and a couple waterskins, and head out into the forest for additional materials to once again expand upon our homestead.

As the cooler season approaches, leaves are just beginning to take on their new colors. Bits of yellow glaze the tips of them, and a few even decide to take an early descent. I notice extra voices up in the canopy today, as if a large assembly betwixt all companions feathered have gathered to discuss this year's flight south. They don't seem to mind us.

Pansa points out some sturdy-looking, younger trees, and so we work at them, bringing one back each time it is felled. We're going to need to replace the main structure's frame entirely if we are to withstand all the weather to come. We accumulate a couple dozen healthy logs over a couple hours, and then spend a couple more digging up clay from the pond—we decided on a brick foundation.

After a short rest, I tear down the slightly decayed walls of our shelter, level the ground a bit more, and outline a large square. Pansa is working the clay into bricks, and setting them in the kiln, one after another. Setting the posts for the new frame, I notch them, and interlock crossbeams.

I work on building a sloped top to set upon the frame, as she begins to carry the bricks over to set a foundation of sorts. She makes a shallow trench along the perimeter, and sets them in, sealing crevices with a thicker mud-mixture. She then helps me settle the roof, and I take up laying the bricks while she follows in my stead to seal them up. It is late in the afternoon, and with the wall at a good start, we head to the pond for a break.

I kneel down at the water's edge to wash my hands, and splash some water into my face to clear the sweat and dirt. I draw my tunic up to dry, and take note that Pansa has already undressed—as usual—for a swim.

Trying to focus elsewhere, I go to rewash my face to cool myself from the warmth surfacing.

Pansa must have noticed. She giggles. "You wash your face too much, and you'll lose fur that way!" She takes a plunge, sending strong ripples careening across the water.

Thinking I'm safe to converse now, I look back up, and forgot that much of the pond is fairly shallow, and although she's a bit shorter than myself, it matters little as she's standing to wash herself thoroughly.

I am unsure what to do with myself, and sit down, resting my feet into the water. I look around, admiring the scenery for what it is—leafy tree tops rustling about in the soft breeze, a squirrel practicing its acrobatics, the sun casting bright rays downward to illuminate the pond. I hadn't been aware that Pansa wandered nearer to me, and as soon as I noticed, she splashes me playfully.

Taken completely by surprise, I almost fall backward, and shed the moisture from my eyes. "Hey, what are you—" I begin, and find myself lost for words entirely.

She has her head cocked to one side. "Does my form embarrass you, Kitso?"

Unable to hide my face this time, I clear my throat, and attempt to look slightly past her. "No... I—well, not entirely."

"You know, I don't think anyone should be ashamed of their body," she states plainly.

Before I can get out what I was to say, she dives under, and makes her way out to the center. She comes back up after a short moment. "You should enjoy a good swim, too!" she says, submerging once again.

I close my eyes. *Now I am certain she's teasing me. Either that, or just testing my integrity.* However I think of it, her jovial spirit fills me with an irrefutable joy.

* * *

Kitso never did join me for a swim yesterday, but it was to be expected. He regards me with a great sense of respect, and I am very fond of him for that.

Though, I can't help but to feel that he sometimes holds himself to a high degree of integrity for whatever his purpose might be. It isn't that I think any less of him for it—I just wish that he'd loosen up once in a while.

We completed the wall late into night, partially due to me enjoying my swim a bit longer than I had planned. I was just enjoying a chance to have some fun with Kitso, and I know he can't argue that.

Thankfully, it hadn't rained during the night, so we made haste on finishing the roof while we had light. I reminded Kitso about the thought of clay tiles for a roof. He instantly accepted such a novel idea, and spent a good part of the day unearthing extra clay.

I drew in the dirt to give him an idea on how he could tie some extra lengths of timber across the roof to support them. Kitso began that while I rotated tiles in and out of the kiln.

When he was done, he took his bow out to hunt. He returned with an adolescent boar, and when I gave him a discerning look, he assured me that it was indeed alone.

We dined on quite the roast that evening inside, a few tallow glims lit, our home ready for the coming frost.

"It's absolutely remarkable, Kitso."

He smiles at me. "It is because we worked on it together, never giving up until it was done."

"Well, yes, but I didn't necessarily mean just our home. It's been almost a week since we've gotten to know each other, but I feel like I've know you all my life. Is that strange?"

"Not at all. I feel the same way regarding you, as if we've been friends since childhood. I believe it has something to do with your playful nature."

She snorts. "Yeah, seems to be something you lack."

"Hey, despite my docile outer appearance, I am actually quite fun."

"Yeah, alright."

"No, really!" he assures me. Then he frowns. "I've just... always been taught to present my very best when coming to know someone. The Vulpani find it considerably difficult to make good friends, let alone retain them. I am unsure whether that makes sense to you or not."

I notice the tone in his voice. I do believe him, but find it almost impossible to imagine someone so naturally pleasant would have trouble with friendship. He makes it sound as if I am his only real friend.

"In fact, sometimes I feel as though you're my only friend..."

As if that wasn't confirmation enough.

I place a hand on his shoulder, just as he always did for me. "I do believe you, Kitso. And I am very happy to know you for life."

"It's just that..." His voice causes me to feel unnerved for some reason. "I am not sure what my tribe would think of you and I. Together, that is."

My appetite is gone. "...What are you saying?"

"I am only saying that I don't know how everyone would react to us traveling together. They might feel put-off."

Rising, I walk toward the door, and stop. "Why would that be a problem?"

I spin around, and dart a cold stare. "Was it all just a ploy?"

"What?"

"Were you just tailing me for your own benefit? So you could at least look successful to your tribe?"

"No, that's not what I—"

"You couldn't manage a proper structure, so instead leveraged me into helping you to survive, thinking you could buy my labor with food and shelter."

"That isn't—"

"You never really needed me at all, did you?"

"I—"

"Did you?!"

"Pansa!" He stood over me, shouting. Before he had even realized that he stood, I was already sitting on the ground, weeping into my hands.

I felt terrible accusing him of such, but even more, I was upset that I had let my feelings get the better of me. Letting my words carelessly wander, I had probably hurt him more than I have hurt anyone before. He was only defending himself because I had attacked him—I had made myself the antagonist.

I try to run out the door—he catches me, and I flail a hand out of shock. He takes an inadvertent blow to his face, refusing to let go. "Pansa, listen to me, please!"

Ceasing struggle, I find reluctant willingness to allow him the benefit of the doubt, and he wastes no breath in senseless justification.

"What I said was wrong. I should not have taken my tribe's feelings above yours. Truth be told, I am not at all sure how they would react to me being with you. But you know what? I am not afraid, and I will not allow anything spoken against us to sever our relation, no matter what!"

I don't say anything, eyes closed, hardly breathing.

"When I promised that I'd not leave you, I meant it with all my heart. And if my tribe would want nothing to do with you, then they would want nothing to do with me. I would sooner abandon my own before you."

I sniff, and wipe my eyes. "I could never ask you to do that, Kitso..."

"I know you wouldn't ask that of me, and that is precisely why I would do it. I doubt your father or friends would be as accepting—"

"It wouldn't matter."

He sounds surprised to here that. "But... I thought your family meant more than anything to you."

I force a short laugh. "They do mean more than anything to me. It wouldn't matter because they wouldn't care either way." I sigh heavily. "I still love them all, and would still do whatever I could to help, but I honestly doubt they would care whether I were alone, or wound up having a rat for a mate, so long as they think that I'm happy."

"Would you still be happy with me, even if we couldn't have a family together?"

Blinking, I stare off into space. "It—I don't… I don't even know if I want one, okay?" I smirk then, eyes glossed over. "Now, shut up before you say something else stupid."

He takes my word as an obvious cue, and makes content with that. Without warning, I embrace him into a kiss—he could do very little else but reciprocate in that moment.

Kitso appears to allow my sentiment to sink in, and that is good enough for me.

Chapter 7

The first frost of the season comes that night, and I wake to a chill. "Ugh, not unexpected, but no less unpleasant."

"What's that, hun?" Pansa went out a little before I got up to replenish our supply of kindling and firewood. She was outside now, beginning a fire.

"Oh, I was just stating how unpleasant this cold can be, especially the early frost."

"Hey, you got to enjoy the nice, hot weather, so now's the time for crisp and cool," she retorts in a teasing manner.

"Yeah, but that doesn't mean I'll enjoy it."

After Pansa got a good flare going, we went out together to hunt to begin storing a supply of rations. The plan was to keep some of the meat to salt and preserve for the cold when it came around. If there was one thing neither of us wanted to run short of, it was food.

I had no fortune this time, but Pansa managed a rabbit and a squirrel. I wanted to eat the rabbit for dinner, but she believed the meat would keep better, so I settled for squirrel. We made a soup from it, seasoned with some mushroom and peppery ginger roots I found while hunting. It was more satisfying than I thought it would be.

She told me she was going to search for some more parupeteng flowers. Although it didn't make me happy, I am just thankful that she bothered to mention it at all. She must have considered my feelings about the matter.

I go off on my own to look for some minerals at the river. I wanted to carve Pansa a new friend for her shelf.

When I arrive, I notice a bear fishing. Taking care not to disturb, I make my way down river, and notice the water moving slightly faster. *Must be a decline,* I think to myself. *There is bound to be great sediment at the base.*

I continue to traipse the river's edge until I reach a small waterfall, and gingerly climb down on the slippery stone. Scanning over the water, a gleam catches my sight. I remove my clothes, set my belongings aside, and settle into the water. It's cold, but I adjust as I can.

I wade over to where I saw the glare, but see nothing. "Huh, I was sure there was something shining over here." I keep looking, but don't notice anything. I begin to shudder, and hop out. Shaking and brushing myself off, I see it again. "Where is that light coming from...?"

Looking the rock face over, I realize that it was a reflection, coming from a stone set into a nook above. I sigh at my obliviousness, and determine how to reach it. I feel for some holds, and after planning a route, I grab a small pick from my satchel, and head up the rocks.

It takes a while, but I manage to work the brilliant, blue mineral from the cliff. Arms sore, I ease myself back down holding both pick and stone in my mouth, but slip, dropping both of them. I gasp a bit too late, and breathe water, but am determined to not lose my prize. I hold what breath I had, lungs burning, and grasp at the stone. It rolled along the bottom, out of my reach. I come back up, clear my chest out, and dive again.

I retrieved the stone, but lost my pick. I lie down on the riverside for a while, resting and drying in the sun before dressing. I admire the stone while I lay there. "Well, that wasn't very fun, Kitso... but it sure was worth it."

I wander back to the camp, exhausted.

Pansa sees me, and runs over. "Oh my, you look *terrible!* What happened?!"

"I... went for an unprecedented swim. I also lost a tool of mine in the process."

She crosses her arms, raising an eyebrow. "I hope it was worth it."

"Oh, it was! It definitely was worth it."

"So, what did you find?"

"A bear that was fishing. And... a surprise." I grin mischievously.

Pansa becomes excited. "Oh, what did you get me?"

I lean in close to her ear to whisper, at which she anticipates with impatience. "... It's a secret."

She shoves me, and I giggle. She pretends to be upset, arms crossed again. "I don't like surprises."

I play along. "Sure you do, especially the secret kind!"

Pansa huffs. "If you loved me, you'd tell me."

"But that's why I cannot tell you! I love you too much to present something that isn't ready."

Smiling with amusement, she goes back to tending the site.

Lately, Pansa has been more inclined to focus on the smaller details of our base, as opposed to the larger ideas we had whilst getting to know one another. I imagine she is becoming more comfortable with revealing her tender nature for all things considered.

I head inside, and set a small light to work by. I size up the mineral, brushing it free of any dirt and dust. It appears to be a deep blue sapphire. Making sure to work on it whenever Pansa distracted herself, I make good progress that evening.

I'm called out to share in another fish dinner, so I set my chisel and gem aside, and join her.

"We've got some trout tonight. The fish have been growing fantastically from the warm season. I also roasted some greens to go with them."

I sample some of each. "It all tastes remarkable. You must know a fair bit more about food than you let on."

"Yeah... I like to be humble when it comes to cooking. Some of your work still impresses me."

"Well, you had better not let me get used to meals like this!" I laugh.

"I'll take that as a challenge." She winks.

I decide to ask her about something that had me wondering since I met her—something that never left my thoughts. "Pansa... if you don't mind my asking, what was it like for you, growing up with your family as a whole?"

She has a distant look on her face. "When I was quite young, my mother had passed away, as I had mentioned. The burden of my own fell mostly upon me since, as my father had difficulty supporting us children by himself. We had many troubled times—sourcing our food, keeping safe from opposing clans, maintaining sanity from emotional distress. It was challenging to try and fit into all roles as mother, sister, daughter, and even friend.

"I was told that my mother used parupeteng flowers to cope with life before she had me, but my own father was primarily the one who maintained that when I came to be. Eventually, everything became too much for me to handle—it was my own body that gave out—and I lost all that I was but my life. I wasn't even conscious to my own doing anymore.

"At that point, father decided he'd seen enough of my destruction, and drugged me with something. I still don't know what it was, but I slept for many days on end. It was then that I felt I had failed my entire line and everything we worked for. So I left, hoping that one day I would become strong enough to help once again." Pansa started to cry into her hands.

I put an arm around her, and she leaned into me. "Everyone has limitations, and I imagine anyone with enough sense wouldn't utterly destroy themselves for the sake of everyone else. That wouldn't do any good."

She speaks through her fingers, sobbing quietly. "But I am supposed to be the strong one, and I left them. That was selfish of me."

"No, you weren't being selfish. You gave more than you expected to receive. And you are strong. Far stronger than myself, and anyone I have ever known. There are not many others in this world that would have sacrificed everything in your situation. It just took you a lot longer to reach your limit than you anticipated, and so you may have believed that you could go on forever, not realizing the outcome of it all."

Pansa stops crying, and continues to breathe heavily, sighing every so often. "You still amaze me, Kitso. You always seem to know me better than myself, even the times you never knew me. I still don't understand how."

"It is because we all need someone who can see the things in our life that we aren't able to. I don't believe we're made to take on life alone. If you were to ask me, I'd find it to be totally asinine to try."

She looks up at me, smiling. "Then I am very glad that I've chosen a mate who takes my feelings into such consideration."

It is night now, and Pansa went for a long walk to clear her mind before bed. I handed over my knife to take with her, and though she insisted her claws were enough, she understood that I felt better to contribute something to her outing. When I was certain that she had left, I went back inside to finish sculpting my gift for her.

I have carved a few gemstones before, but this one was challenging to work with. Not only was it larger than any other one I've done, but it was also pretty tough. It would last for life if I did it correctly.

This time, I went for a depiction of a panther standing with a fist held overhead, as though she were proud for being victorious. When I got all the angles done, I started polishing it.

Pleased with my work, I went into her room, and set it along with the other two. I smiled to myself. "I wonder if she'll notice..."

I take a little walk myself afterward, and find the night air to be quite soothing. I don't care for the cold at all, but I do enjoy a quiet night walk now and again. Whether part of my daily schedule, or if it is because the night is so peaceful, I couldn't say.

I look up to the sky—the trees are silhouetted against the clear, star-filled night. The moon hides amongst the treetops as I walk. Maybe she, too, enjoys an occasional private stroll across the night.

It is becoming more brisk with each passing night. I spot the fishing bear returning from another trip by the river. He lumbers along, and wanders into his cave, content for sleep. I find myself wishing to be that bear, preparing for an extended rest throughout the cold season. However, it would do me no favor to let my survival skills slip away in favor to a long, uninterrupted sleep.

I am grateful for this time to test everything that I am. From setting up a decent abode, to taking every measurement in ensuring survival for this trial, I feel that I've come to a crossroads in my life, and am free to take whichever path besets me.

My experience will be my trodden road—my desires, the light I travel by. What is determined will decide what is had.

I can make no wrong decision.

* * *

I've returned from my night walk, and Kitso isn't here. He may have also gone out. I set a small fire for his return, and head inside to sleep.

I enter my room, and sit for some meditation, when I look up to the shelf bearing my figurines. A faint, blue light catches my sight, and I stand back up to investigate. Sure enough, there was a third figure betwixt the others.

She sported a lovely blue finish, and stood there, reigning over her new domain. She was proud, like myself, to have made new friends so easily. *He really is incredible. I look forward to all that we'll share together.*

The morning dawns, and I rise early this day. It is very cold—dew has formed upon my fur as I slept. I shake off, and peer into Kitso's room. He looks restful and happy as he sleeps.

I step outside, and breath deeply to greet the dawn. I don't remember having any dreams, but I have an odd feeling that I spent all night thinking about today and what it'll hold.

Giving the fire pit a decent start, I prepare a small breakfast of vegetation, feeling that a good dose of fiber

and greens would set my morning off well enough. I am certain that Kitso would prefer something a bit more hearty, so I go out for a hunt.

Though I have never given much thought to a future involving a family to call my own, I did consider very much the possibility of a mate, and what they might be like.

Someone who would cherish and care for me, and would consider all I have to say, however minuscule. Someone that could love me for who I was, and not what I did, or how I lived my life. Such a mate would appear as only a dream to anyone with enough sense about them.

Now that I have found a mate who seemingly matches all my desires, I wonder if it really is all but a dream. If so, I don't ever want to wake.

I happen upon a rabbit hopping about in the woods, and track it for a short time. When I find its run, I set up a trap, and continue to seek more game.

I find a buck not much farther, and brace myself. My adrenaline begins to build as I prepare for the thrilling chase that is about to ensue. Though he does not expect me, he'll very soon notice me, and I will be there to race for his life.

Slowly, I encroach on his territory, and flex my hands, claws shining in the morning light. "You're mine," I whisper.

I burst out from cover, sprinting full force after my prey. The buck inevitably decided not to stand around waiting for me.

It leapt clear from my path, dashing to and fro amongst the trees. I kept pace with my own acrobatic display. Around boulders, over streams—through the woods we ran, headed in the same direction, but toward totally opposite goals—his was to live, and mine to kill. Edging ever closer, I prepare for closure, and pounce off the next rock he bounds. I sink my claws into its back, and finish with a swift bite.

"You were fast, but not quite fast enough," I say to my prey, washing blood from my fur at the river, my adrenaline just beginning to recede. "You'll make for a fine dinner, and several rations thereafter."

I return with my prize slung over my back. Kitso notices me, and runs over to help. "Impressive, Pansa! Did you catch that on foot?"

"I did, and he gave me quite a run! That ought to be enough exercise for the day. I had also set a trap for a rabbit, but it was empty." I hand him my kill, and roll my shoulders around, feeling tensed up from my excursion. "I am going for a splash in the pond to relax."

"Alright, I'll begin preparing our dinner."

I cleanse the remnant of sweat and dirt from myself, and find the waters to be much colder this afternoon. The first hoar is nigh, its frigid touch upon the atmosphere. I quickly finish up and head back.

The air is laden with the scent of game, and I began to hunger. The rush from a successful hunt is extraordinary, but enjoying the fruit of your bounty is so much more satisfying. This was only exemplified by the work of such a wonderful cook.

Kitso is hunched over the fire pit, incredibly focused on a pair of steaks he's prepared. He seasons them with some herb mixture, watching the flavors take to the meat. I don't think he notices that I've returned.

Fervently, he tends to the meat as grease drips from the tips, sizzling on the open flame. The aroma is overwhelming, and my stomach chimes in with expectancy. This seems to get his attention.

Kitso looks over to me with a grin. "I bet you could sense it from the pond. It is just about finished, so feel free to relax some more while I furnish the last touches." He turns back to the steaks.

"I am perfectly contented with watching you at work. It amazes me what you can do with what you're given." My comment seems to make him blush lightly.

When the meal is done, Kitso hands me my cut on the plate I made, a few sprigs of fresh herb upon it. I nod with appreciation. "What will you eat yours with?"

He looks his steak over, presumably checking the quality of his work. "I'll be fine eating it as it is. I enjoy savoring the taste of the meat."

I pick mine up and take a bite, the juices running from where I bit. As I chew, my eyes begin to water. The flavor is absolutely indescribable.

"Is it okay, Pansa?" Kitso asks with grave concern. "I didn't use too much spice, did I?"

I swallow, and wipe my eyes. "No, not at all!" I assure him. "It's… it's so good! The flavor and aroma make me feel at home again." I can't stop feeling like I want to cry from the ecstasy it fills me with—I take another bite, before my body has time to do so. My mouth absorbs every ounce of taste as I mull it over.

"Oh, well thank you. I was afraid that I might have over-seasoned it. Seasoning isn't something I utilize very often, so feedback is helpful."

I place my hand upon his. "I promise you, you've got your method well-established, Kitso."

We talk about my hunting experience—I share with him many adventures I've had with my clan as we provided for family and friends alike.

"We were prided from many others for our hunting prowess. There were those who would travel just to witness what we were capable of first-hand. Ambassadors have been sent on behalf of their lords to offer a number of dowries to the women of our clan solely for their abilities to provide.

"Of course, every one of them were turned away. Our bonds could not be broken for gold or silver. That isn't to say we haven't accepted offers from merchants to procure the freshest of meats for their caravans. We're more than willing to turn a few good deals for the betterment of everyone as a whole, so long as our families aren't put to risk."

"I would very much love to see your kin in the thick of a magnificent hunt."

"I am sure you will some day, Kitso. I'd even go so far to say that us women would be thrilled to invite you along with us." I extend a nail. "What you lack in… felid equipment, you more than make up for in speed and athletic ability."

He bows his head slightly. "I would be honored to be had along for such an opportunity."

I giggle. "And I'm certain that we would also be honored to have you join us." I eat more, and wonder about Kitso and his tribe's history. "What about you, then? What sort of feats has your tribe accomplished that you are proud of?"

He finishes chewing before speaking. "I would say that I am proud of all that my family has endured."

"What do you mean?"

"From the time my parents had begun to head our family, Vulpena instilling what she could at my young age, we resettled from the tribe to reside on a great expanse of plains. My mother, father, brother, sister—It was just the five of us, enjoying life as it were, making the most of every day. I led a mostly happy life, and was content with what we had at the time. But eventually, we had to travel to retain sustenance. Despite us being in a decent place, it couldn't provide entirely all we needed as we grew older.

"So we moved on to another location, hoping to find that which could support our needs. We happened across several decent places, though none were to our liking. Finally, it was decided that we'd live amongst others from afar, so we settled in our new home. Our surroundings were more structured, what with other locals more involved in the lives of fellow inhabitants. But it suited us by making things easier to manage.

"Not long after we were settled, my parents had been met with many struggles together, and so my father had left for a time. I never knew all the details of the situation, but I knew that it was abnormal for a family to undergo such, particularly of Vulpani origins. We made do with the events at hand, and though we did our very best, it wasn't enough to maintain our homestead. It was inevitable that we moved on."

I had a distant look on my face. "It sounds as though your upbringing wasn't much more stable than mine."

Kitso nods lightly. "We ended up moving several more times before we wound up living amongst ourselves again. My brother made his own way in the midst of our transitions—it was disheartening to see him leave. Since we weren't with the tribe then, he had not undergone his trial, but it was believed to be for his betterment. My mother, sister and I continued to live together in years to come. Becoming increasingly stable over time, we all felt it was time to relocate once more.

"We were discontented with our seeming isolation from family, so we resettled amongst the Vulpani tribe —it gave us great comfort with renewal of stability. Mother became the lead huntress, and the head of our provision. Vulpena picked up on her mentorship with me as though we'd never left. She's my godmother, you know. She'd vowed to always be there for me should anything happen to my own mother."

I give him a friendly smile. "She must be a wonderful caretaker of a woman."

"Oh yes, very much so. I regard her second to my parents, and would do anything for her. She has ensured my upbringing was filled to the brim with the utmost care and tutelage. I know that she'll be sad when I return from my trial, only to leave again."

"I am sure that she supports you fully on your decision," I say.

"Yes, she does. I hope that she finds another to raise in my stead just as soon."

After we finish our food, I wash my plate and set it back inside. I peek in my room to check on my little friends. "I'll be back soon. Kitso and I are going to spend some time out together."

I grab our fishing spears, Kitso's satchel, a couple waterskins, and go back outside. "Kitso, do you want to go fishing with me?"

He looks over, smiling. "I'd love to, Pansa. Just let me finish up here."

We arrive at the river, each of us holding our spears. I give him a refresher course, and let him go first. After a few attempts, he doesn't manage to get anything, and we trade places. He watches me as I spear one, and hand it to him to pack away. I get another, and let him try again.

This time, he gets one, and shouts excitedly. "Got it! I was sure I'd not get anything this time."

"Great job, Kitso! Will that do it for you?"

"No way," he remarks. "I want to get as many as you do today!"

I laugh. "Okay, good luck!"

He gets another fish, and swaps with me to take a short break. "That's two for two," I say, and take a sip of water.

I get two more before I go back to the riverside, and Kitso takes another turn. He successfully nabs a third fish. "Three for me, so one to go."

About five minutes later, he's panting.

"Want to call it a day?" I ask him.

"No... I want to try one last time."

He stretches, and readies his spear, scanning the water intently. *I wonder what's taking him so long to strike.*

Finally, without so much as a blink of an eye, he stabs downward, and draws back up. There are two fish flopping wildly on the end.

"Alright, I did it!" He jumps and throws a fist in the air, and almost slips.

I clap with glee for him. "Awesome! I got to hand it to you Kitso, I think you've pretty much mastered the art of spear-fishing! I consent to your victory today."

He hops back over, and stuffs his catch in his satchel with the others. "Thank you, Pansa, for teaching me with patience and perseverance. I don't like to give up on anything."

"So I've come to notice. It makes me happy that you picked up on it so easily. I'd better be careful what I teach you, or we just might end up competing on everything!" I give him a playful shove, and he pushes me back.

Okay, you asked for it! I slowly let him walk a few paces ahead, set my spear down, and tackle him from behind. He drops his gear, and we roll a few feet, tussling on the ground. He tries to flip me over, but I have him pinned, arms above his head. I giggle. "Just because you bested me in fishing today, doesn't mean you can best me in wrestling!"

He gets an arm free, and tickles me, causing me to loose my grip just enough. He grabs my arms, and rolls me on my side. "I may not be as strong or experienced as you, but I can hold my own, too!" Trying to hold my arms with one hand, he continues to tickle me.

Laughing, I wrench my hands free, and wrap him in a tight hug, disabling his ability to reach me. I flop back onto him, and press him into the ground. "Okay, give!"

"Never!" He gasps, trying to free himself.

After a moment of desperate struggle, he sighs and lies there. "Alright!"

"Yes? What is it?"

He breathes sharply out his nose. "I give in..."

I let him up. "You gave up so easily. And here I was thinking you don't like to give up on anything."

He sticks his tongue out, and laughs. "So I am not as strong as I thought."

It's evening now, and the fish are grilling over the fire, sending small billows of smoke upward. A brisk wind has picked up, making its way throughout the woods.

Kitso is working on the hide from the deer I brought earlier. He appears to be fashioning a sort of garment.

"What are you making?"

"I am working on a couple mantles to help keep us warm for the coming cold."

"That sounds wonderful. I have seen a few before, adorning the occasional merchant, but have never worn one myself."

"You're going to love it, I promise you."

I let Kitso work in peace, and head inside to relax. I pick up each of my three figurines adorning the shelf, kiss each of them, and replace them. "Kitso is such a great guy. If he's not careful, he'll spoil me." The statuettes stare back at me, complacent with their setting. "Oh, don't get me wrong. It makes me happy to know he values us enough to invest all he can." I sigh. "I just don't want him to feel like he's obligated, and wind up being turned away." I fish out a parupeteng flower.

As the evening fades into dusk, the sky becomes clearer, and stars begin to poke through the treetops. They sparkle to greet the growing darkness, reminding it that even in the night, the light still prevails.

Kitso has kept the fire going, his craft set aside. He's begun to salt the fish, the fire's warm glow illuminating him against the shadows of the trees.

"That ought to keep for quite a while," I mention.

"I am hoping so. I imagine it won't be easy to gather any after the frost. I am not fond of the thought of fishing in the ice and bitter cold."

He wraps them one by one in parchment, tied off with the fibers we made together.

"Where'd you find that parchment?"

"Oh, I had brought it with me since I left the tribe. I wasn't sure what to use it for until now."

"It seems to have some quality—a shame to use it for food preservation."

"I agree," he replies. "Though sometimes, I find sacrifices just have to be made. It was a gift from my mother last year. She was surprised I hadn't used it. I suppose if the things you have never get used, it's a waste all the same."

"That makes a lot of sense. There have been times where a good meal has been made that I wanted to wait on eating, only to have it spoil. I guess it has to do with my nature of trying to preserve everything I can. But not everything is meant to be held onto for so long, I guess."

Kitso wraps the last fish. "Yeah, you're right. But then, some things are meant to be kept, even if nobody else holds the value in it that we do. I will admit that I am a pack-rat at times."

I smile. "I am glad that we share a keen sense of preservation. There are so many good things in the world that don't deserve to be forgotten."

I bid Kitso a good night with a hug, and head to bed.

* * *

I see Pansa off to her slumber, embracing a warm hug as she makes her way inside.

She is always so passionate about every interaction betwixt ourselves. It is as though every situation is graced with a prismatic perspective and a breath of fresh air.

I sit in silence for a long while, meditating on my everything that has become. *I am so thankful that Pansa has come into my life. I honestly doubt I could imagine life without her presence after I conclude this time of mine.*

I've long decided to adventure beyond my time of trial, and I have chosen an unorthodox mate to share my future with.

Now, there is only one thing left to discover—where it all will lead me.

Chapter 8

The following day brings with it a brisk wind—it is slow-blowing, but cold. Surely another frost is besetting.

Pansa has gone off to hunt the morning away. I believe that she is adamant about our provisions lasting us beyond the first snowfall, which she says may be within a few weeks. She has traveled far more than I have, and has seen many varying weather patterns across the lands, so I have plenty of reason to believe her claim.

I bring out the mantles to continue my work. I want to get them done by the day's end, as the sky is bright and clear. The sun provides a great amount of light this early afternoon. Its shining rays help fend off the wind's bitter chill.

With a good fire taking, I evaluate my progress and pick up where I left. A songbird keeps me company overhead, and I wonder to myself why it hasn't gone south yet. *Maybe there is unfinished business to tend, or perhaps family to raise.*

The cold season provides many challenges to fauna everywhere, no matter the specie. The birds both prepare to take flight for warmer climate, and others come to settle in for the season. Rodents rework their burrows and store up sustenance for the cold. Bears are making their way about, maintaining an exceptional diet to endure a long hiatus of dormancy. And we Vulpani do our best to fortify our settlement and preserve all the food we can.

Some of us exercise a warrior's diet. Though I tend to have a voracious appetite, I understand the necessity of such a diet, adapting it well into my life. Pansa thinks it strange that I do such a thing, commenting on how this season should hold just the opposite for someone of my stature.

Speaking of Pansa, I wonder how the Panteo manage their seasonal preparation. Now that she is apart from what she has known all her life, how will that affect her plans? Does her clan have a collective effort toward longevity, or does everyone focus on their families? Will she consider how I have prepared for my trial a viable means to prevail?

Before I know it, her mantle is finished, as the sun grazes the upper tier of the canopy. I take a small break, set my work inside, and decide to hunt also. I withdraw my bow and quiver from storage, and head out deep into the forest. If there is game to be had at this time, they will not be near settlement of any kind.

A while later, I cross an elk. Quite like the one Pansa had found the day before, although a bit smaller. I go to nock an arrow, but before I can take aim, he spots me, and runs. I let out a small sigh, and continue onward.

I come to a small clearing amidst a marsh, and see two quails hiding amongst the brush. I wait until they distract themselves, and loose an arrow after one of them, causing it to drop in place. Before the other takes notice of what had happened to its companion, I let another arrow fly, and it too falls abrupt.

As I wander over to collect my prizes, I see a wild jaguar several yards off. Before it happens upon me, I gather the quails up, and make haste for our site. Now was not the time to attempt to make a new "friend".

I approach our base, and hear what sounds to be rummaging. Pansa must have found some game to store.

As I near, something drops and shatters. "Get *off* of me!" My heart jumps, and I drop the quails as I dash around the back of our home. I quickly draw an arrow and set it, quieting my breath.

"Well look at this! A fine pair of mantles, and a fine lass," a guttural voice sounds. A second voice, deeper and bolder-sounding, chimes in. "Hey, I saw her first. Besides, her pelt is much finer—*very* smooth..."

"Unhand me, you brute!" A sharp smack follows, and it seems Pansa made way for the door. I round a nearby tree to get a better view of the front.

"Playing hard-to-get, girly? I love this game!" The deep voice belongs to a man resembling a grey wolf. He goes after Pansa as a second figure exits.

A younger voice with a slight rasp belongs to this one, appearing to be a large bilge rat. His brown fur is rough and smudged. He stands a few feet out from the door. "Don't harass her too much! We wouldn't want any company."

I am unsure who the first voice is—I don't wait to find out. The wolf pins Pansa against a crag of the hill. I take my aim, and send an arrow into his left thigh.

"Aargh!" He falls to the ground, grasping his leg.

Before the rat manages to turn, I am running at him with my knife. He barely notices me in time, and jumps out of the way, almost tripping. I lunge for him, and get the wind knocked out of me from my right side. I am sprawled on the ground, and look up. A looming figure stands before me, two blunt tusks protruding from his boar-ish face. The rat regains his step, and runs to the boar's side.

"Very unwise of you to meddle with us, lad," his guttural voice drawling from his mouth. I glance over to where Pansa was pinned, and find that she is missing. The wolf is tending to his leg on the ground.

I glance up at the boar intently, out of breath. He continues. "A few inches lower, and my tusks would have run you through. Don't you know these woods are dangerous to little girls, and wandering *heroes*?"

The rat laughs—they're obviously mocking us.

"Pansa... is not... a little girl." I manage to say.

"Oh, so you know the lass? Is she a friend of yours?"

"He's my mate!" Pansa flies off the roof of our home, digging her claws into the boar's back. He uproars in a rage, knocking her into the doorframe, but she hangs on. I jump up, and grapple the rat around his waist, sending him into the ground. He retaliates, ramming a fist into my stomach, and I fail to keep hold of him.

The rat then grabs Pansa, and pulls her from her perch.

The boar reels, a rapier held overhead. He stabs at my head, and I dodge, the blade grazing my cheek. He goes after Pansa. I quickly slash his ankle, causing him to scream and drop his weapon. I toss it from his reach and roll away,

jumping back up. A sharp pain rises throughout my front side, throwing me off balance.

I turn around to face the boar's gaze, a deadly leer. "You'll not live to see her die!" He charges, and I leap from his path. I throw my knife into his back, and he halts in his tracks. He lurches back, deeply gasps, and collapses. I crawl over to his body, and remove my knife.

I hear a scream, followed by a raspy howl, and find that Pansa had slashed the rat's face. He holds both hands over half his face, drops of blood finding their way through his fingers. "How dare you!" he shouts, as he runs off.

I find myself not far from the wolf, and walk slowly over to him, trying to ignore my pain. He finishes tying off his leg, looks up, and glances frantically around, before he spots the boar lying face-down in the dirt. He gasps, and stares up at me, uncertainty in his eyes.

"Unless you desire a like fate, you'll leave us immediately." My voice is dry and direct.

He darts off, a limping gait carrying him beyond our sight.

I lean over, hands on my knees, sighing heavily. I look over to Pansa—she is clutching at her head. "Hey, are you alright?"

She rubs her eyes. "He bit me..."

I notice a thin streak of blood drawn down from the side of her head—a portion of her right ear is missing.

* * *

"I'm ugly..." Pansa says, weeping into her arm.

"Oh, come now. It's hardly noticeable," I lie. I feel bad about it, but seeing almost half her ear missing makes me want to cry, too.

"I doubt that."

I rub some salve across the gash, and she flinches harshly. "Sorry," I whisper, and spread it very gently.

My chest is bound in straps of leather. A terrible pain rises with each breath I take. "We took quite a beating from those three."

She laughs, and seizes from pain. "You think? You nearly got killed. Twice."

"I know, and I truly am sorry for being so reckless. I was fraught with a bitter hatred for them treating you that way."

"My hero..." She pokes my ribs gently, and I double over. "Yeah, that's what I thought. You've got yourself at least one cracked rib."

"Alright," I say. "I won't endanger myself out of spite."

She looks at me, unconvinced.

"I promise."

Smiling, she breathes out, and turns over the coals, pressing a couple flames out of the pit—they instantly cast a glow about the shadows of the trees. "We had better rest a good deal tomorrow. The cold will not take kindly to our injuries."

Chapter 9

I come to the next day, and see that the sun has already begun to climb atop the canopy. I must have slept in, and the shorter days have only brought the night sooner.

I cross into Kitso's room, and sit beside him, my mantle draped over me. He is sprawled along his fell, as though he couldn't get comfortable last night. His half-finished mantle is covering his legs. As he dreams, his tail twitches slightly, and I can't help but to giggle.

Drawing a hand up to my ear, I notice that the wound isn't as terrible as I had thought. The part that's missing is noticeable, but only if I compare it with my other ear.

I decide to let him sleep in a little while longer, help myself to one of the preserved fish, and go outside.

Most of the leaves have fallen from their trees, and the ground is covered in sheets of reds and oranges, yellows and browns. It looks as though the forest has painted herself a fresh coat of protection to bid the transition a passing farewell, anticipating the bitter cold-to-be. Nearly all of the birds have gone, and the lively chorus that once adorned the treetops has now fallen silent. A chipmunk comes from under some brush, and runs over to our fire pit before taking notice of my presence, and stares at me for a good minute before moving on.

I finish my breakfast, and lounge about for a while, breathing the chilly air—the cold feels good to my aching body. I withdraw a parupeteng flower.

Going back inside, I kneel before Kitso. I softly pet his head, and his ears twitch. I run my hand along his side, and notice that most of the swelling near his ribs has gone down. I continue to stroke him, and purse my lips. *Be a good girl, Pansa—he respects you.* Before I realize it, my hand is on his waist, and I quickly draw back.

He comes to slowly, and looks up at me. "What time is it?"

"It's a fair bit into the afternoon. I'd say perhaps a couple hours before evening."

He sounds sluggish, but alert. "I feel as though I had slept the whole day away."

"That's probably because your body is just taking extra time and energy to recover. I probably could have slept the whole day if I wanted to."

"So why didn't you?"

I sigh. "I can't just sleep all day long. Even if I decided to, it would just be a waste of precious time."

He smirks. "Well, you were the one to say we could use the extra time for rest."

I chuckle. "I didn't mean to sleep! I meant to take the day easy while we tend to whatever needs doing." With another sigh, I get up. "You can sleep some more if you want to. As for me, I gotta do something with the day, or I'll go crazy."

I leave our home, and glance around the camp to see what might require doing.

The fire pit is laden with a few ashes from the night before, but nothing serious. A few bones are strewn around it, but Kitso had asked me to leave them out to dry so that he could craft with them.

The kiln and my earthenware are fairly clean—I am sure to keep up with that on a regular basis.

Kitso's waterskins are mostly full, and we have plenty of food preserved for a good ten days or so.

I sniff to myself. "Oh, come on, Pansa. Is there really nothing that can be done around here?"

My ears pick up on movement. I turn to face the door, and realize the sound was Kitso settling back to sleep. *He really must be worn out from that scuffle.*

I let him be, pick up a large pine branch, and begin to sweep our site clear of loose brush and leaf.

Evening approaches, and I rest after a couple hours of clearing up the forest floor. *I'm sure she appreciates all my hard work, if nobody else.* I smirk, and think it silly that the trees would care at all.

The bright sun slowly crawls along its endless, predetermined path without a thought to spare for my impatience to await the day's end. I throw my hands up, and go back inside. I cannot figure out why I am so frustrated about having nothing to do. *Am I really so busy all the time that even a single day of lazing about stresses me out?*

Going into my room to meditate, I hear Kitso waking again. *It's so easy for you Kitso, to sleep the day away, only to wake up to the eve's call for a quiet night.*

I push him and all else out of my mind, close my eyes, and steady my breathing. A gentle breeze makes its way into the seams of my walls.

The sound of silence is peaceful.

The sight of darkness calms me.

The thought of nothingness… is.

I am Pansa. Who I am is what I am made to be, and what is made is what I have become. It is my own doing that determines what becomes of my destiny. No one can control me but my own. Nobody can alter my path. Not a single entity has the ability to upend my serenity…

A soft rap sounds against my door.

Except Kitso.

His voice whispers. "Pansa… are you asleep?"

I breathe out slowly. "No, Kitso, I am not."

He steps in. "Sorry if I disturbed you in any way. I just woke up, and noticed it was getting a bit late."

"Indeed. Did you happen to sleep well? You've been out for most of the day."

He scratches behind his ears. "Yeah, I guess I did. I don't recall any particular dreams, though. Mostly just peaceful rest."

I open my eyes, and turn to him. "I'm happy that you got some good sleep. I was just relaxing after, well, not doing much of anything."

He smiles.

"What's so funny?"

"I don't know. It just seems like you're really stressed out over it. I can hear it in your voice."

I huff. "I am not."

"If you say so."

"So I guess you'll be up for some time now?"

"Yeah, I suppose so." He stretches. "I won't bother you though if you don't want me to."

"No, it's fine," I tell him. "I was kind of hoping you'd be up soon anyway. I've been a little bored talking to trees and myself."

He sits down by me. "Alright then, what would you like to talk about?"

I gaze up, trying to think of something to discuss. "What about your plans to travel? Where do you want to go? What do you want to see?"

He looks off to the side, and appears to space out. "I'm not totally sure. I was expecting it to be a surprise, but I suppose I need some direction, don't I?"

Kitso goes to fetch a couple waterskins, and hands me one, continuing. "I want to see the edges of this world. Every plain I cross, a new experience, and every mountain and valley, an adventure. I'll see new places and who lives there. Hamlets, villages, towns—each place holds exciting things to see and learn.

"I've heard great bodies of water expand beyond the horizon. I want to see them for myself, and perhaps even go as far as to traverse those waters. I want my travels to have no limitations, and no boundaries."

I cock my head to the side. "Will you ever consider settling anywhere after you've seen what there is to see?"

Kitso looks back at me. "Of course. What would a life full of new experiences be without being able to settle with my mate, reaping all the joy of what I come to see and learn that can procure such good things thereafter?"

I smile at him. "Despite how I have come to know you Kitso, you still remain an elusive mystery, full of surprises at every turn."

He hugs me, and gets up. "I'm going to do a bit of crafting. You go ahead and try to get some good sleep yourself."

"I'll do that."

As he leaves my room, I ease onto my back, staring to the side. I trace the grain of the wood lining my walls with my eyes, and notice that as each line branches off into another, it never really ends.

Chapter 10

As I sit by the fire, the bone I'm working with begins to vibrate slightly. It catches me by surprise, and I drop it, my body tensing up as I watch it roll sporadically across the ground.

The remaining bones follow suit, and they twist about each other, forming a small creature. It meanders in my direction, and sits down, looking up at me.

"Um, hello?" I look around, and see nothing else moving in the dark woods. I glance back down at the odd creature, unsure of what to make of it.

It gets up and walks in a circle around the fire, before resettling in front of me.

"I don't know what you want," I tell it.

It rattles a bit, exuding a creaking rasp from its body. "I... want..."

"What is it?"

It continues. "I want... your soul."

A massive blast of wind unexpectedly erupts from it, knocking me backward, shrouding me in total darkness.

My eyelids tear open in a flash, and I find myself gasping, as though I just surfaced from drowning. My fur is laden with sweat.

The front door flies open. "Kitso, what's the matter?! I just heard you shout a moment ago."

I lie steady. "It... nothing... just a bad dream."

She reclines on her side next to me, and touches my face. "You're cold. Do you need anything?"

"Maybe a bit of water..."

Taking the waterskin handed to me, I sit up and drink from it until it's empty. "It was just a bad dream. Nothing more."

"You look awful. Are you going to be okay?"

"Yeah, I'll be fine. Thank you, Pansa."

She nods. "You're welcome. By the way, it's pretty nice outside, almost like a heat wave. It must be a last reprieve to the approaching freeze."

"That sounds wonderful. I'll be out in a little bit."

After a while of silently meditating, I pull on my tunic, and go out to meet Pansa, who is sitting quietly on a rock near the hill.

"Oh, hey Kitso. I'm just soaking up some of the sun's rays."

I glance upward to see the light peering through the trees. "You're right, it is pretty nice out today."

"Told ya!"

I begin clambering up the hill.

Pansa calls up to me. "Hey, where are you going?"

"Just up to the top of this hill. I have never actually been up there yet."

She follows in my stead. "What do you think you'll find?"

"I'm not sure. It is more of what I hope to see from it."

As I near the top, I slow down to relax my chest, minor pain still poking through. I see a large stump, and decide to stand on it to get the clearest view I can manage.

"Wow..."

Pansa nears my side, and looks in the same direction. "Oh my gosh," she remarks, clearly stricken with similar awe. "This view is amazing."

The treetops that once held a fuller canopy appear to draw a prominent line across the horizon, rising and falling with tender waves to accent the land's structure. Dense branches and foliage shadow the trees perfectly along the ground, the sky casting a highlight along the crowns.

"I wish I could capture this image forever, Kitso..."

"I know what you mean. It's gorgeous," I respond. "It's rather too bad that I am not skilled with paints, but I fully intend to come up here more often."

She continues to stare off into the distance. "It's a great spot for meditating. I might make my way up here on occasion as well."

We head down the hillside, taking note of a clearer path.

As I head back toward our home, Pansa stops. "Hey Kitso, do you want to go for a walk with me?"

"Where to?"

"No place in particular. I think it's a nice afternoon to go for a leisurely stroll through the forest, since there's little else that needs doing."

"It sounds great. I'll pack a couple things to take along."

I empty my satchel, and replace the inside with a couple waterskins, my knife, the finished mantle, and a couple of the preserved fish. Pansa suggests we take the other waterskins as well, since the day is warmer.

"How long did you plan on us walking for?"

She giggles. "It doesn't matter. I just don't want us to be left without water, that's all."

I let her decide on the direction, and we head out.

As we go along through the woods, I admire various sights with Pansa. Many more of the trees continue to loose their leaves, as though they are offering tribute to our procession. Overhead, a squirrel follows us, piqued with curiosity. Several minutes later, it runs off to join a friend. I spot a doe wandering several dozen yards from where we're headed, and she soon disappears with the scenery.

"There isn't much company out here today, despite the beautiful weather," Pansa says.

"They all must have gotten a good start on preparation." I take out my knife, and make a mark on passing trees now and again.

Pansa laughs. "It isn't as though we're going to lose our way out here."

"Well, you never know," I reply.

She quickly retorts. "I am pretty sure we'll be fine with our combined sense of direction."

I sniff out at her, and pick up a pine cone to carve away at. Pansa continues admiring everything around us.

"Did you hear that?" I ask her.

"No. What is it?"

"It sounded like a low growl."

She stops, listening intently for a moment. "I still don't hear anything."

A couple minutes later, I hear it again. "There it is again. Wait, that's not a growl... that's a rumble."

"Oh, there it is. Sounds like thunder."

"It seems like a storm is passing overhead, off in the distance."

We press on for some time, the evening beginning to show its colors high above. I feel a droplet on my nose, followed by another.

"Hey Kitso, I just felt a few drops on my ears."

"Yeah, as did I on my nose."

Without warning, a light shower drops a sheet of rain on us, followed by a fine mist.

Pansa perks up. "Whoa! Where did that come from?"

I wipe my head clear of the water. "I've seen it happen last year, and a couple before that. It's a spontaneous shower, usually followed—"

Whoosh! My words get drowned out by another sudden rush, the rain coming down in droves.

"Ahh!" Pansa shrieks, and laughs as she runs for cover.

I run after her, and we notice a large pine to shield us from the surprise storm.

"I can't see five feet in front of me," I shout, and duck under the tree.

Pansa is brushing off her face. "I'm already soaked!"

I wipe my face into my tunic, which I find didn't help much. "As am I. But it isn't so bad once you're used to it."

We sit beneath the branches, waiting for the rain to let up, but the moment it appears to slow, it just as quickly returns with more.

I laugh to myself.

"What's so funny?"

"I guess we weren't left without water after all!"

She scoffs, and shoves me off balance. I hit the mud, still laughing. Sitting back up, I flick my hand toward her, splashing her with muddy water.

"You jerk!" She says, grinning.

"You're not very convincing with that smirk."

No sooner than I finish my sentence, she tackles me onto the ground.

We both lean up against the tree trunk, cleaning dirt from ourselves. "You got my fur all dirty," Pansa pouts.

"It'll wash out."

"Yeah, well, I don't wanna have to wait to get back to go for a swim." She gets up, walks around the tree, derobes, and heads out into the rain.

I continue to brush myself free of debris, somewhat thankful that the rain's mist is too thick to see very far.

"This feels great, Kitso. You should come out!"

I sigh, and clear my throat. The cool rain feels good against my warming face. "Alright, I'm coming," I tell her.

I splash my face from a nearby puddle, and begin to make my way out, raising my arms up to let the moisture drench me completely. My garb lies flat against me as it soaks.

Pansa is dancing in the rain, and I can't help but to stare. *She looks absolutely beautiful.* "More than ever..."

"Did you say something, Kitso?"

My skin tingles with bumps. "Uh, no, nothing at all. You're right, though, this is totally refreshing! It isn't often I get to enjoy such an awesome storm."

"Right? I'm glad I'm not the only one who loves rain."

I join her, prancing about in the thrushes of moisture brushing all around us. It feels as though I'm swimming and flying simultaneously.

Pansa laughs, and slows down. She takes my hand, and begins walking again. "Thank you for walking with me. This was a pleasant surprise, and I am happy to share it with you."

I gaze at her. "As am I."

She stands still, looking into my eyes. "Do you love me, Kitso?"

For a moment, I am without words. "Of course."

"Tell me so." Her leer holds me with a particular intensity.

I breathe deeply, and hold her gaze. "I love you very much, Pansa. More than I can know."

She slowly leans in, and I can almost feel the warmth of her own face merge with mine as she kisses me. I embrace her with a passionate hug, feeling her own love encapsulate my being as the thunder roars.

Chapter 11

The following morning was an unpleasant reminder of the ever-nearing freeze, as it was very cold. Most of the leaves had stuck to the ground with a bitter frost, and any pool of water not more than a few inches deep was reduced to a brittle sheet of ice.

Yesterday was indeed a very nice reprieve from the bitterness, and although the storm has thoroughly drenched the landscape with enough moisture to coat the ground with patches of frost, I am only thankful that there was no wind today.

Kitso did not want to move at all. I told him that even though we had plenty of food, we still needed to work a bit more on our shelter if we were to keep the freeze out.

"Ugh, I despise the cold so much," he moans, determined to stay put the entire day. I could see furls of steam rise through the air as he spoke.

"Don't be like that, Kitso. You know well enough that if we don't get this taken care of, you're going to be met with the cold regardless."

He shifts beneath his fell. "Alright, just grant me a few more minutes, and I will get up."

"Alright. I'll be outside waiting for you." I head out, and tense a bit from the temperature shift.

We scavenge the land for some moss, dry grasses, and other soft materials we can make use of. Afterward, I set a good fire to warm my collection of loose clay.

Working the mass into a malleable state, I sift plant matter into it. I then hand it over to Kitso, who proceeds to cover any cracks in our structure that the cold air might find its way through.

I go to strip large pieces of bark to layer against the outer walls, as he fashions an inner fireplace from big stones and more of the clay. Kitso says his chest is feeling fit enough to chop wood, and so I permit him to stow away what he can until evening. I tell him that he really needs to rest afterward, and though reluctant, he understands.

"I was just getting into it all, too." Kitso reclines by the inside fire, stretching his feet toward the warm, open flames.

"I know," I reply. "But the time you start feeling better is the most critical time to ensure that everything heals properly."

He is working on more weaving while I stir some water in the jug near the heat. I flavored it with tallow and herbs.

I pour a small amount into a cup I had made, and offer it to him. "Try this."

He does so, making a strange face. "It's kind of... odd. It feels as though I am drinking meat. But it does taste pleasant."

"Hmm." I add more herb to it. "This broth should push the cold from ourselves, so savor it well."

Kitso finishes what I've given him, and hands me the empty cup back. "I wouldn't mind another few sips in the meantime."

"Heh, so you do like it."

He chuckles. "I said *odd,* not *bad.*"

I serve him another portion, and cover the jug to put away.

"Hey, what are you doing?"

"I'm storing it, silly. If you drink it all now, there won't be any left for when it gets really cold." I stick my tongue out at him.

He looks down at his cup. "If I manage a fresh rabbit some time today, will you make us a stew?"

I ponder for a moment. "Well, I'll have to make another pot for cooking it, but yes, I think I can do that."

At that, he gets up, and fetches his bow and quiver. He dons his mantle, and readies himself to hunt. "I'll be back before dusk."

When Kitso leaves, I take out what's left of the clay, and begin to work a cooking pot into order. *I know that he doesn't like the cold, so I am happy that he can get outside for something he wants to do. I hope for his sake that this freeze isn't as bad this time around.*

I fire up the kiln, and gingerly settle the cooking pot. I look toward the sky, and see a flock of geese flying south. "It's so easy for you birds, being able to take flight for the sake of your own convenience." I know that they cannot hear me, but it doesn't make me any less jealous.

I go back inside while the clay fires, and decide to lie down for a rest. Despite not having exerted myself, I feel a bit fatigued from healing the last couple days.

As I lie there, wind starts to pick up. I can feel it finding its way through the door from my room. "Ah, so much for that. I do hope Kitso is staying warm out there."

I look to my side, and notice that the light has mostly left. "Oh no, it's already dusk. What could be keeping him?"

I get up to open my door, and smoke curls from beneath. I step back as it nears my feet, and it gradually becomes darker, until it takes on the appearance of soot. "Well then, we meet again, Pansa."

"What do you want with me?" I fiercely glare.

"I want for nothing but only to share some news with you."

"Well I don't want to hear anything you say."

"You will if it regards your mate."

My throat seizes, hardly leaving me passage to speak. "What have you done with him?!"

"I have done nothing to him. I only observe what transpires..."

I shout. "Don't play coy with me! Tell me what's happened!"

"If you so insist."

The smoke clouds up half the room in complete darkness, displaying an image to me—it is Kitso, lying on the ground, his legs maimed. He reaches for his knife as I see a wild bear swing a massive paw at his face.

With a horrid shriek, I burst through the smoke screen, breaking the door off one of its hinge points. It's almost completely dark, and I run through the trees, my heart racing.

The tears streaming down my face feel icy to my cheeks. As I try to make my way into the woods, I trip on a rock and hit the ground hard.

My neck begins to tingle. I go to lift my head, but cannot. The darkness overwhelms me entirely.

A brief silence later, I open my eyes. I am lying in my room, just as I had before, and I realize I had dozed off.

My head pounds from a headache, and an unsettling thought crosses my mind. *You may not accept them any more from me, but so long as you indulge, I will be bound to you.*

I wipe tears from my eyes, and pound a fist into the ground.

Kitso returns as he said he would, just as the sun decides to set out for the night. I hear him come into the front door. "Pansa, are you in here?"

I clear my throat, and wipe my face into my mantle. "Yes, Kitso. I am just resting in my room."

He comes in, bearing two rabbits in hand, talking as he hangs them up. "I traveled quite a bit, and found these two looking for food out past the river."

I jump up to hug him, and almost knock him over. I hold him firmly.

"I said I'd be back by dusk, didn't—" He gasps.

I furrow my brows."What's the matter?"

"You've got a cut on your forehead. How did that happen?"

I release him, and draw my hand up to touch it, wincing from the pain. There's a small bit of blood on my finger. "I'm not sure."

"I've never known anyone to get a cut while laying down."

I breathe deeply, letting a long sigh escape. "I wound up taking a short nap, and had a disturbing dream." My chest feels tight as I recall the image.

"Oh. It must have startled you to graze your claw. I had a pretty bad dream myself the night before."

"What of?"

Kitso scratches the back of his neck. "I don't really want to talk about it. But it was quite unlike anything I've ever dreamt before. Almost surreal, and dark."

I can feel the fear in my expression. *Just leave us alone…*

"Oh, I noticed that you made a large pot for cooking. It was done firing, so I brought it in for you."

Never…

I hug him again, and start to cry once more. "I'm so sorry, Kitso."

He sounds half-amused. "For what?"

"I don't know. Just hold me. Please."

Kitso reciprocates my embrace, his arms holding me softly but surely. I can feel his breath run down my head and neck, and it brings me an endearing comfort. I nuzzle into his chest, rising and falling with each breath he takes.

We lie down next to the fire so he can warm up from his trek. As we lay there, he pets my head slowly, and I let out a low purr. I go to stroke his tail, and it flops to the side.

"Sorry."

"Nothing to apologize for. My tail is just sensitive to touch, that's all."

He swings it back over to me, and I gently hold it, stroking its long pile. His tail feels like a small fox, and the warmth makes me smile. My own tail sways to and fro, and Kitso softly grabs it to hold when it brushes across his legs.

"There, now we're even. And I'm not sorry."

I can't help but to giggle, causing him to also laugh.

* * *

We lounge lazily by the fireplace, without so much as a care to the world. I continue to stroke Pansa's soft, warm fur on her head. "We'll get through this season of cold, Pansa. You'll see."

She glances up at me from my lap. "I know. But it isn't going to be easy, even if it isn't as cold this year, what with all of the struggles we have faced the last few days alone."

"So long as I am with you, I am confident."

"I'm happy that I provide a sense of confidence."

I stretch, settling my arms under my head as I lay down. Pansa sits up to let me adjust, and sets her head back onto my lap, resting her eyes. "I have experienced a great deal of enjoyable moments, and have garnered experience I wouldn't have otherwise, had it not been for you. Yes, a few bad things have happened quite recently, but I also know that it is no cause of our own.

"I get the feeling of someone wanting us to fail, but I refute any thought of it. I know that we will see these situations through. All we must do is stay by each other, and everything will turn out right."

She appears to be sleeping, but she replies to let me know that she still hears me. "I trust your instinct, Kitso."

"It's more than mere instinct, Pansa. I cannot really explain it, but there is a driving force that moves along with our efforts. I sense it almost daily, and it gives me strength to do whatever I can."

"I am happy to be with you. I feel like I have a greater purpose to life beyond my family."

"So long as you care for yourself, you'll be able to care for them also. Just promise me you'll do whatever it takes."

"I will. I just need a lot of time, that's all. I only ask your patience in return."

Chapter 12

*J*ust *promise me you'll do whatever it takes.*

I know that he inadvertently refers to my consumption of parupeteng. It isn't as though I had decided to maintain this burden. If I believed that I had the ability, I would have dropped it long ago. I only hope he knows what he's gotten himself into…

I retreat into my room for evening solace. I asked Kitso to not bother me, and he agreed, understanding my being mentally distraught. Settling into meditation, my mind is cleared from any distracting thoughts of the world. The bitter cold flees my mind—the pain I felt is no longer relevant. Time itself ceases to exist in my consciousness. Only I, in and of myself, am.

Then, a thought makes its way in. *If I am not what I do, then who am I? He loves me not for what actions I take, but proclaims his love is for myself.*

You are nothing if you do nothing.

That simply isn't true. I was there before I was capable of doing anything for myself.

You have no recollection of that.

I may not recall it, but it must be true, as no one passes into this world any other way.

Are you certain of your own perception on reality?

I must be, or I wouldn't be aware of anything.

Is he even real? Is your awareness your own? Maybe you are not anything. Perhaps you do not even exist.

I shake my head, snapping back into full consciousness. "No, that can't be right. This is all real... isn't it?"

I get up, and step over to my inner door. I crack it open slightly, peering into Kitso's room.

"Kitso?" I say, half-whispered.

"Yes? Are you alright?"

"I think so. I just... needed to hear your voice."

He smiles warmly, but the concern remains in his eyes. "Would you like me to tuck you in for sleep?"

His suggestion causes me to feel strange. Is it unusual for someone as old as I to be tucked in? I quickly dismiss the thought, and nod.

I go to lay down. Kitso grabs my mantle, and drapes it over me. I ask him to fold the edges under, and he does so with gentle regard. I expect that he's finished as he walks away, but find he's circling around instead.

He sits by my head, and softly strokes behind my ears. I cannot help but to emit a contented purr, and he hums, resonating with my vocalization. I'm bewildered, and momentarily cease, only to find he silences himself. The instant I begin again, he continues also.

I am completely without conclusion as to why, but his harmonization with me fills me with an absolute sense of tranquility. Before I am aware of it, I find myself within a most beautiful dream.

* * *

I gently ease myself up from Pansa's company as she drifts off into a peaceful sleep, and silently make my way back into my own room.

I don't know what had me hum alongside her purr, but it pleases me greatly to know she finds comfort with my voice.

I've always loved vocalizing in artistic ways beyond mere singing. It isn't often I find myself singing or humming lately, but Pansa encourages me to share this ability of mine in ways that even I am not fully aware of yet.

The night has gotten quite late, but I find that I'm not as tired as I should be. I rekindle the fire a little, and keep busy with more weaving. We don't really need any more clews of fiber, and though I am energetic, I also feel somewhat lazy.

As I weave the night away, a draft begins to find its way beneath the outer door, and causes me to shiver. I get up to put away my needless work, take a spare hide, and press it up against the door's base. "Alright Kitso, time for bed," I tell myself as I ease out the fire.

I come to for another day, wrapped thoroughly within my fell, and see Pansa standing over me. I raise my head slightly to see her looking down into my eyes.

"Good afternoon, Kitso. You look comfortable."

I drop my head back down. "I am very comfortable, thank you. And I am *not* moving."

She giggles. "I don't blame you. A little bit of snow fell early morning—it came sooner than I expected."

"I cannot wait until the hot season returns."

Pansa laughs. "It only just left us a little while ago! Now it must wait its turn."

I groan, very much against the notion that each season must take place accordingly. If it were up to me, we would all do without the cold entirely.

Pansa has set out to admire the new sights, mantle around her. I have decided to sleep a little while longer.

* * *

The woods have taken on an entirely new appearance. They've donned a white dress in waiting for the groom of cold, content with the first layer for now.

As I walk through the trees, I see little blue and red birds congregate for today's gathering. There must be a few dozen, all searching for tasty berries and seeds. I help myself to a small, round red berry from a nearby bush—it tastes sweet. I return for a moment to our home, and grab a bag. Kitso is sleeping soundly, so I let him be.

I return to the bush, and start to fill the bag. I place them gently so as to not accidentally end up with juice.

With most of the bush now barren, I move onto another. These ones are a different shade of red, but no less delicious. A smaller batch of deep black berries lie beneath the bush, and I gather those, too.

Discontented with a half-full bag, I continue to search for other treats. I allow the birds plenty of space to keep from disturbing them and their foraging.

I find a handful of mushrooms that have stiffened from the cold—they can be thawed later. There is an abundance of herbs that survived also, and I help myself to a few. I find a nook in a large tree, housing a little pile of an assortment of nuts. There appears to be no squirrel in sight, nor any tracks, so I scoop them up.

"This should suffice for now." I wander back to the base, and notice a couple parupeteng flowers. I consider passing them, but ultimately give in.

When I return, I notice the front door ajar, and see Kitso a fair distance in the trees—he's relieving himself.

I head in, set the bag of goodies to the side, and add tinder to the fire. It flares up, when Kitso comes in.

"Hello, Kitso. I found some treats for us today."

I hear him ruffle around the bag. "They look great!"

"Yes, just don't eat them all at once, as the birds have gotten well ahead of us."

"I won't." He sits beside me, a palmful of each type of berry, and an herb. "How does it look out there?"

"I know you may not be of the same opinion, but it honestly looks remarkable. I imagine it'll be all the more stunning as the snow accumulates."

"Hmm…" Kitso snaps up a berry. "I believe I am content with as little snow as possible."

I smirk at him, and tend to the fire. "A blizzard is inevitable. It's just been too cold to not expect one."

He gets up, and brings out a hide from the storage. "I am going to prepare my mantle with an additional layer. This talk of snow has me shivering."

I snort with laughter, shaking my head. "I have never met someone with such disdain for the cold. How did you even survive all these past years?"

"Oh, well I used to love playing out in the snow when I was younger. I enjoyed throwing balls of snow at my siblings, and the occasional other member of the tribe. I even built a formidable fort or three."

"It sure sounds like you used to have lots of fun. Whatever happened?"

"I got older."

I draw a hand up to my face.

We bring out a couple fish to warm over the fire, and season them with the fresh herbs. Kitso also thaws a mushroom to have with his portion.

The both of us relax near the warmth of the open flame, and start talking about whatever comes to our minds for the evening.

"What about you then, Pansa? Did you always enjoy the freezing cold of this season?"

I pick a bone from my teeth. "As best as I could. I often took a walk to purvey the surrounding scenery, its beauty in presenting a clean slate for nature. Of course, I was charged with keeping an eye out for danger of any sort, but I made the most of it."

"And were you ever met with danger?"

"A number of times. Be it a hungry bear, a wild jaguar, or ravenous wolves—I would have to say the latter most being the worst of all."

Kitso's eyes grow wide. "That must have been undoubtedly rough."

"It was." I take a bite of fish. "I almost didn't make it back to my clan. Thankfully, a couple other members were readying themselves for a hunt, and so were already prepared to fend the wolves off while I and a few of the others did what could be done. Six wolves followed me back. By the time we were finished with them, only one had managed to run off."

"I am glad you were alright."

I draw my right leg forward, and drag a finger along the side, lining a scar under the fur that Kitso apparently had not noticed before. "I couldn't walk for three days. In fact, I find myself incredibly fortunate to be able to walk at all."

Kitso finishes his meal, almost surprised that it's gone. He grabs a few more berries. "Any pleasant memories to share with me?"

I think for a moment, and smile. "There was a doe that had crossed my path when I had gone out one particular afternoon. She was without fawn, and was grazing at whatever grasses poked through the snow.

"When I noticed her, neither of us moved for the longest time. She was hesitant to look away, and eventually conceded to wander over to me. I held out my hand for her to take my scent from, and from then she took to me as though I were her own.

"Every day I was to go looking about, she was there to keep me company. It was more or less passive, but she was willing to sample any plants I came across for food. Perhaps she simply thought me a mutual source of food, but her presence was nonetheless an exciting highlight to my otherwise normal day. It was only that year that I saw her. I never will know what became of that doe."

Kitso is grinning. "That is incredible. The only friendly wildlife I've come in direct contact with have been foxes. Go figure."

We both break into laughter.

Kitso is working on lining his mantle, while I prepare more of what he has decided to call "tallow soup". It has since become a favorite of his, and he has requested that I make it at least once every other week. I tell him that I will happily oblige, so long as he can provide me fresh game each time.

As I stir the water, I hear a gentle tap against the walls of our home. I glance at Kitso, who is listening intently. I send him a puzzled look, to which he replies with a shrug. He arms himself with his knife.

I ease off the floor, and walk over to the front door. "Who's out there?"

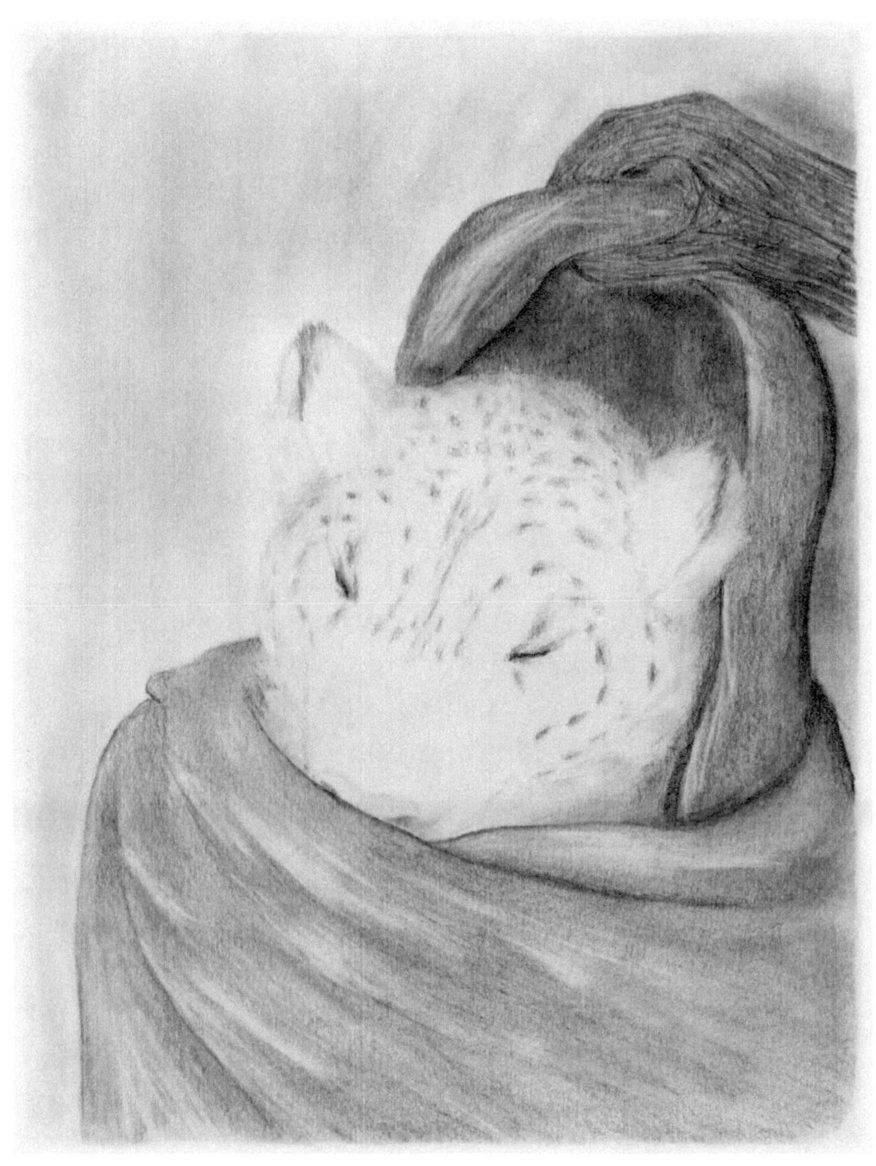

A short spell of silence is followed by a strained voice, sounding both frail and young. "I'm sorry... to bother you, but... have you a heart to let me in... please?"

I look back to Kitso. He breathes slowly, and nods. I gently open the door, and we see a short figure wrapped in a deep brown cloak shuffle in. They stand still for a while, shuddering stiffly. I reach to draw back the hood, and a couple of small, round ears coated with bluish-grey fur poke out. Black rosettes adorn their head, as their eyes appear to be staring down at the floor, shut tight.

After a few long breaths, the figure speaks again. "Thank you..." She seems to have thawed enough to present her true voice, and begins swaying with a shiver.

I offer support, and help her to sit near to the fire. Kitso pockets his knife, grabs the cup, and pours water from a skin, setting it betwixt her and the fireplace.

For what felt like forever, we all sit silently. Then the girl eases her eyes open to a narrow glance, as she reaches for the cup. Holding onto it with both hands, she speaks again. "Thank you so much..." She shuts her eyes once more, a few tears trickling downward.

I get back up again, and grab my mantle. I drape it over the girl, which startles her, eyes flashing open. They slowly close again.

I whisper to Kitso. "She isn't entirely conscious of what's going on around her. Stoke the fire more."

He fetches some additional kindling, and the flames brightly blaze, before settling back down into steadiness.

A good twenty minutes pass by with the girl easing sips from the cup, and Kitso engaging his craft. I become restless at the silent nature they both put on.

"So," I begin, unsure of where to finish. "What brings you out here?"

She says nothing.

"Are you out on an adventure of some sort?"

Nothing still.

I huff. "Do you at least have a name?"

The girl gently sets her cup down, and slowly pulls a locket out from her cloak, drawing it over her head, and hands it to me, never looking up from the floor.

It has four letters inscribed on it: Krys.

"Krys, huh?"

She nods gently.

I return it to her, and she loosely tucks it back into her cloak. I refill her cup, and she continues drinking.

I grab the bowl, fill it with a little broth, and offer it to Krys. "Would you like some tallow soup?"

"No... thank you."

Kitso glances at me with a wide smile, and I hand it to him, sticking out my tongue.

I ladle out a bit for myself, and sip from it. "You're welcome to stay with us if you'd like for the time."

Krys sets the cup down again, and puts her hands up to her face. She starts to silently cry.

I go to kneel by her, and stroke her head lightly, at which she leans into me, crying more audibly. I softly hush, putting an arm around her.

* * *

Pansa is reclining on her side by the fire, stroking Krys, who is asleep and wrapped up almost entirely in Pansa's mantle. Only her closed eyes and ears are visible.

I whisper quietly. "Where do you suppose she's from?"

She replies equally quiet. "I couldn't say. Her cloak appears to be of cheap cloth, but her locket suggests royalty. It's encrusted with a jewel on the back."

"Do you think she's run away?"

"It's hard to tell. I would guess that she's more or less heading toward somewhere rather than away from. She was tired, but not winded or panicked. I imagine she's either lost, or wandering freely with some sort of vague idea as to where she wants to go."

"What should we do if someone comes looking for her?"

"I think we'll keep quiet for now, until we figure out what's going on. Someone could be sending a search party on her behalf, but her life could also be in jeopardy. Unless she tells us more, there really isn't any way to know."

I sit quietly, thinking to myself. I wonder how long Pansa intends to keep her here. Not that I don't care, and I would just as well she stay with us as long as necessary, but eventually we'll be returning to my tribe in the warmer season. I am sure Pansa is ahead of me on this—she isn't one to make such types of decisions involving others directly.

"We'll all sleep in here tonight to keep warm and safe," says Pansa. "Tomorrow, we can ask her about her travels."

She gives these kinds of situations plenty of forethought. That is one of the things I love most about her.

Pansa is curled up against Krys, the both of them fast asleep. I stayed up just a little longer than I normally do to finish my lining job, and also to keep my ears open for any sort of suspicious sounds.

Thankfully, nothing else happened tonight, and so I put out most of the fire, letting the hot cinders burn out for themselves over night. I drape my finished mantle over Pansa, and she subconsciously pulls it tight around herself. I smile, lay down to wrap myself into my fell, and sleep.

Chapter 13

Another day begins, and both Pansa and Krys are up and out. I roll over and consider my option of staying put or getting up. As far as I know, there's nothing much to be done. Or at least, nothing Pansa had mentioned to me.

Stretching with a yawn, I think about all that has transpired thus far. I live within a formidable home, I have successfully put my survival skills to full use, I've housed a friend and practiced my social relations beyond mere friendship, was able to fend off dangerous opposition, and now I was a part of potentially saving a life. My tribe would certainly deem this excursion a great success, and it hasn't even come to an end yet.

I begin a fire. *I am anxious to see what else will happen.*

The front door resounds with a loud, sharp knocking, and startles me out of my thoughts. I do my best to rise quickly, and go to the door. "Who's out there?"

"The guard of Telios. We demand entry at once, lest we force our way inside."

"One moment, please." I pull my tunic on, and open the door partially. A large hand pushes it the rest of the way.

Three bulky canids stand before me, laden with metal armaments. I can see little more than their faces and hands. They stand confidently, each with hand on hilt.

"We've come for a young girl—a snow leopard. Have you seen one pass through here?"

"No, I have not."

One of them cocks a glance behind me. "There's a second room back there."

"I enjoy having extra space to move about."

"We saw tracks leading from here."

"I see the occasional beggar."

The back guard lifts his snout. "I sense a strong, feminine presence in the air..."

I give him a stern look. "As a bachelor, I like to entertain once in a while."

They all look at one another, and back at me. "If you cross this girl, send to inform us immediately. You'll find a post approximately four-hundred yards south of this area. A messenger will be at-the-ready. Good day."

They take their leave, and I close the door, shaking the cold off. "I hope those two don't run into them. Please be okay..." I say to myself, sitting down in silent prayer.

A little while later, Pansa and Krys return. They come in, remove the mantles, and Pansa sets them up to dry, while Krys sits down in front of the fire.

"It snowed a little this morning. I took Krys out to get some fresh air, and to see the sights of our woods."

"I hope you two had fun. Did you happen to see any large, armor-clad beings around?"

Pansa puts a hand to her mouth with a gasp, looking at Krys briefly. "We did see them. Have they come by here?"

"Yes, but I was able to see them away."

"Krys and I hid ourselves as soon as we saw them—"

"They're from Telios, a city not overly far from here that oversees the citizens under my uncle's guidance as head councilman."

Both Pansa and I look at Krys as she says this.

"Why didn't you say so, Krys?" Pansa asks.

"I didn't want to mention it. I hoped they wouldn't bother stopping here, but it seems that this matter is being treated very seriously, so you might as well know."

I chime in. "Are they looking to take you somewhere?"

"They want to bring me back to my uncle's court. I thought the letter I left behind made it clear enough that I had no intent of returning. The guard being sent out openly admits otherwise."

She draws her legs up, puts her arms across them, setting her chin—her mature demeanor leaves suddenly. "I'll be sixteen this year. My uncle had intended a mate for myself. When I told him I didn't want to bear a family with a foreign prince, he became livid. You see, most of our family isn't royalty, but he wants to be, and will go to any length in using me. Since my parents passed away, I was sent to him for my care, but he only saw me as an opportunity."

"He can't very well force you to be wed to royalty outside of your province. It would have to be approved by council in these lands," Pansa says.

"I have a cousin who is of royalty. My alternative was..." Krys drops her head into her arms and legs, and starts to sob.

Pansa kneels by her, offering a hug. "I'm sorry that he's treated you like property for his selfish gain. There's absolutely nothing just about that."

Pansa looks up at me, beckoning me to add something supportive.

I speak. "We won't let anything bad happen to you. Wherever you want to go, we'll see to it personally that you arrive unharmed."

Krys wipes her eyes, gets up, and comes over to hug me. "Thank you. Both of you." She looks up into my face, her large eyes full of both joy and sorrow. "You're like a brother to me, and Pansa my sister. I don't have any siblings." She tucks her head into my chest, nuzzling me.

Pansa quietly giggles, and I place a hand upon Krys' head. "Don't worry, little sister. We'll protect you."

* * *

We all spend a fair bit of time in silence, absorbing the warmth of the fire. Krys opens up about her scenario, and expresses that she wishes to travel with a very direct motive. "It's called Adleborough. I have another cousin there who is also of royalty. She is quite older, and has children of her own. Her parents founded the place with the ideal of helping anyone in need, and I am certain she'd have me."

"It sounds amazing," I remark. "Where is it located?"

Krys bears a look of uncertainty. "Well, it is kind of hard to find just from looking around. There is no real sign of exactly where it is, because it's underground."

Pansa sounds intrigued. "That's impressive, if not a little inconvenient. How would we find it?"

"I'm not really sure, but I recall seeing the place once when I was younger. My parents had brought me to go see it when it was being developed. The place we entered from was... very unique. I would know it when I saw it."

I pace around the room. "Hmm, it certainly sounds like the ideal location for you to reside whilst your uncle makes his rounds. Though, it may take a while to find a lead to its whereabouts, much less make our way there. And it would take time to prepare for setting out, and of course it'll get colder still."

Krys begins to sadden, sounding desperate. "Please say you'll take me. I promise I won't ask of anything beyond your escort."

Pansa looks over at me. "Please say you'll take her, Kitso."

I almost smile with bemusement. "Hold on, now. You'd be coming with us, Pansa!"

"So we're decided then?" she retorts. "Great! We leave tomorrow."

Krys beams with ecstasy. "I'll help pack what we can!" She runs out the door with an empty bag in hand.

"What? But we—wait... what?" I am lost for words.

Pansa comes over to me, and gently pats my head with a grin. "You're such a good brother, you know that?"

"Pansa, wait. You know I—we—are only out here for a certain time." I maintain a serious look.

"I know, Kitso, and I would not jeopardize that for you I promise that if we cannot find Adleborough by the last week or so, I will help Krys find it myself." She kisses my forehead. "I have every intent for us to stay together as you yourself do, but you also know as well as I that this is one promise we cannot break."

I hug her. "Thank you for your understanding."

Chapter 14

It is noon. Kitso is just waking up as Krys and I take account on what we've gathered for our journey. We all spent most of last night discussing our plans on how to go about finding this place from Krys' memory. I had her sketch a rough idea of what she could recall, and although it appeared vague on parchment, she was certain about the more prominent features.

"The only things I know I'm not mistaken about are a cascading river, and a large, fallen tree it runs over, making its way down slate-like steps. Things like that don't just change over a handful of years."

"Unless they were discovered, and wanted to get rid of any signs," says Kitso.

I huff. "*Discouragement* aside, this seems very promising, Krys. Maybe we'll ask a couple others from towns nearby."

"But what if we ask the wrong questions?"

Kitso responds. "I know it sounds risky, but it's our only chance of finding somewhere to start. There's just far too much land to cover on our own."

I continue. "He's right about that. I have been to a lot of places over my years, and have never seen or heard of anything like this. We just have to trust others."

We all bundle ourselves up, each toting what we can carry comfortably. Bearing little more than food, water, and warmth, I step outside and turn to look at our home one last time. Kitso comes out last, shutting the door behind him. I notice an extra bag hanging from his satchel.

"What've you got there, Kitso?" I ask him, pointing to the little burden.

"It's your collection of figurines."

"Oh, come on now. Those are hardly necessary to our survival."

He looks sternly at me, but ends up smiling. "I know that, but this is one thing I simply won't leave without. They're too precious."

Krys adds her own thoughts. "They really are very pretty, Pansa. You should take them with you wherever you go."

I acquiesce. "Alright, then. At least allow me to carry it, them being mine and all." I reach a hand out, at which Kitso hands the bag over.

He turns back toward our home. "This is it, then. Time to bid our abode farewell. It has become quite the sight, hasn't it?"

I nod. "I am sure whoever happens upon it will take very good care of it. Maybe they'll even add something, such as another room, or additional storage."

After a moment of admiration for our work, we abandon our homestead, and make our way north, leaving behind any worries of being found.

It isn't long after we begin our journey that the weather decides to challenge us.

"Of all the times it begins to snow…" Kitso moans.

"It was inevitable," I say. "Better now than later, when we would already be colder."

"I don't think it's all that bad," says Krys. "What's the matter?"

I snort. "Let's just say that Kitso isn't fond of the cold weather."

He laughs. "That is quite the understatement there, Pansa. I don't suppose you'll tell her how I like the snow a little less than some, or that I am a tad unfavoring of icy wind."

Krys giggles. "I see what you mean, Pansa."

Our lighthearted derision seems to irk Kitso after a short time, so I find another subject to discuss. "How did you use your time before leaving Telios, Krys?"

"I usually kept busy with my chores, if only to keep my mind off of my uncle and his business. If I had some spare time afterward, I'd go to the market often, trading goods and learning about merchant trends."

"Hm, you don't seem like the type that would enjoy such activities."

"Yeah, but one thing I really enjoy is studying the economy, and how it works together to serve everyone's needs. Most others frown on that kind of duty as far as I hear, but it provides me a sense of comfort and better understanding on how others are affected."

"You seem to exude a great deal of concern for the general welfare of others," Kitso states.

"Oh, I very much do. I may not be of royalty, but I was told that I'd make an excellent queen by many others. I am sure they were just being nice."

I pose a curious question. "If you were ever granted such an opportunity—via realistic means, of course—would you take up the throne?"

Krys spends some time in deep thought. "I'm not really sure, to be honest. I don't know everything that involves ruling, and even though I care about others, I don't feel comfortable giving orders."

She probably had to experience a lot of orders through her uncle. I decide to not pursue the topic.

We settle for a short time in the afternoon with varied activities—Kitso is building a fire, Krys watching him intently. I am fashioning a new fishing spear, so that we all may fish together some time.

When the fire is started, Krys begins to prepare one of the thawing fish. She seems to have exchanged her awe with Kitso, as he is now watching her.

"I had no idea you could work so well with food," he tells her. "Remarkable!"

She smiles. "One of my many chores was to prepare dinner for the council every night. We would have anything from soups and stews, to vegetables and meat. Sometimes even bread and fruit, too."

"Did you learn on your own?" I say.

"Yes, I had to teach myself everything I know about food. Nobody had the time to work with it, and I had a little experience from my mother, but other than that, all I know comes from practice."

I grin. "Careful, Kitso, or you may have a rival for your delectable fish meals!"

He smirks at me. "I suppose you'll be the judge?"

"Naturally."

Krys shakes her head at our silly banter. "You both sure argue a lot. Next, you'll tell me that you two are mates."

When we don't make so much as a breath, she puts her task down, and glances at us one by one. She jumps up and points. "Kitso's got a mate!"

Kitso gapes in astonishment, before jumping up himself. Krys squeals with excitement as she runs about the trees, taunting him.

As they run by, I grab at him, bringing him to the ground. We wrestle for a bit, before I pin him down.

"No fair!" he shouts. "Two against one."

"Oh, don't be like that. It's plenty fair." I kiss him.

"Ewww!" Krys exclaims.

Kitso looks up toward her. "Hey, be careful what you say. Someday, someone may take interest in you."

She crosses her arms. "I hope he would know what he gets himself into. I don't take relations lightly."

He looks back up at me. "Are you sure you two aren't actually related?"

As the night has fallen upon us, we lie settled under a travel shelter. The snow hadn't accumulated enough to make much of a bother, but the night air has gotten a fair bit colder.

Our fire begins to retreat for the night itself, as Kitso and I whisper the remainder of our energy away. Krys is nuzzled beside the both of us, sleeping soundly.

"She sure has taken to us quite a bit, Kitso. Of all those I've cared for, no one has adapted to the situation at hand as quickly as she."

"I agree. She's an impressive individual."

"Do you think we'll ever find Adleborough?"

He shifts to recline, an arm propping his head. "I am certain we will. Something tells me that with her enthusiasm, my insight, and your stubborn streak, we'll find it eventually."

I scoff at him. "I am not stubborn!"

"See?"

Sticking a tongue out, I glance down at Krys, and slowly stroke her head. "I know she will be very happy there, wherever it is. Undoubtedly, her cousin will take her in and appreciate the help. Krys is just the type to lend a hand without inquiry. And all that she has been through under strict demand, it'd be like an eternal relief to offer her service so freely."

"I really am convinced that you two are related somehow."

I resettle myself, and yawn. "Maybe we are. Who could really say?"

Kitso relaxes his arm to lie down. He asks me something, but by the time I register it, I drift off.

I awaken to find myself staring up at a soft glow. I ease myself up, and realize I am settled on a bed of moss. The glow is cast upon me from a group of bioluminescent fungus.

"Oh, yes, how could I have forgotten? I came down here to see Krys off to her new home. It's too bad we had to leave Kitso behind so he could return to his family with such a successful trial."

I get up from my bed, and wander over to the window. I look out, and admire the brilliant blue sky over a fresh green pasture. "Um... since when does the underground feature its own sky?" It dawns on me suddenly. *Of course, Pansa... it's a dream.*

But it is a wonderful sight, isn't it?

I sigh, and turn to see the shadowy figure sitting on the mossy bed. I am too tired to talk anymore. *And why shouldn't it be? It's my dream, after all.*

It shifts from the bed to a wall, and takes on a more solid form that appears to recline against the dirt. *If this dream is your own, then your reality is mine.*

You stay out of my life! I am not going to deal with you, especially not with Kitso and I now caring for Krys!

When the shadowy figure doesn't respond, I draw a hand up to my mouth, a cold shiver running through me. My eyes start to tear. *...You wouldn't!*

Wouldn't I...?

A soft finger gently caresses my eyes, and I suddenly come to, barely able to see through my tears.

"Why are you crying?" Krys cocks her head. Though I can't make out her expression, it's obvious she must have a concerned look upon her face.

I dry my eyes with a hand. "It's nothing. I was just having a sad dream."

She lays down to hug me, and sits back up. "It's okay. I sometimes have bad dreams, but they never come true."

If only you knew.

Uncertain of whether the thought was my own or not, I push it out of my mind, and grab for a waterskin to quench my arid mouth. "Where has Kitso gone?"

She yawns. "He said to let you sleep longer when he saw how pained you looked. You got up, telling him how you felt sick, and went back to sleep."

"I did?"

"Yeah, but he said you wouldn't remember, and that he saw you do that many times before."

Dismay washes over me, realizing that Kitso had never mentioned this to me. "Oh. Well, I feel better now. Thank you." I don't feel at all better. In fact, I feel far worse than I ever have before.

I find a private area to relieve myself. My stomach hurts greatly, and I can't seem to rid myself of the pain. I ask Krys to watch the site as I go look for Kitso. By the time I wander from her sight, I wind up looking for something else entirely.

I stare down at the plant, the large flowers in full bloom. It's a wonder that they can grow at any time of year, in the harshest of conditions nonetheless. *How could a plant that's so bad grow so well?*

Its worth lies within the individual who uses it.

I try my best to keep a blank mind as I cut the flowers.

Your will is strong as ever, but you are still vulnerable.

Pocketing two of them, I consume the third. It doesn't do much for my head, but my stomach begins to ease.

There, now don't you feel much better already?

I resume my search for Kitso, but fail to find any trace of his whereabouts. I sit on the ground, and begin to cry, my face dropped into my hands. I lose track of time entirely.

"Pansa?"

I almost startle, but my face remains covered. *Why does he find me when I don't want to be found?*

"What are you doing way out here? Is Krys alright?"

I sniff. "She's fine. I had her watch the site while I went out to look for you."

"I hope she wasn't found with you gone!"

"She's a big girl. She can take care for ten minutes!"

He breathes as though he were about to shout, but only exhales. I feel a cloth pressed against my hands, and I fold it to my eyes.

"Dry your eyes, and we'll go back together to make sure, alright?"

He gives me as much time and space as I need, and I get myself up. My stomach begins to feel uneasy once more. My sense of balance fares no better.

"I hope you were able to sleep some more. You complained about feeling sick the first time you woke."

I recall why I wanted to find him. "Krys told me so. I mentioned I didn't recall, but apparently that wasn't the first time I woke up without remembering."

He stops for a couple of seconds, and continues walking. "You've awoken many times in the midst of your sleep since we met. Sorry, I thought you knew."

I sigh heavily. "I suppose there's no way you could've known for sure."

"Your brief conversations are seemingly vivid, albeit strange on occasion."

"Could we please talk about it later?"

Kitso heeds my request, remaining totally silent.

Krys has found means to entertain herself in our absence. Gathering up fists of dead leaves, she throws them into the air, trying to catch them as they float down. She is giggling all the while, and I wonder how I can feel so sad in the midst of such a carefree spirit.

I absentmindedly clear my throat, and she stops to look over. She runs up to us, embracing me in a hug. "I'm so glad you both are okay! I was worried."

She was worried.

Kitso pats her head. "You were concerned for us?"

Of course she was.

I put a hand to my forehead.

Why wouldn't she be?

Was that your own thought?

"Just because you both are older, that doesn't mean I wouldn't care. Adults have problems, too."

What type of problems do you have?

"We're just glad that you're okay too, Krys," Kitso remarks. "I am sorry that we left you alone."

More problems than you know.

"Stop, please…"

Kitso stares at me. "Pansa, what's wrong?"

Everything is wrong.

"Nothing. I'm fine." I reply, both hands now on my head.

Are you sure?

"Are you sure, big sis?" Krys releases me, and looks up at Kitso. "Is my sis gonna be okay?"

Of course not.

"Of course she will. She is strong."

No, Kitso, you're wrong.

No, you're wrong.

Stop it!

Make us.

I drop to my knees, both my hands as a vice to my head, screaming. "Leave me be!"

Krys almost chokes on her words. "Pansa, what's—?"

I feel Kitso's hand on my shoulder, and I push him away with my arm. "Just leave me alone!" I run off into the woods.

* * *

"Pansa! Come back here!" I shout after her, but she shows no sign of returning.

Krys is holding fast to my side, an arm around my waist. She sounds as though she is about to begin crying. "What's happening to her?"

"I don't know, Krys." I say, breath shallow. "I don't know."

Krys and I sit by a fire, saying nothing. She is leaned against me as I weave some roots without purpose. It has become evening, and Pansa has yet to return.

"I'm scared, Kitso..."

I don't say anything.

"I'm scared, even though I'm not in danger."

"It's okay to be scared."

She seems to accept this answer to her comment, but soon asks a question. "Do you get scared for her?"

I cease my hands, and lower them into my lap. "I worry about her every day, Krys. There isn't a single day that's gone by since I met her that I don't concern myself with her well-being. She has been nothing but strong most of the time, but I still feel as though she hides her own fear, solely for my sake, and now yours, too."

"Why do others do that? Hide their fears, I mean?"

"That is one question I haven't found the answer to yet."

"Are we going to continue without her?"

I close my eyes at the thought, fighting back tears. "No, Krys. If there is one thing we'll do for her, it's wait."

She hugs me, burying her face in my side. "I'm so glad you said that. I don't want to go anywhere without her."

Night has fallen, and Pansa remains missing. Krys begins to fall asleep sitting next to me, and I urge her to go lie down. She resists at first, afraid to be apart from anyone, but when I mention to her that I must keep looking out for Pansa's return, she reluctantly goes.

Please come back, Pansa. Krys needs you. I need you.

As I sit, I look skyward. The trees have thinned in this part of the forest, and I can see a great deal of the sky above. The moon has hidden herself from our sight tonight, for she fears the stars may expose her flaws. But whenever I do see the moon, I see only her natural beauty. Her soft glow caresses my eyes, and I miss seeing her tonight.

A sound catches my attention. I thought I heard a rustle of leaves, but as I focus my ears more intently, I realize it's a voice behind me.

"Psst... Kitso."

I look toward the sound, and see Pansa beckoning me, hands signaling my silence as I get up. I walk over to her, and stare at her with such intensity, she must have felt it.

"Please don't do that. I'm so sorry for running away."

I walk passed her, and stand still. "Why in the world would you do that? You caused both Krys and I a great deal of stress with your retreat."

"I know I did, and I'm sorry."

"You mustn't have liked it when I went off this afternoon."

"No, I didn't, and I—" She sighs. "I really am sorry! I don't know what else you want me to say!"

She cups her hands over her mouth. She must have wanted me to come over so as to not awaken Krys.

"Krys is fast asleep. She won't hear us."

Pansa releases her breath.

"But, I refuse to sleep until you tell me what is going on."

She blinks. "I felt sick today. I had to get some fresh—"

"The truth, Pansa. The entire truth."

She frowns, and her eyes start to water. "A voice, Kitso. It's an evil voice, and it won't go away."

I sit with Pansa for a long time. By the time she finished telling me about this evil voice, she got sick. It continued for several minutes, and she almost passed out from the lack of oxygen. I did my best to calm her down, but it was apparent that she had no control over her body's reaction.

When she finally was able to stop heaving, I slowly rubbed her back. I unhitch a waterskin from my tunic, and give it to her. She rinses her mouth out, and thanks me for staying with her.

"Like you said, you felt sick today. I can't very well leave you alone feeling like that."

"This is serious, Kitso. It frightens me."

"I know. But I also know that we are going to get though this together."

She leans her head on my shoulder.

"What is it with you girls and your leaning on me? I cannot be that comfortable."

"Sorry." She sits back up suddenly.

I gently ease her head back onto my shoulder. "I didn't mean that negatively. It makes me happy. I was just curious."

"I don't know how to explain it. You're just comfortable to be around. I just... don't know what to do. It torments me almost every day. Even when it doesn't speak, I can feel it watching my every move, waiting to trip me up. I don't want to be around you two when it bothers me. I'm afraid it—"

"That it might attack us through you."

She wipes her eyes. "Yes."

I put my arm around her. "I do notice that you take on a different air about yourself sometimes. I don't know how I can sense it, but it's almost tangible. Though it is attached to you, it isn't enough to drive me away, but you cannot run away every time it bothers you, either."

"I just want it to stop..." She yawns.

"Well, until that happens, you'll just have to let me help however I can, and the first step is to get you to sleep."

Chapter 15

Pansa and I agree that it's best if we say nothing in particular to Krys. We don't want her to worry about something she may not be able to comprehend.

"She's just too helpful." Pansa whispers.

Krys rolls over, yawning and rubbing her eyes. "Too helpful for what?"

It is day. The sun is directly overhead, and as we watch Krys sleep, she hears us talking.

"Oh, nothing." I say. "We were just saying how helpful you are, how you do whatever you can to lend a hand, and that it's almost impossible to convince you otherwise."

She sits up, and smiles at us. "I want to help as many others as I can."

I smile back at her. "We know, and that's why we want to help you find your cousin and her refuge—so you can assist her and all those who come your way."

Krys fidgets, as though she has some sort of puzzle in her hands. "I don't remember very much of Adleborough, but I remember it being quite small. It had maybe a few tunnels connecting about five or six rooms, all freshly dug. There were others who were sick or injured. We tended to them."

I nod. "It sounds like the perfect place for you to be."

I ask Krys to make a nice meal for the three of us from whatever ingredients she chooses, and stretch my legs with a short walk around camp.

Pansa is meditating to herself. I sit beside her, remaining silent, and notice her smile slightly. The smile fades as quickly as it showed, and I settle into my own peace of mind.

There was no telling how long we sat there in solemnity together—it could have been an hour or more. I only came to with a hand on my knee. Easing out of my state of mind, I looked into Pansa's eyes, but my consciousness remained unfocused. She must have sensed my absentmindedness as she spoke to me.

"You can stay here if you like for a little while longer. I'll be heading back now."

I had felt my head gesture in agreement, though I cannot remember what for. I only know that the next moment I opened my eyes, she was gone. I breathe deeply a few times before heading back myself.

"Oh, there he is." Krys points over to me as Pansa glances over her shoulder.

"We were wondering if you'd make it back before we finished eating."

I softly rub a hand across my temple. "Yes, thank you for not eating all of it."

I help myself to my share of a rabbit salad.

"I hope you enjoy it!" Krys bears a grin with anticipation. After sampling a few bites, the flavors work their way throughout my senses.

Only two words come to mind. "Absolutely satisfying."

Feeling sated from our meal, we pack our equipment and shelter, readying ourselves to set out for the rest of the day.

The sun eases itself toward the horizon as we ease ourselves back into our journey. The warmth of its light keeps our backs warm as we trek eastward. We have no particular bearings in mind, other than a progression of logic.

"Well, Krys mentioned that it was founded by a cousin of hers, so word must have gone through family at some point."

"We also know that she couldn't have been there from Telios, as her mother brought her when she was younger. Where did you say you were from, Krys?" I ask.

"I didn't say. I don't remember the name of our village."

"Did you head for Telios by water?"

She thinks for a moment. "Not exactly. I was brought across a river from the village, but it was all ground from that point on. I have never crossed that river before then."

Pansa reasons further. "So your village was near a river. Adleborough must have been on the same side. If we find some cartography of the rivers around here, we can work from there. We find the river with your village on it, and we are that much closer to locating Adleborough."

As we wander through the trees, they become less dense than I had expected. Spanning out from where we stand, I can see a few distant hills to the north. I look in the opposite direction, and remember being told about the messenger's post. I tell Pansa and Krys about this, and we edge a little farther north before continuing eastward.

What little snow there was has been mostly dissipated by the bright sun. Grasses run a gamut from green to beige, as if nature couldn't decide on which color to go with, and has decided to lazily spot a mix of the two.

My ears twitch, and I signal the others to wait. I pull my bow out to nock an arrow, and they fall silent, following in my steps as I track something.

A wild buck is feeding on some moss not fifteen yards from myself. I kneel, steady my aim, and release. The arrow flies perfectly, and punctures the buck in its side.

The moment he collapses, Krys gasps. "What an amazing shot," she whispers, as though the slightest sound might arouse the dead buck.

"Thank you," I say. "Using a bow and arrow is one of the greatest skills I honed through my mentor, Vulpena."

"Do you think I could learn to shoot so well?"

"I'm sure I can find some time to teach you what I can."

Pansa interjects. "I'll make a bow for you tomorrow, Krys. Perhaps we can all carve out a little time to practice."

"I would like that very much," says Krys.

With a fading evening, we settle down in a little valley. Krys and Pansa work on building a bonfire as I prepare the buck for dinner.

"I hope we find shelter soon," Krys exclaims. "I don't know how much longer I can sleep on the ground."

"We're sure to cross one by the next couple days," Pansa replies. "I came from the other side of the northern hills, and I've heard of many settlements in these parts."

"Did you hear if any of them are by a river?"

Pansa frowns. "No, I don't think so."

I finish preparing what I can before my hands get any colder. "It sure is cold tonight. Pansa, could you please help me skewer and set some of this by the fire? Krys, do you have any experience preserving meat?"

"Yes, I've learned to salt all sorts of meat."

As the remainder of the buck gets packed for later use, Pansa and I begin setting portions out to cook.

"I gave us each a thigh and some cuts of fat," I say.

Krys makes a face. "I'm not so fond of eating fat..."

"Honestly, neither am I, but it will help us to get through the cold season."

As we eat, we talk about whatever comes to mind.

"What was your family like, Krys?" Pansa asks her. "Do you recall any fond memories?"

"My mother was a very sweet lady. I don't ever remember a time when she wouldn't sacrifice something for me. When we ate, she would give me a greater portion of food. Whenever we went to the market, she would always treat me to something small.

"The clothes she had made for me used some of the finest materials around. I couldn't take them with me when I was sent away, but they were very colorful."

I express my curiosity. "Did either of your parents specialize in any trades?"

"My mother connected those who sought to complete a task with those who were skilled to do them. She usually earned a bit from the work that was done, along with a little money just for connecting. My father was a merchant. He found all sorts of goods at decent prices, and traded them to other traveling merchants for what they felt fair. He'd always seem to turn a profit no matter what was traded."

"He must have been a very savvy man."

"Yes, I think so. He always put our needs first, and liked to give very good deals."

Pansa further inquires. "Does your interest in economical research come from his experience?"

"He would always share his stories about his trades from the day when we settled down for the night. Sometimes, he would show me how he kept track of it all on paper, and would let me keep the old records. I kept all of them up to the very day I had to leave home."

Just then, a thought sparked in me. I smirked at the smallest glint of hope. "Krys, did your father ever trade in any goods with regard to your cousin's preparation for her refuge?"

"Um... now that you mention it, he did spend some time with her to discuss what she needed. She knew he could get just about anything, knowing when certain goods were traded during the year."

"Do you think that when we find your village, your records might indicate merchants who possibly remember their transactions with your father?"

Pansa can't help but smile widely. "Kitso, that's brilliant!"

It takes Krys a moment to catch on, but when she does, her expression makes it blatant. "Oh my gosh, that would tell us all we need to know!"

We finish our meal, just as the sun hides its face for the night. I set up the shelter, and no sooner than I complete it do I find Krys tucked in for bed. I lay my fell over her, and softly stroke her head before retreating back to the fire.

I tell Pansa about it as we sit next to each other. "I have never seen anyone so anxious for sleep before."

She giggles. "Well, with her mind filled with such hope and excitement, it's no wonder that she wants the next day to begin sooner than later."

I poke at the fire. "So, how are you feeling?"

Pansa seems to know what I am asking. "Uneasy, to be honest. Sometimes, I just want to cry without ceasing."

I put my arm around her. "Just know that it's okay to cry whenever you feel you must."

"I need to be strong for Krys' sake."

Turning to her, I gently hold her cheeks in my hands, looking into her eyes. "You are very strong, Pansa. Too strong, sometimes. You cannot retain your emotions forever, as they make you who you are. I think that Krys would feel a lot closer to you if you'd resonate your feelings with her."

Without warning, Pansa begins to cry, hugging me tightly. "I don't know how you make so much sense when I can't even think straight. How do you always go out of your way to care so much for me?"

I smile, my own eyes beginning to glaze over. "Contrary Pansa. I never, ever go out of my way for you, as you are my way. My life has only become more adventurous with your presence. I aim to make the very most of every experience."

We slowly draw our faces together, engaging in a kiss that deepens in a matter of seconds. Pansa doesn't seem interested in letting up, so I reciprocate as long as she desires. I didn't think it was possible, but she embraces me closer, wrapping her arms around me as far as they go. Her hands find their way beneath my mantle, fingers tracing my back along each curve.

I hold her just the same, and caress her back also. Her fur is exceptionally soft, and I wonder despite the fact if her back ever actually touches the ground when she sleeps. I draw my hands around, and up to her shoulders.

Without my realization, she shifts her arms, causing my hands to graze the sides of her breasts. The moment I notice, my breath shortens. She hesitates, and hugs me close again, sliding her face into my neck with a sigh.

"I'm sorry, Kitso."

I try to gather my thoughts. "I... nothing to be sorry for."

She kisses me on the cheek. "We'd best sleep now."

Chapter 16

I don't remember much of last night, and remember nothing of my dreams. I only know two things: I slept incredibly well, and I've made Kitso feel incredibly uncomfortable.

At least, that is what I believe. He didn't say anything about what had happened, so I assume he mustn't want to talk about it. If he doesn't mention it, I would just as soon forget about it myself for his sake.

As I'm carving away at a bow limb, Krys watches me with her big, round eyes. I briefly glance up at her, and smile. Her face always cheers me up, a seemingly boundless source of joy.

"How does Kitso sleep for so long?" She asks of me.

"He actually doesn't sleep much longer than we do. Just later, that's all."

"Doesn't he get lonely at night?"

I mull her question over as I continue to carve. "You know, I never actually considered asking him that."

"I'll ask him when he gets up."

I chuckle. "You should give him at least an hour or so before engaging in conversation with him. He does take a bit of time to wake up fully."

I finish after a long while, and test the flexibility of it. The bow seems to hold well. I dig through Kitso's satchel for some string to finish, and find a bundle.

"Aha. I knew he had some in here. I wonder if he kept any of the wax I gave him." I continue rummaging.

Krys has an odd look on her face. "Do you think Kitso will be okay with you going into his bag?"

I think about it. "Well, sure. When you are mated to someone, you tend to get special privileges in mutual understanding. Besides, it isn't as though he'd keep anything embarrassing in here."

The moment the last word leaves my mouth, I see a small book.

"Hm, no wax it seems." I set the satchel aside.

"What did you find in there?"

"Um, nothing really. Just... a book of some sort."

"Oh. Maybe he's keeping a record of our supplies or something."

I somehow imagine she is wrong.

As noon approaches, Kitso awakens with a bout of yawning. He appears to be considering whether he should go back to sleep.

"Morning, Kitso!" I say to him.

Krys gives him her own greeting. "Hey, sleepy!"

"Oh, hello you two. Would you mind terribly if I went back to sleep?"

"Yes, we would mind. Krys wants to try out her new bow. I figured we could also go fishing afterward."

Kitso narrows his eyes. "Fishing? In this weather?"

"Believe it or not, there are fish who remain active in the cold season."

He shakes his head. "I'll believe it when I see."

"Great! They should be mostly active in an hour."

Flopping back down with a groan, Kitso pretends to sleep. I leave him be for now.

"Do you think I'll do well with a bow?" Krys asks.

"The best way to find out is to try!"

I finish up with the bow, and hand it to her. She examines it carefully, running a hand along its curve.

"What do you think?"

She looks at me, mouth ajar. "It's beautiful."

"Thank you. I've made a few bows before, some being for my siblings. They didn't make use of the bows much, but I was just happy to carve them. At the least, they make marvelous decorations."

Krys lifts it up in the sun, as if to show the world. "It'll never become a decoration. I'll use it every day."

When Kitso finally rises for the day, he readies his own bow and quiver. "Are we set then?"

"Certainly," I respond. "I could use some practice for myself."

"Yes, let's go!" Krys jumps up, excited to learn.

We trek into a clearing with lots of space around us. There are a dozen or so trees within a ten yard radius, a couple of them fallen. There are also some boulders, ranging in height from half of Krys, to Kitso's chest.

He purveys the grounds. "This is the perfect area." Turning back to us, he tells both Krys and I each to pick out any one of the standing trees.

I cock my head. "What for?"

"It'll be your 'base', so to speak."

I exchange a glance with Krys, and we go to separate trees. When we arrive at our selections, Kitso goes to each one and marks an initial in their bark—a 'P' for me, and a 'K' for Krys.

"Okay, let's see you shoot an arrow at that one there." He points to the nearest fallen tree. He draws his bow, nocks an arrow, and shoots. It sticks squarely into the trunk with a hollow thud. "Pansa, you're next. Krys, watch closely."

I stretch my arms for a bit, and follow suit. My arrow also hits the trunk, although with a less satisfying sound.

"Not bad at all. Okay Krys, let's see you now."

She looks to be a bit nervous, but does her best to ready an arrow. After a few attempts, she takes aim, and releases. The string snaps her across the arm.

"Ouch!" She almost drops the bow as she holds her wrist.

I rush over to her. "Are you okay?"

"I think so. It just burns."

Kitso sighs. "That's alright, it happens. Try not to pull so hard, and steady your arm when drawing."

I take a strap of cloth from my tunic, and wrap Krys' forearm. "There, that should help a little."

Kitso proceeds to go over a few simple exercises in stance and technique. I also observe him and practice alongside Krys so she doesn't feel singled out.

When we resume with shooting, Krys successfully lands an arrow into the ground near our target. She seems content that the arrow flew at all. After a good twenty minutes of drills, we rest and drink.

"I think you're getting the hang of it," I tell Krys.

"I must agree with Pansa. You certainly picked up on using a bow rather well. Good job."

Krys smiles at our praises. "When I improve, I'd love to go hunting. Then I'll be able to provide food for us."

"That would be an excellent notion. Let's focus on practicing every day for a while. Use most of your spare time during daylight, and I believe you may be ready within a month."

I note the concern on Krys' face. "You think it'll take her that long?"

"I didn't go on my first hunt until three months worth of practice. Then again, I was studying many things."

Krys stands up, a determined look in her eyes. "I will spend every day learning what I can!"

Kitso grins. "That is what I like to hear! Now, let's discuss navigation methods."

"Well, that makes sense. It's no good if you're seen before you even nock an arrow," Krys proclaims.

A half an hour later, Kitso explains the details of why he had us weave throughout the trees and rocks, hiding.

"Yes, it is essential that you make the most of every little opportunity. You must keep yourself hidden when tracking your prey."

He had us go to our chosen trees, and attempt to make our way to him when he wandered away from us.

"It isn't so much about just keeping hidden, but also mapping an efficient path to your target's range. You want to get within reach as quickly as you can, as quietly as can be, and without being noticed."

"Isn't your prey sometimes unpredictable?" I ask.

"Absolutely, and you must also be ready to redirect yourself on a whim." He ponders for a moment. "Of course, there's a chance that you will lose sight of your prey, or it'll wander into an area where it is impossible to remain hidden. Inevitably, you will fail at times."

"No matter the effort, there are times the effort won't matter," Krys recites.

This piques Kitso's attention. "That's completely true. Where did you hear that?"

"Um, my father used to say that all the time."

"Very peculiar. My mentor has only mentioned that phrase on a couple of occasions, but it appears to be undoubtedly widespread." He turns to me. "Have you ever heard that saying, Pansa?"

"I can't say that I have, until now."

"Hm. Anyway, it is a very good phrase to live by. Just remember to never wallow over your imminent failures. If you give up, you cannot succeed, but if you persist, you cannot fail."

Following the philosophical discussion, I loose the fishing spears from my burden, handing a couple to my friends. "Are you two ready to go fishing?"

"Not really," whines Kitso. "Though, if you insist, I suppose I'll tag along."

"I really do insist!" I stick my tongue out.

Krys ponders aloud. "I wonder what kind of fish enjoy the colder waters."

"Only the tastiest kind," I reply.

"I hope the water isn't overly cold."

I shrug, smirking. "I don't plan to swim. Do you?"

We near a pond, its clear water reflecting the bright sunlight. There are few trees about, and they all seem to have decided to shed their leaves almost entirely, making our view of the landscape all the more brilliant.

"Wow, look at those gorgeous mountains."

"We're not here to sight-see, Kitso," I remind him.

"Now, there is nothing wrong with admiring the beauty of nature during a fish."

I sniff out at him. "Would you like to begin, Krys? I'll show you some of my techniques, and we can get a start on the best fish in the pond while Kitso stalls."

"Does he not enjoy fishing?"

"Oh, I believe he does. He simply has some bad experiences involving—"

"If you two are going, then get on with it!"

I laugh as I run toward the water with Krys, Kitso poking at me with his spear.

Another evening belies us, gracing our company with a bitter chill as we wander back to our site with a dozen fish in tow.

"Not bad, Krys. Even Kitso didn't manage half this when he went with me."

"Thank you. I had a lot of fun today."

I leer at Kitso. "Did you have fun today?"

He sighs. "Yes, very much so. It was nice to get out for the day, practicing with bow, and even fishing."

"I would say it was a successful day then. Your tribe will be entertained with all the stories you'll have for sharing."

He looks upward with distant eyes. "I am sure they will be quite thrilled to hear of my adventures."

Wandering into our camp, I hand the fish I'm carrying over to Kitso, and work on a fire. Him and Krys start to prepare a few of them. We decide to let Kitso cook tonight's meal as Krys and I preserve the remaining fish.

"What will you make for us tonight, Kitso?"

"Oh, I was thinking of a nice stew. Do we have that cooking pot about?"

I nod, and fetch it for him, filled with water.

"Thank you. Do you like stews, Krys?"

"I love stews. They are a favorite of mine for the colder seasons."

"You know, I have always admired your mature outlook, despite your age."

"I was taught to put forth my best with company."

He smiles. "As was I."

Well fed, I stare up into the sky, beholding the stars. They shine brightly to bid us a good night with their protecting light, softly illuminating the landscape.

We are settled in for the night, Krys tucked betwixt Kitso and I as usual, sound asleep. I'm gently stroking her head, and notice Kitso smiling at me.

"What is it?"

"One of the things I adore most about you is the care you express to everyone you hold dear."

"It just comes naturally to me. It's how I would always want to be treated."

"I am sure it only encourages Krys to do her best when she makes her way to Adleborough."

"That reminds me of something I wanted to ask you. When we started back from fishing, I noticed that you had a distant look about you when I had mentioned your tribe. Is something the matter?"

He looks down to Krys. "Was it that obvious?"

"You aren't the only one who picks up on subtle detail about others."

Shifting, he looks back to me. "This trial has become far more than I ever could have imagined. It's almost become less about my survival, and more about wandering the land with a mate and a new friend in search of a hidden sanctuary. It's unlike anything our tribe has heard of regarding trials. Yet, however odd it seems, I almost don't want it all to end."

"You know, that doesn't necessarily seem to be a bad thing. If anything, it would sound amazing."

"No, I wouldn't say it's bad… but I am unsure how they would perceive it as a test of my own mettle."

"If you were to ask me, I think that it would only prove you are more than capable of anything that comes your way. So far, you've taken on so much more than anyone else might expect of you. You bear a deep relation in spite of your upbringing, you've tackled a few foes that threatened our well-being, and have provided a means to support us and another selflessly. And I will be honest: handling me alone is more than anyone should have to expect in life."

Kitso grins. "You are not as bad as you think."

"Everyone else seems to agree otherwise."

"That's because everyone else has their own agenda to fulfill. I've only made mine about you for the most part since we've met, and thus far have yet to regret my decision."

I close my eyes, trying not to show my emotion. "I am really happy to hear that you think so."

"I know so."

Chapter 17

I had a strange dream about Pansa and Krys that night. Pansa had decided to return to her family, leaving Krys in my care. She told me that despite our feelings for one another, it wouldn't work out in the long run, and bid Krys and I a fulfilling life together.

I felt that it was probably one dream I could live without sharing, and dismissed it from my mind.

Pansa is hovering over my face as I awaken, looking intensely into my eyes.

"Oh, hi."

She kisses me briefly, and sits up. "I was just admiring you in deep sleep."

"I don't imagine there is much to admire."

Giggling, she places a hand on my shoulder. "You looked quite pleased as you dreamt. Was it anything exciting?"

"No, not particularly. Nothing I remember, anyway." I also sit up, stretching my arms. "Where has Krys gone?"

"I sent her out to pick some berries."

I cast her a concerned look.

"Don't worry. She isn't more than five yards from us." She points off to her left, and I see Krys moving amidst the bushes, as though she consistently finds little surprises in the foliage.

"She seems to be enjoying herself," I say with a smile.

"Yes, well I sent her to do that for a reason. I wanted to ask something of you."

I feel my stomach drop, but try to ignore it. "What is it you want to ask?"

"Well, I was looking around in your bag the other day for some string and wax as I worked on the bow for Krys, and I thought I saw something peculiar. A small book, to be more precise."

I saw the side of her mouth perk ever so slightly as she finished speaking, but offered her benefit of the doubt.

"Did you happen to notice what it said on the cover?"

"Not really. I wasn't trying to be nosy, so I didn't take a direct look."

"Alright, well feel free to ask for something from my satchel the next time you need it."

Pansa appears neutral to my response. I could only assume that though she may be slightly discontented with my secret, I also know that she respects me enough to not inquire further.

Then again, it is possible that she lied entirely about not seeing the book more clearly, and is merely testing me.

Krys returns with a little bag stuffed full of assorted berries. "I found so many of them, Pansa!" She hands the bag over.

"Wow, that certainly is a lot of berries. You may have to eat a few handfuls as we pack up to lighten the load."

Krys accepts the bag gleefully, and begins to do just that.

With our belongings set, Krys, Pansa and I continue our journey across the land, hoping to find whatever information we can to help aid in locating Krys' point of origin, and from there, finding the sanctuary of Adleborough.

"Oh, I know these parts. This is an area I passed through before I met you, Kitso. There's a town very near to here."

I am thrilled. "That sounds great! I'm more than ready to be indoors before the next snow."

"Does it have any informative resources?" asks Krys.

"I don't know," Pansa responds quietly. "I haven't been there myself, but heard about it from another traveler."

"They're bound to have a nice inn though," I proclaim.

Pansa huffs quite audibly. "With your constant talk of the cold, I am surprised we're not freezing by this point."

I grin mischievously. "If you prefer, I could turn you a... cold shoulder."

She shakes her head, saying nothing.

"Your smile is unconvincing."

I duck my head as a snowball flies by.

Thankfully, we approach the settlement by mid-evening. My feet feel numb, which is only further impressed by the cold stone trailing from the town's gate.

"This place looks amazing," comments Krys.

Pansa adds her thought. "I am fond of the entry. They've made good use of timber for the fence."

Extending from either side of the gate, several beams of timber run vertically about five feet from each other. Many stripped branches intertwine with one another betwixt the beams, making for an intricate design, as though someone has woven fibers in a beautiful pattern around their fingers. As far as I notice, the fence runs for a distance either way before being stopped by a structure.

Walking through the opening, I spot a nicely shaped beam of timber overhead. It features a fancy carving of which I presume must be the town's name. Just as I read it to myself, a jovial individual greets us, whom I swear could almost pass for a sibling of mine.

"Hello to you, cousin, and fellow travelers! Welcome to our humble town of Timbervale!"

That is to say, if it weren't for his eccentric display to complete strangers.

Krys is the first to speak. "Thank you, sir. Your entryway is so pretty! I can't stop admiring it."

He laughs. "Thank you, young lady. Timbervale prides itself utilizing wood for the entirety of the structures, save for the fire pits within our homes. That'd be simply foolish."

"Indeed it would be," I remark. "Say, you wouldn't happen to be familiar with the Vulpani Tribe, would you?"

"No, I haven't heard of them. I was bore and raised here. I do have an aunt who grew up in a tribe, though. I forget which tribe, as she doesn't speak of it much."

"Since these two are obviously too enthralled for a proper introduction," interjects Pansa, "I may as well speak for us all. I am Pansa, a member of the Panteo clan, and this is Kitso, my mate from said tribe. And this is Krys, who is particularly outgoing, as you've witnessed."

"You all are a very nice family. We like family here!"

"Oh, we're not family," Krys says nonchalantly. "I only just met Pansa and Kitso a few—"

Pansa intervenes. "A few months ago, we adopted Krys when we heard that her parents passed away. She was left in care of a rather hostile associate—we couldn't stand for it." She gently places a hand upon Krys' head.

It takes Krys only a moment to catch on. "Yes, mother, that's correct. You aren't upset with me speaking hastily, are you, father?" She glances up to me.

"Not in the least. We know you've been unable to express yourself in former company. I am proud of you."

Apparently, we had little trouble convincing our greeter.

"Oh, that is precious. My own mother would welcome you all with open arms! By the way, my name is Byron. Please, follow me."

Byron leads us through the town, the path of stone coursing amidst every structure as though they were built with the path's design in mind. As I take a closer look at the homes, I note that indeed everything is fashioned purely from wood—not a single piece bound by fiber or metal—carved to lock together in such an impressive way.

"These buildings are absolutely brilliant," I speak with awe. "They have me look at crafting in a whole new way."

"Thank you. That means a lot to us from travelers. Many who come through only criticize us for our... primitive nature. They don't realize how much time and effort is spent in planning alone, much less building."

"I must say that it is undoubtedly remarkable what you can achieve with such craftsmanship. I myself love to work

TIMBERVILLE

in many ways with nature's finest materials, albeit with much less grandeur."

Pansa chimes in. "Aside from wood, does your family delve into other trades, Byron?"

"Certainly. My mother comes from a line of fishermen. She is the first female in her line to master the art, and has gone so far as to trade with fisheries abroad. My father was an artist, learned from generations of such. Sadly, he's passed as of two years ago."

"My condolences," I murmur.

Byron nods in appreciation. "He carved Timbervale's namesake in the timber you saw initially. It originally graced our home's wall. Our council raised it in honor of his passing, as he was a head councilman. It is partly the reason I welcome everyone that makes their way through."

As the night befalls Timbervale, we're shown to the inn. "You all must be very tired. Thank you for taking the time to admire our works. I hope that wherever you head in the morning, you don't soon forget us."

"Actually, we were considering staying for a day or three," I tell him. "We are in no particular hurry to see the world."

"Ah, casual wanderers. I can appreciate that. Then please make yourselves at home as though it is your own town!" Byron calls out to a figure I only just noticed, sweeping a corner of the inn. "Gwen, would you kindly fetch our guests some sumacade?"

"Yes, I'll do so," Gwen replies with a small bow.

We all sit at a large, rectangular table, benches running along the sides. There are no others present than the maid.

The only sound I note is the faint crackling of the nearby fire pit. As suggested, it's formed from roughly hewn stone blocks, set into a fairly large circle. Flames cast dull shadows from our movement, and cast the entire place in a soft glow.

"I wonder where everyone has gone," Pansa wonders aloud. "Come to think of it, there wasn't anyone else outside."

"The town is engaged in a council meeting," remarks Gwen. "You happened upon us during our monthly rapport."

"How long does it last for?" I ask.

"Usually no more than a few hours. There should be another half-hour or so remaining at most."

"It doesn't sound like too much fun," comments Krys.

Gwen brings over a small, wooden tray bearing three goblets, also made of wood. She sets each one in front of us. "You're welcome to see for yourself, if you'd like. The council hall is outside the inn to your right, two buildings down. It bears the emblem of an oak leaf on the front."

"Thank you for the drinks, Gwen," I comment. "Perhaps we'll take a look."

She bows lightly, and returns to sweeping.

I turn back to Pansa and Krys. "Well, what do you two think? Should we go see what everyone is about?"

"I think it may be a good idea," responds Pansa. "We might even hear about some helpful information."

Krys moans. "Must we?"

Pansa smiles. "You don't have to come along, Krys. If you want to, you can get a head start on resting in our room." Pansa thinks to herself, and calls over to Gwen. "Gwen, which room will we be staying in?"

"Whichever you like, as we have no other travelers tonight, what with the recent snow. Though, I recommend the one to the right of our bar. We restuffed the bed recently."

At the mention, Krys gets up, and stretches with a yawn. "Good night, you two."

"Good night, Krys," I say to her.

Pansa gets up and hugs her. "Sleep well. We'll be there within the hour."

Krys then heads to the room, goblet in hand.

"This really is a fantastic place, isn't it, Pansa?"

"I couldn't agree more, despite you being a tad irked with that fellow Byron."

"What do you mean?"

She laughs. "I could tell his exuberance annoyed you."

"Alright, I will admit that, though I found him less annoying as we talked with him. I believe he may have simply been deprived from greeting others for some time."

We hear a giggle come from Gwen. "You are right. We've not seen much activity as of late. The last one to pass through Timbervale was about three weeks ago."

Warmed from the fire and the sumacade , we make our way over to the council hall. As we approach the dim glow of the doorway, I hear inaudible banter, which quickly becomes more clear as we step inside.

"... Which I, for one, find to be preposterous. We can't very well begin outsourcing our firewood. As soon as the next storm comes, the caravans will cease entirely. Timbervale is simply not going to survive by—"

The voice stops suddenly, a brief moment after we walk in. Heads slowly turn to us a few at a time, until almost the entire congregation is staring at us. Byron is standing near the door, and he gestures to us, followed by pointing to himself.

The discussion commences just as quickly as it ceased. "As I was saying, at the rate we've declined in passersby, the trade caravans won't be any more encouraged to continue with us."

Another voice from the council table speaks. "We need the additional timber from the storehouse to repair some homes before the coming storm. It has been put off for too long."

"Five weeks isn't too long. What is another three?"

Yet another speaks up. "The last three weeks haven't seen but one traveler, aside from those two, of course. Katara is right. No one is going to want to invest their time coming all this way with some measly coins to exchange for firewood."

Someone amongst the crowd stands up. "Can't those who are in need of home repair stay at the inn? I mean, you said so yourself that few come here nowadays, so why can't we use the extra space in the meantime?"

As they sit back down, the previous voice replies. "That isn't a bad idea. We'll surely be able to use the excess wood we've gathered to keep warm beyond the storm for a good month. Should anyone find themselves against this motion, speak now, please."

Not a sound was made.

"Good. We'll see to it that everyone in need can settle at the inn. Now, what was next?"

A prominent figure presents a short trail of parchment, scanning it intensely. "We must discuss the development plans for a greenhouse... and then plan our excursion over to Tinderburg next week."

At the center of the council table, a large being rises slowly, clearing his throat. "We shall commence tomorrow evening. I tire from the excess argument, and find the air to carry a chill tonight. I want everyone who is needing to board at the inn to see Katara for book-keeping. She will follow up with Gwen for necessary arrangement and preparation as you pack some belongings. Everyone is dismissed." He sounds a small hand bell. At the sound, almost everyone stands simultaneously, conversation ensuing.

Byron comes over to us. "What did you think of that small taste of our council meetings?"

"It was astoundingly drab," I remark.

He chortles. "Not all of them can be exciting, I guess. Did you get a room set up with Gwen?"

"Yes, we did. She suggested a room that had its bed restuffed."

"Good, because the inn will be nigh full once we're all finished here. Are you headed back now?"

I shake my head. "Not quite. We were hoping to ask someone about your town's archive."

"Ah, that would be Katara. She is directly involved with anything that has to do with Timbervale's record-keeping and history. She is my grandmother's sister's cousin's daughter."

We stare blankly at him, as Pansa cautions a response. "Your family has... quite a history with this town, I imagine."

"My father wasn't a head of the council for no reason," he says with a wink.

Pansa and I wait around for a chance to speak with Katara. We find a bench to sit on after several others leave. I hold Pansa's hand in mine, and smile at her. She returns a smile, and we watch as the hall becomes quieter.

It doesn't take too long for the line formed by the needy townsfolk to end, and before we know it, Katara makes her way over to us, and sits down beside Pansa.

"Hello, you two. I am Katara, the head of Timbervale's archival efforts. I heard that you became acquainted with my relative, Byron. He had mentioned that you are interested in our history."

"More or less," I said. "We find Timbervale to be an exceptional town, more unique and friendly than most places we've been. We've come a long way with our daughter since we adopted her, and haven't found a decent place to rest until now. The last place we saw had not been so kind to us. What was it called again, Pansa?"

"Telios, I believe. I've quickly forgotten the name."

Katara nods. "I have heard a few unfortunate things about Telios last year. Nothing monumental, though."

I continue. "Anyway, we wish to enrich ourselves with information about this place so that we may grace our travels with regard to Timbervale. Perhaps some history, a little bit of its culture... possibly some trade records."

Katara withdraws a pad of parchment and a writing utensil, and begins to make notes as I speak. "Yes, I am sure we can lend you a hand in finding out all you would like to know. I profess in our historical culture and background. As for records of trade, you'll have to refer to Sybol."

Pansa smirks. "Let me guess. Sybol is also a relative."

Katara looks down, trying to hide a smile. "I suppose you are no strangers to our family's extent. She is my elder sister." Looking back up at us, Katara continues. "Though, she is already asleep by now. We live next door from this hall, to the left. You can find the inn one more building over."

I scratch my cheek. "That's easy to remember."

"Sybol will be up first thing in the morning."

"I'll meet up with her then," says Pansa.

By the time we return to the inn, everyone who saw Katara before us has already begun to settle in. About a third of them are sitting in the common area, most of them having one form of drink or another.

We retreat to our quarters. I notice that, like the rest of the buildings, there are no windows whatsoever, presumably to keep the cold out and heat in this season. The center of the room has a table bearing a lit candle. We find Krys huddled to one side of the bed, hugging a pillow. She is snoring softly.

"She has the cutest snore," Pansa tells me.

"I find yours to be cuter."

She scoffs. "I do not snore!"

"If you say so."

Pansa draws a thick, burlap curtain over the doorway, then proceeds to a nearby nook bearing three shelves vertical to one another, where she removes her mantle to place within the middle. "It is good to be inside, safe and warm." She also removes her clothing, and I promptly wander over to the bed to sit, unpacking my satchel to keep busy.

Pansa chuckles. "You are still quite shy, despite your proud demeanor."

"I just harbor a great deal of respect for you."

"If you say so," she retorts. I can hear the grin in her voice. "You know, we will have to sleep together with Krys hogging one side, so try to keep your paws to yourself, okay?"

I cannot help but to look at her abruptly. "What are you going on about?!"

"Are you really unaware?" She tries to read my face, and discovers my ignorance. "You do know that your hands tend to wander a bit while you sleep by me, don't you?"

"No, I really had no idea. I'm sorry."

"It's nothing to shame yourself for," she says.

I look off to the side, unsure of what to say.

She sits beside me, and strokes my cheek. "Sorry for teasing you. I'm not offended by it. If anything, I am flattered." She sighs. "Let's just get some sleep, shall we?"

I nod, and she tucks herself in beside Krys. I put out the candle and follow suit. "Good night, Pansa. I love you."

"I love you too, Kitso."

Chapter 18

I awaken to a soft chatter. It takes me a moment to recall where we are. I am so used to waking up with the sun before anyone else that I found myself a bit confused to hear others talking when I came to.

I can't see a whole lot, as there are no windows, but what little light there is coming from under the curtain, I should have little trouble making my way around the room.

I try to roll to my left, and bump into Kitso, almost waking him. His arm is around me, partly under my breasts. He is hugging me, and only tightened his grip when I shifted. Krys hasn't moved an inch since we went to bed, and I realize that I won't be going anywhere.

I suppose that I'll have to catch Sybol at a later time.

Just as I am about to drift back to sleep, Krys begins to move, and slowly sits up. She whispers, "Pansa, are you awake?"

"Yes, Krys. How did you sleep?"

"I slept pretty well. I have to relieve myself, though."

"Give me a moment to get up, and we'll see Gwen."

It doesn't take us long to strategically get up without waking Kitso, and I find that I am still surprised at how he can sleep through it all.

Krys and I find Gwen talking with one of the townsfolk at the bar. She greets us with a warm smile.

I walk up to her and whisper our little situation, at which she excuses herself from company, and has us follow her to a back room.

"Take your time. I empty the pot regularly."

Krys looks at me. "What does she mean, Pansa?"

I try to find words. "Well, some places lack the luxury you may've been used to, or the... freedom of nature."

She gets a disgruntled look on her face, but concedes.

When Krys enters the room, Gwen looks over to me. "She is so adorable. You and your mate are fortunate to have adopted such a girl."

"Thank you. Have you any of your own?"

"No... I cannot bear one, unfortunately, and have no mate. However, I am content as I am, and I am happy to serve others who may need me in their own way."

"Yes, I imagine many a traveler seeks warm food and drink, as well as shelter."

"Amongst other things..."

I nod absentmindedly, and then realize what she meant. I glance at her, unsure of what to say, and she looks down, blushing.

"There are perks to being barren, I suppose."

Krys comes back out, and thanks Gwen for her kindness. I encourage Krys to catch up on sleep while I tend to business.

She heads back to the room, and I sit to dine with Gwen for the morning.

As I step outside, someone asks me to spare them a parupeteng flower. I offer them one, and have one myself. When I finished, I thought it strange that someone might ask me for something they couldn't have known I had. *They were probably just chancing it, Pansa. Don't be so paranoid.*

I enter the building next door, and find who I presume to be Sybol sitting on a stool at a desk with a large book in hand, back turned to me. She sports long, grey hair.

I clear my throat. Nothing happens.

I attempt it again, but to no avail.

As I begin coughing, she speaks. "You should probably have that checked out. Our doctor is out the door, straight across, three buildings to your right, second room to your left."

"Thank you very much for that wonderful advice. Are you Sybol?"

She doesn't flinch the slightest, and seems totally absorbed in her reading. "Well, that all relies on what kind of information you seek."

"I am interested in the history of Timbervale and some of its cultural background. Oh, and perhaps trading documents."

"The history and culture I can understand, but why on earth would you desire records of exchange?"

I carefully consider my approach, but find myself a little irritated. "I want to completely undermine your progress, and establish a route of success for my own lofty desires."

Surprisingly, she bursts out laughing, and sets the book down. She turns about on the stool to face me. "Finally, someone with a quick wit and appreciation for dry humor! You must be Pansa. Charmed."

She extends a hand, which I shake cautiously. *Humor, huh? Glad you haven't met Kitso yet.*

"Are you surprised to find word travel so quickly in such a small town?"

"Not particularly."

"Of course, that would not be saying much in the presence of someone like myself who makes everyone else's business her own."

I now know why I found myself to be irritated.

"So you and yours have come quite a way to interest yourselves with us. Surely you possess ulterior motive, no? Nobody just comes asking for such. Nobody."

I give her a cautious glance.

"It is okay, darling. Just because I make it my business, it does not mean others hear about it all. I am a historian, not a busybody. But you must understand that sharing delicate details of our affairs is no light matter."

I've decided it was better to open up to her, rather than having her find out on her own. I clear my throat once more. "Kitso and I have known each other for some time. We are mates, but we haven't officially adopted Krys. She happened upon us one night, frozen to the core. We invited her to stay with us, and over the next day, she told us about her situation, involving the passing of her parents, and being sent to stay with her uncle to live under his rule in Telios. She was pressured to marry into a foreign family, that he might gain a foot into royalty to presumably exercise his unruly nature."

Sybol sits and considers all I've spoken, a finger curling at the tips of her hair. "Very intriguing. I imagine you are wanting to help Krys go somewhere, and so you and Kitso have taken it upon yourselves to bring her there."

"Yes. We want to help her find a place from her earlier childhood."

"I suppose you have no idea about the name or general location, or you would have asked for a map."

"We only know about some details of the landscape, but nothing we can go off of yet."

"Hmm…" She takes a long look at me. I get the feeling that she is trying to find out all she can without asking me directly.

I really hate it when others do that.

"Well then, since you are obviously not at all interested in our background, you could at least humor me, and take a couple of books with you to read about it nonetheless." She holds out a sizable book. "This one will introduce our history—naturally there is an encyclopaedia dedicated to the remainder." She hands me another larger, surprisingly lighter, book. "And that is a collection of various letters and documents regarding the background of everyone who has lived here since our beginning. Oh, and of course, record of every exchange, trade and traveler." I receive a heavy, leather binder.

On my way back to the inn, I settle the load of information upon a nearby bench, and take a seat. I pull out another flower, and sit back, sighing.

Well that was an enlightening trip. It's a good thing I love to read.

Don't worry, Kitso will help you sort through it.

I lean forward, hands on my head. *Please... I really am not in the mood.*

That's the wonderful thing about it. You needn't be in the mood for a conversation with yourself.

Just go away already! I almost lash out, when a couple walks by. They nod at me, continuing by.

Really, now... I am being totally civil. It is you who is lashing out at yourself.

"Yes, I know that I can count on Kitso to help with all of this. Even Krys may be happy to help."

That's more like it. Kitso has always been there for you. He is faithful like that.

I smile to myself, staring off into the distance.

It's probably just because he has a great interest in you. Of course, he also shares the same notion for Krys.

I lurch upright, and almost shout. "That—" I catch myself, and tense up. *That simply isn't true!*

Are you so sure of yourself? She is a fair bit younger, and healthier, too.

Kitso cares little for those things! He loves me for who I am, not what I am. I almost begin to cry.

She's in perfect condition for a mate. In fact, she could probably bear children, despite their—

I jump up, shoving any loose thoughts out of my mind with such ferocity that my temples strain. I grab the materials. and head off to the inn, trying my best to hurry without seeming hastiness.

I step inside, and to a small relief, find everyone but Gwen has left the inn. I ask if Kitso or Krys have left yet, and she says she hasn't noticed. I request if she wouldn't mind taking a look around town while I go through the materials loaned to me.

"I'll go and ask Byron if he has seen them. He regularly patrols the town, noting anybody going about their business." She leaves.

I take a few deep breaths, inadvertently bracing myself, and walk over to our room. Slowly, I push the curtain aside, and step in.

I allow my eyes to adjust in the incredibly dim light before moving any farther. I take a couple steps and peer over at the bed. Both Kitso and Krys appear to still be sleeping. Then, I hear a faint ruffle from Kitso shifting, and a giggle from Krys.

My face burns, and I slam the books onto the table, startling the both of them.

"Whoa, what's going on?!" Kitso asks, nigh shouting.

"I want to ask the same thing!"

"Pansa, is that you?" wonders Krys. She is quite alarmed at the situation.

I feel bad for waking her, and extremely upset at Kitso. I am not sure if I want to scream or cry, but I do neither as I rush out, almost tripping over a chair.

I pray that no one sees me run outside of the inn, and thankfully, pass nobody as I round the building, heading for the gate.

I pass the entrance, and graze my heels on the stone. Running farther, I slow down, and stop at a tree. I punch it, scraping my knuckles. My ears pound with pressure.

Pansa, why are you so upset?

I punch it again, causing a cut to begin bleeding.

Please, stop. This is no way to vent.

I hit the tree over and again until my arms give out, and kneel to the ground. *Shut up! Shut up! Shut up!!*

"Pansa! Please stop!"

Instantly, it occurs to me that what I had heard wasn't in my head. I look up, eyes straining to see beyond the tears flooding my face.

A soft cloth graces my eyes, as a gentle hand holds my chin in place. The voice belongs to Gwen.

After what seemed an eternity, I begin to regain a semblance of sanity. All I did was sit with Gwen on the ground, crying and shouting incoherently, as she hushed and held me. I felt terrible then, unsure why, as I hadn't asked her to stay by me.

"Are you feeling any better?"

I nod shakily, sniffing. She offers another cloth.

"Now, tell me again what has happened."

She says "again" as though I just told her, but I can't recall saying anything. I sigh, tears edging in. "I went into our room, and saw Kitso and Krys there in bed."

"So they were still asleep after all. That's good."

"I saw Kitso slide an arm over Krys, and she giggled in such a way that…" I feel no breath in my lungs, and I gasp so heavily I begin to seize. Gwen calms me down, rubbing my back.

"You believe that Kitso was—"

"I know he was!"

She places a gentle but firm finger on my lips. "No, you do not know."

"But how can—"

She breathes, and huffs. "Honey, I will be blunt with you. I know a number of males, and I can say beyond a doubt that Kitso is not that type. I won't pretend that you didn't see anything, but for your sake, I hope you at least provide him the benefit of the doubt."

Gwen says nothing else on the matter, and makes sure I am stable enough to sit up before rising from the ground. "Take a few moments for yourself to calm, and return before dark." She places a hand on my head, whispering something before walking away.

I sit for several minutes in silence, hearing little else than my own breathing. *Why do I feel like I've done something wrong? She couldn't be any older than me, and I feel as though my own mother just scolded me!*

Feeling terrible about everything, I pity myself a little while longer before heading back. *Or, as it would seem, if I had a mother…*

* * *

I am sitting with Krys at the bar, attempting to gather my consciousness. After Pansa had awoken us, I found it impossible to relax. I have no idea as to what might've happened, but whatever it was it has obviously upset her so.

Krys had asked me what was going on, but I admitted that I didn't know.

"Is it because we over-slept?"

"No, I don't think so. You're typically up with her in the morning, so I doubt she would be unhappy with you catching up on rest."

"I had to relieve myself the first time we got up, and she told me to go back to sleep."

I nod. "It sounds like her, so we know it couldn't be that."

"There you two are." I turn around to see Gwen, Byron close behind, as they enter the inn. "We've been worried about you."

"We haven't left since last night. Is Pansa about?"

Byron speaks. "Krys, I want to show you where my mother and I live. Will you come with me, please?"

Krys hops down from her seat, and follows Byron to the door. "I'll be back by nightfall, father."

I smile at her, and turn back to the bar. Gwen walks around to stand in front of me. She waits patiently for me to say something first.

"Is she alright?"

"I found her outside of the town about a hundred paces, punching a tree."

I stare at the grain in the bar top, tracing lines with a finger. "Whatever it was, it must have been pretty awful."

"Kitso, Pansa believes that you were engaging with Krys."

I shoot up. "What? That's outrageous! Why would she—"

"Please." She raises a hand. "Don't shout. I am not accusing you of anything. I am only relaying what I've heard."

"Sorry." I sit back down. "I just... don't understand why she would think that. Pansa sent her back to sleep. Why would she consider that if she thought I would do something with Krys?"

Gwen speaks in a soft voice. "I don't know, Kitso. I only know that whatever she witnessed led her to believe such."

"... What is it that she saw?"

"She said that your arm moved over Krys, causing her to react in a way that seemed as though you were awake."

Wandering hands. That must have been it. I feel both sick and relieved. "Thank you for telling me about this, Gwen."

"You're welcome. I told her that you do not seem to be that type. The last thing I want to see is you two leave each other over a misunderstanding."

I stand once more. "I've every intent to clear this with her."

"That makes me happy to hear. If you would like, I will make myself present as a mediator."

"Thank you, but I want us to sort this out on our own."

She gives me a short hug. "My blessings upon you both."
As Gwen returns to her duties, I go to find Pansa.

As was mentioned, I found her outside of Timbervale. I have my mantle on, and brought Pansa's along, just in case the eve decided to get colder.

When she sees me approach her, she turns her back to me, almost as if she plans on running away.

"Please don't run, Pansa. I only want to talk."

"I... don't plan on running." Her voice is choked.

I sigh, finding it difficult to begin. "Gwen talked with me a short while ago. She mentioned that you were out here."

Pansa doesn't respond. I am not even sure that she is listening to what I say.

"I know that you came into our room as Krys and I were sleeping, and I am certain I know what you saw, despite our being unconscious." My heart quickens as I continue. "Remember how you mentioned that I have wandering hands when I sleep?"

"How can I trust you?" Her voice sounds to be on the verge of yelling, but she never speaks any louder. "How do I know for sure that you were asleep?"

I glance at my feet. "There is no way I can prove that. The only thing I can do is speak the truth. Whether or not you believe me... that is up to you."

Pausing for a moment, I begin to walk away. Not three steps later, I hear shuffling behind me, and I stop.

"Please don't leave me, Kitso." Her voice cracks into a whine, and I find it increasingly difficult to stay calm.

"I was headed back to the inn."

She grabs my arm, only to release it suddenly. "Please don't leave me... forever. I'm sorry that I thought you did anything. I just don't know what to think..."

I turn around, casting Pansa's mantle over her. She grabs at it to pull it tightly against herself, and cries. I touch the side of her head, and she leans into me, gently pounding a fist onto my chest. I flinch, but let her do so.

"You should not be the one apologizing," I say. "My lack of awareness is no reason for you to hold any responsibility. I am sorry for what happened."

She hits my chest again, a little harder this time. "Stop being so calm about it! Don't you ever have emotions?!"

"Yes, I do. Just because I portray emotions a little differently, that doesn't mean I don't experience them." I hug her close, and stroke her head. "I am not ever going to leave you. I love you very much, and have no interest in being with anyone but you."

Her crying lessens to a sob. "I hope not, because I don't think I could live without you."

I think to myself. "If it makes you feel any better, we'll have Krys sleep on the opposite side of you. Okay?"

Chapter 19

The sun begins to hide from view as Pansa and I return to the inn. It veils its face from the world, feeling ashamed for keeping nature awake for so long today, as I shame myself for causing Pansa to feel what she does.

I know I cannot control myself in my sleep, and although I do not logically find reason to blame myself, I still feel awful.

The inn is quiet tonight—everyone has taken in early as the air grows all the more frigid. A storm indeed approaches.

Upon entering our room, we find Krys kneeling at the side of the bed. She notices us, and jumps up to run over to us.

"I was so scared, Pansa!" Krys exclaims as she hugs Pansa. She then hugs me. "Thank you for bringing her back safely. What happened?"

"Pansa just needed to take some time out for herself. She was feeling very stressed."

Krys walks back over to the bed, and crawls up onto it to sit. "Sometimes, I find a quiet place to sit and pray to myself when I feel that way. I was praying that you were okay."

"Thank you, Krys," Pansa replies. "I am okay now."

I can tell by her tension holding my hand that she isn't okay, but I know better than to say anything.

"Why don't you go ahead and tuck in for the night, while Kitso and I take a look through all these documents and books?"

"But I'm not tired. Besides, I want to help!"

I see the spark of enthusiasm in Krys' eyes. "Why not let her stay up with us, Pansa? She obviously really wants to help us, considering it's her past we're after anyway."

Pansa sighs. "Alright, you can help. Just be honest with us when you begin to feel tired."

Krys nods excitedly, and shifts over to the end of the bed. Pansa sits down at the table, and I drag a chair from outside the room to join them.

We had divided the materials amongst ourselves—I began with the book on Timbervale's history. Pansa took the book on the town's culture, as she found it to seem more fun. Krys happily worked through the papers documenting trade history, as she has experience in that department.

Throughout our paper-filled journey, Gwen frequents upon us with refreshments, occasionally chatting to see what we've discovered.

"I never knew that a town's roots could impact its development so much," I mention.

"Yes, I can say that many of us are proud to have helped in founding it all."

Pansa chimes in. "These traditions are remarkable. We Panteo are familiar with a few of them. Do they stem from Byron's family, or are they adopted from various tribes?"

"Some of our traditions are derived from his aunt's former tribe, and other ones Timbervale has picked up from a few travelers over the years, mostly in recognition of his family's lineage."

"Is it true that you're responsible for distribution of over seventy-three percent of this province's wood supply?" Krys asks with both amazement and disbelief in her voice.

Gwen flashes a smile. "That's right, dear, and although that number has decreased over time, we haven't given up on sustaining our growth with other trade, as you'll see."

As Gwen steps back out, Krys settles the papers in front of her, and slides under the covers. "I guess I'll read more about it tomorrow."

"Krys, would you mind sliding over to one side? I'd like to sleep next to Kitso again tonight."

"I don't mind. You two probably miss being next to each other with me always in the middle. I feel safe enough here."

"Thank you." Pansa turns to me. "Should we also head to bed for the night?"

"Yeah, that sounds like a good idea after such a long day. I will read for a little while longer as I relax."

We tuck in for the night, and I bring the book to bed with me to continue reading until my mind can settle as well.

Timbervale's history is truly fascinating. I am not sure how any of this will help us discover anything of Krys or her past, but I know it will lead us somewhere.

I set the book under my pillow, and put out the light. I watch its glimmer fade into the dark as I drift off, pursuing my own sense of nothingness.

* * *

Pansa, Krys and I are enjoying lunch in the common area. Well, lunch to them. For me, I consider it breakfast.

Byron has decided to join us, and has brought his mother to introduce Pansa and I. She is a very kindly lady, deliberate in her demeanor, and I am reminded of the times when Vulpena would dine with me.

We discuss our venture into the heart of Timbervale, much to my expense.

"Seriously, he had the book under his pillow, as though we'd have run off with it," Pansa proclaims with laughter.

Byron joins in commentary. "It's rare to witness an outsider fancy themselves with our history. Cherish it!"

"I'm pleased to know my son has found such good company in you three," says Byron's mother. "Your family's presence warms this woman's heart."

"We are happy to get to know you all," Krys remarks.

"Thank you, child. Had your guardians not beaten me to it, I'd have adopted you when you came by the other day."

"If she ever becomes too much to handle, we'll send her your way," I say.

Pansa slaps my arm, giving me a nasty look.

"What? I was only joking!"

"You are a nice family, albeit strange at times," Byron announces aimlessly.

They both bid us a good day, as we return straight to researching.

As we continue our pursuit of more information, I feel a small draft begin to pick up. I walk to the front door to see snow falling.

"I cannot believe it has already begun to snow again. It isn't even the start of the coming storm."

Gwen comes over to see. "I imagine this year is going to be particularly bad. We're due for an awful one."

I chuckle, shaking my head. "What is it with you females and your fascination for the worst weather?"

She laughs as she goes about her business, tending to the townsfolk.

I wander back to Pansa and Krys. "It's snowing..."

Pansa teases me. "Since when did you become interested in the cold weather?"

"I just want it to go away!"

"Well looking at it won't encourage that."

Sitting back down, I continue to ponder the history book.

Krys cocks her head as she shuffles through various papers, setting them in some sort of order. "Huh, that's interesting."

"What did you find, Krys?" Pansa asks her.

"Oh, nothing too exciting. It just seems the spice trade is gonna be less prominent as the weather warms this year."

I furrow my brows. "How do you figure?"

She responds, pointing to a few papers. "Well, according to these dockets here, wild growth is increasing for more southern towns, as indicated by their surplus trades. If that trend continues," she goes on, as though the papers are puzzle pieces designed with her in mind, "then there'll be a bumper of spice production, causing prices to drop.

"I also noticed that there's a drought coming the year after, based on the weather patterns. It'd be a great time to buy up all the spice, and store it to trade again later."

I stare off into space, completely astonished.

Pansa seems to have little to say herself. "I suppose there's more than just trade documented there."

I perk up with an idea. "Perhaps we may get her an audience with the council. I'm sure they'd love to hear this."

Krys glances at me. "Do you mean to have me speak in front of everyone?"

"Kitso, she's only a child."

"That doesn't mean they won't listen!"

"That's not what I meant."

I look at Krys. She is glancing down at the papers, looking considerably disturbed. Her face tells the small tale of someone who may have gotten into trouble.

I place a hand on her shoulder, causing her to become alert. "You don't have to speak in front of everyone, Krys. I apologize for the suggestion. But, if you decide to, it would likely help immensely. Pansa and I would be there, giving you our full support."

Her eyes wander back to the documents. "It would be a nice thing to do, but what if everyone thinks it's silly?"

Pansa speaks up. "Nobody could ever deny that you have exceptional skill for this kind of thing. They would be sure to listen to what you have to say."

"May I think about it?"

"As much as you like. Here, why don't you take a look through this book of culture? It's sure to clear your mind."

Krys accepts the book, and begins to finger through it as Pansa gathers up the scattered trade documents into their respective binder.

"Wow, they sure do some weird things during the cold weather," Krys says with glee.

Pansa giggles. "I thought the same thing when I read it."

Late into the afternoon, we finish up with all that we've been given. Much to our dismay, we find nothing that stands out as helpful or important to our adventure.

"Well, that's too bad. It did make for a nice learning experience, though," I remark, as I settle it all together.

Pansa nods. "I expected it to take us at least a full day, but across the mandatory law papers, family trees, and the illustrations, there was a lot less to actually read."

I shrug. "Perhaps it'll serve a purpose at a later date. You never know when something you've read comes up somewhere else."

"Kitso," Krys says as she gingerly places a hand on my forearm. "I decided that I want to help Timbervale."

Excitement fills me. "Really? That's great!"

"I just don't want to talk in front of everybody."

"Maybe we can have you meet with the council only."

"Will you still be with me?"

I smile as I pat her head. "Of course. Both Pansa and I will be right there by your side the whole time."

I have Pansa and Krys go to meet with Katara and Sybol to express our interest in procuring the documents, while I speak with Byron on behalf of our intentions.

* * *

Krys and I enter into Katara and Sybol's home to return what was lent to us. Kitso suggested we mention which documents we need for Krys' presentation as we discuss our potential discovery.

We find Katara sipping from a cup as she lounges lazily by the fire.

"Oh, hello you two. Find anything interesting?"

"Very much so," I tell her. "Sadly, nothing overly helpful to us."

"Oh, that's too bad. If you're done with everything, you can find Sybol in the back room. She's likely ready for bed."

I step into the back room with Krys right behind me, and get taken aback momentarily. Sybol apparently is quite ready for bed, as she is almost entirely unclad. Her back is turned as she straightens the bed.

"Pansa, I presume?" She turns about to face me. "Indeed! Oh, company. This must be little Krys."

My face is warm. I try to not show embarrassment. "Thank you for lending us everything, Sybol."

"Please, darling. It is nothing you would be unfamiliar with. We are all women here."

As my vision is focused elsewhere, I notice big blue eyes looking up at me. *Now I know what Kitso must have felt in a sense.* "What is she talking about, Pansa?"

Does this child know no shame?

"It's nothing, Krys. How did you know it was me, Sybol?"

"Considering the time of day, and the recent events, I suspected you would have finished with the materials that I furnished for your enlightenment. On top of that, you tend to step quite noisily."

The last thing I want to consider is how I walk.

"Anyway, we've come to talk to you about something that you might find intriguing."

Sybol sets a couple of chairs out for us, and flops onto the bed, reaching for a notepad and quill. Despite her professional etiquette, she certainly surprises me.

"It must be something to talk about if it is to intrigue me. Well then, let us hear of it."

Krys goes on to reiterate what she discovered in the paperwork. Sybol seems absorbed with what she is told, and, after asking a few questions and writing several notes, seems contented.

"You are quite the little informant, Krys. Tell me, where do you derive such extraordinary skill?"

"My father used to trade in the market all the time. He traded with many types of merchants, learning what he could about all types of goods and trends. He also shared what he learned with me—even his records."

"Remarkable. Pansa, would you be at all opposed to me borrowing Krys for a time as you travel abroad?" Her face offers a friendly smile.

"Sure. Just get in line, and we'll let you know when your turn comes up."

Her laughter is contagious. I only cease myself when Krys appears to think that I am serious.

"Nobody could ever take you from us, Krys."

Sybol clears her throat. "I figured as much. In any event, I will happily speak with the council, and retain a set of documentation from our records."

"So, will we have time to talk with them?"

"That will not be necessary. Matters such as this are handled entirely in private."

Krys seems more than accepting of this fact.

"Oh, Sybol, do you know of any nearby locations that might provide us with maps of the area?"

"As a matter of fact, I do. Though, you are not going to appreciate where to find them."

I become unsettled. "Telios?"

"Precisely. There is a small but profound library there, housing many atlases covering the lands to every province within several dozen miles of it. However, if you are determined enough otherwise, you may find a traveler or two with copies of these maps. For the right price, of course."

I get up and shake Sybol's hand. "Thank you, Sybol, for your time and willingness to help us."

"It is the least I can do. Now, if you will kindly excuse yourselves, I have an early morning tomorrow, what with this newfound information."

We meet up with Kitso outside of Byron's home, and reflect on what we've all been told.

"Oh, well that's good to hear. Byron said that the council will hear us out, but it seems unneeded."

"Yes, Sybol told us that they prefer to handle these matters on their own terms."

"Do you think it'll make a difference?" Krys asks.

"I think you'll make a very big difference, Krys."

Heading back to the inn, I tell them both to go on inside while I take a short walk to relax. When they're gone from sight, I wander along the path, parupeteng in hand. After some time, I begin to head back.

I wish I could drop these altogether.

But then you would be without your ability to cope.

After a few nibbles, I discard the remainder. *When we find Adleborough, I swear I'll be done with these for the rest of my life.*

I return to find the others at a table with Gwen and a couple townsfolk.

"Isn't she the most adorable thing you've seen?" Gwen says to one of them.

Krys is fiddling with her tail, looking abashed.

"Certainly is. She makes me want to have another."

The male, who I assume must be her mate, gives her a look of surprise. "You must be joking."

"Why? You posed no problems with the first three."

I almost choke, laughter bubbling in my throat.

"That's because they weren't more than a year or so apart. A fourth would be five years!"

"Oh, I see how it is. A man who is afraid of such commitment. It all makes sense now."

It's normal, Gwen mouths to me silently, as the couple continues in their silly banter.

The male finally speaks to me. "Stay with one. A second only leads to more."

This seems to end the conversation, with his mate getting up and leaving the inn, at which he chases after her, apologizing profusely.

"Well that was unexpected," I say.

"You should have heard their talk of her parents. It was far more amusing!" Kitso mutters.

I cannot tell if he is being sarcastic.

Gwen bids us a good night, expressing that she probably won't be able to see us until tomorrow afternoon, and rounds the common area to clean.

When we head into our room, Krys hops onto the bed and settles under the covers. She seems thrilled from the day's events.

I slide into bed next to her, and Kitso follows after me. I face him, and hug him against myself, offering a kiss, which he reciprocates.

Krys rolls over to face the opposite wall, giggling at our display.

* * *

We all slept in until about noon. I woke up hugging Krys. She must have settled against me in the cold night. Her ears twitch as I breath, and I smile.

She awakens not long after me, and we both ease out of bed slowly.

When Krys is off the bed, I set my feet on the floor.

"I am glad to know you both slept so well."

I turn to look at Kitso just as he rolls over. There is barely enough light for me to see him grinning. "I'll be up in a little while."

Krys and I wander out of the room to find most of the residents sitting around, quietly enjoying warm drinks.

We notice Gwen at the bar, and go over to sit down. "I see that everyone here is enjoying a good Sumacadra this year."

"And I see that you've read quite a bit about our culture." She smiles, offering up a couple servings to us. "Care to join?"

"Gladly."

We take up our cups in silent prayer, and drink.

"The storm hit early this morning, settling an hour ago," Gwen tells us as she rinses cups in a bucket.

"At least Kitso will be glad to know that it passed."

"Yes, he seems to dislike the snow a fair bit."

I smile to myself, as does Krys.

"If you three head out today, be sure to bundle up. There's no telling when it'll begin again."

When we finish our drinks, we return to find Kitso slowly packing our loose belongings.

"I suppose it's time for us all to go, then," I mention.

"Yeah, there doesn't seem to be much else we can do here. Did you two happen to get any sort of additional information from Sybol?"

"Yes. We'll talk about it on the way."

"So," starts Byron, "have you all conceded to moving into Timbervale yet?"

His mother taps his shoulder, scoffing at him.

"Sadly, we must depart." I reply. "There are many wonders in this world, waiting to be admired by us as we pass through."

"We will certainly tell many others about your wonderful town," Kitso tell him, which straightens Byron's frown a bit. "Your kindness shan't be forgotten any time soon."

Byron draws a hand up to his eyes, and appears to be massaging the bridge of his nose.

He isn't very good at concealing emotion.

"That really means a lot to us. You three are the most wonderful individuals that have ever graced our town with your company. We will be forever grateful."

"We'll be sure to come back some day to see you!" Krys beams with excitement.

Chapter 20

As our departure brings us out of Timbervale, I look back to see Byron, his mother, and a few others watching us leave. I don't care for lengthy farewells, but appreciate it when others take some time out for us.

It was very nice to relax for a few days without worry of ration, or of being discovered by forces from Telios. Since Krys had stepped into our lives, this concern has always sat in the recesses of my mind.

I don't know what I would do if that were to happen.

"That was a most excellent excursion," announces Kitso. "We really ought to return some day."

Krys bears an extra bundle. "They're very kind to send us off with this food, too. I wonder what's in here."

Kitso turns his head toward it. "I sense fish."

I give him a look of disdain. "As though we don't enjoy enough fish."

"Hey, I never turn away a good meal!"

I poke Kitso on the nose. "I've noticed. I'm surprised you didn't eat them all out of home!"

"Just because I love food, doesn't mean I'll go eating everyone's portion."

"Yeah, just the leftovers."

He stands proud. "Never let good things go to waste."

We find ourselves nearing a valley. It cradles a magnificent array of white that appears to fold itself throughout the land. Though almost every foot of the ground is covered in snow, it seems much of it has gathered here to make a statement.

I look out into the horizon, a vast rolling ocean of white and brown, speckled with varied hues of orange and green. "Gwen said it'll be particularly bad this year. Should we aim to take shelter at another town?"

Kitso directs his gaze out toward the sky. "I don't know. If we hurry to another settlement too soon, word might spread quickly of our whereabouts. We have no idea where Telios will be tracking, nor are we aware of their affiliates."

"At least Timbervale was kind enough to help us."

"Perhaps by chance. For now, I don't want us taking too many risks."

"Pansa? I'm a little hungry," says Krys.

"Maybe you'd best let me carry that," I reply, as she hands me the bundle of fish. "We'll eat when we settle for the evening."

"Can we go hunting tomorrow morning?"

"Sure. If anything, it'll be good practice for us."

The sun moves across the sky, casting its brilliant glare about the icy lands. Crystalline hills reflect a sheen from their faces to show gratitude, knowing that they can only expect more cold to follow.

There's a rock face not too far from the valley. Its crags form an intricate structure that weaves along the ground, lending for a concave form. Nearby, there are several evergreens, awaiting the creation of our shelter.

Kitso and I gather several sheaves, while Krys starts to pile together all the driest of wood she can find.

With strong branches set into the snow, we all weave together the boughs against the rock, layering them.

"It's like a giant lean-to," expresses Kitso.

Krys nods, and helps him to set up a fire pit.

I set my arms against my chest, resting a hand on my cheek. "The wind is coming from that side. Shouldn't we move the fire to the other?"

They stop, and Kitso looks up toward me. "As you insist, your highness," he sneers playfully.

"I was only making an observation."

The evening finds us sooner than I imagined, its brisk winds only becoming stronger. Though the rock cuts out much of the draft, any air that finds a way through our shelter feels intensified.

Krys huddles against me as Kitso opens the rations that were given us. He prepares them on a set of skewers—two for each—and sets them by the flame.

"I am quite grateful for these mantles. How is yours holding up, Pansa?"

"Beautifully, Kitso. Thank you for making them."

"I'll have to fashion one for you, Krys. I hope you two find a nice buck tomorrow."

She smiles at him. "I would like that very much."

I yawn. "I am going to try and sleep a little early tonight. You two can stay up and chat."

Kitso sounds concerned. "Aren't you going to eat your fish?"

"I am not overly hungry. You can have them."

"If you insist…" I can hear the disappointment.

I am not really sure why I suddenly lost my appetite. Maybe I am just too tired to eat.

* * *

"It's too bad that Pansa didn't want her fish," I speak with a mouthful. "It really is very good."

"Maybe she's sad that we had to leave Timbervale so soon," Krys responds while looking down at Pansa.

"Maybe so." After eating my two, and one of Pansa's, I wrap the last fish and set it into the snow. "Perhaps she'll hunger in the morn."

"You must love her very much."

"I do. I try to take care of her whenever I can, but she doesn't always allow me to. She retains a lot of pride from growing up and having to take care of so many others."

"I want to be like Pansa when I get to Adleborough, and to care for many."

"Just be sure to mind yourself also, or you'll burn out."

Krys nods in agreement, and lies down in Pansa's arms.

Letting out a yawn, I huddle to myself up against the rock. I feel quite tired, though the dark hasn't even made its way over the land entirely.

I watch the long shadows of prominent figures extend from above the ledge, swaying with the wind, and wonder if there aren't guards waiting to capture us in our slumber.

Awakening to a new day, I rise, and find that much of the snow has receded. It is unusually warm, and as I get up, I find that Pansa and Krys aren't about.

"They must still be out hunting. At least the weather has warmed quite a bit."

I stand and stretch, and find that it's mid-afternoon. "Have I really slept that much of the day away?"

As I walk out from under the ledge, I find that the sun has begun to set. "What is going on with—"

"Kitso, quick!" I hear Krys shout from around the ledge. "Something's wrong with Pansa!"

I run toward where I heard her shout from, the light fading fast. I find it increasingly difficult to see where I am going.

"Kitso!"

I open my eyes in a flash, and roll over to inspect. I see Krys kneeling over Pansa, who appears to be breathing heavily in her sleep.

Squinting toward the sky, I find it overcast, and am thankful that it isn't so bright.

"What's the matter," I ask, as I ease from the ground.

"I don't know. I woke, and found her breathing like this. She feels very warm, and whenever I try to wake her up, she groans and pushes me away."

I rest a hand against Pansa's face. She is indeed warmer than she should be.

"Krys, go into my satchel and find a small, green bag."

I pull Pansa's mantle tightly over her, tucking the edges beneath. "If she is sweating this much, her body must be trying to get rid of something, and the last thing we want is for her to freeze."

Krys brings back the bag I sought, and I open it up to find some ground leaves. "This herb ought to ease her breathing. Hold her head up slightly."

She does so, and I attempt to feed Pansa the herb. After a few minutes, her breath finally recedes into an easy stride.

"I'm scared, Kitso."

"It's okay, Krys. You did the right thing." I hug her as she nuzzles me. "She's going to be alright. Just you wait and see."

Pansa manages to recover a fair bit, and wakes to find Krys and I sitting on either side of her. I am gently stroking the side of her head.

"Kitso? What're you—"

I rest my hand against her lips. "You've come down with something. Krys found you unwell in your sleep."

She leans her head to look at Krys, and then returns focus to me. "I can't be sick. Not when we have to go hunting."

I look into her eyes intently. "Don't worry about that."

"I have to worry about something..."

"Don't be silly. Worry won't do us any good."

Pansa sets her head back onto the ground. "Fine, then let me go back to sleep."

I almost laugh at her remark. "That is just what I wanted to hear from you."

As Pansa finds rest again, I sit back against the wall, closing my eyes.

"What should we do now?" inquires Krys.

"Now we just sit and wait. It's apparently important to her that she take you hunting. You haven't really gotten the chance yet."

Krys draws her knees up, hugging against herself. "I hope Pansa is well soon."

"She's strong. Whatever it is, it won't keep her down long."

I whittle the time away with carving. I found a very nice block of wood in Timbervale, and was permitted to keep it. Gwen said that I should make something nice out of it, and so I have decided to add a fourth figure to Pansa's collection.

This one is going to be sitting cross-legged, as she finds peace within herself.

Krys watches me closely. She finds fascination with just about any craft that I engage with. It makes me happy to know that someone is genuinely interested in my works.

"It's remarkable, Kitso, how you can take anything, and turn it into art."

"I believe that there's a natural beauty in nigh everything. It needs only to be found by someone willing to see it, and then brought forth."

"Do you think that there's any beauty in me?"

I very carefully consider my answer. "Certainly. I think there is a wonderful spirit within you that strives to see the good in others."

"If someone does take an interest for me, I hope he sees that in me."

When we first met Krys, I was certain that she would choose to be alone for the sake of putting others first always. Now I am quite sure that she is more open to the idea of a mate when her time comes. I like to think that my relation with Pansa had something to do with that.

"He will see what you have to offer the world, and he'll want to be a part of it all."

"How do you know?"

"Well, he would have to be, or it likely wouldn't work out in the end."

"I guess that makes sense." She gathers up the wood shavings, and tosses them into the fire, admiring the little sparks they send up.

To find enjoyment in such simplicity is one of the greatest traits of a pure heart.

"What will you and Pansa do afterward when I find my cousin's refuge?"

"For my tribe, it is customary that we either continue amongst our kin, or we set out to travel in pursuit of our own tribe. I've chosen the latter."

"Do you have to have a family to start one of your own?"

"Yes, it's essential that we begin a family together."

"But, aren't you both... um... different?"

"Naturally. Family needn't be biological, per se. For one, we consider you a form of family by how we relate to you."

"I am happy to know you two. You give me lots of things to consider in life."

I continue to work at the wood for a while, and eventually decide to try and rest more. I express to Krys that she is free to do as she sees fit, so long as she doesn't wander far.

Setting aside my work, I lay down on some loose brush, and draw the mantle over my head.

* * *

Slowly, I open my eyes. The overcast weather makes adjusting my vision a little easier.

My head feels of lead, and makes getting up difficult. Aside from a migraine and general fatigue, I feel pretty normal. I hope whatever has decided to befall me won't be staying long, as I've much to do.

I know that Krys must be disappointed in me for not being able to take her hunting.

"Hi, Pansa," she whispers. "How're you feeling?"

"I'm feeling alright. I am so sorry that we didn't get to go on a hunt this morning. You must be terribly upset."

"Not at all. I'm just glad that you're okay."

I was sure she would be unhappy.

She is. She's just reassuring you with kindness.

"Are you sure? It's okay to be disappointed."

"I really am sure—honest."

I find that I am too tired to think. I give in to sleep once more, feeling my consciousness fade from me.

"Poor Pansa…"

When I open my eyes again, I see the sun poking out of the clouds, casting its rays of light through any openings. It looks as though it may rain tonight.

It takes me a moment to notice that Kitso is cooking something. It sends a most wonderful message to my senses.

He puts some finishing touches in it, and lets it cool a bit before transferring a portion to a cup that resembles the ones we drank from in Timbervale.

Krys accepts the portion, and he then pours another in a similar cup. Noticing my awakening, Kitso hands it to me, in which I receive it after sitting up.

It is definitely from Timbervale.

"Kitso… you didn't take these cups when we left, did you?"

"Oh, not by any means, except that they were given to us as gifts."

"When did that happen?"

"Gwen left them amongst my belongings with a note. She said that she was thrilled to share mementos of you and Krys partaking of their Sumacadra."

"That was awfully sweet of her."

"It must have been quite the ceremony."

"Nothing extravagant, but it was nice to sit in silence and enjoy a hot drink. It was very peaceful, really."

"I wish I could have been a part of it. Perhaps I have a reason to actually consider traveling during the next year's cold season."

I refrain from loosing the broth in my mouth.

"Did I put too much salt in it?"

"Not at all. I just found it funny, that's all."

He smiles, and sips a bit from the remainder. "Hm, that should do it."

"What's in it?"

"The fish you didn't eat, along with a mix of mushroom and herb. Something simple to warm the chest and help you to recover."

"I'm not feeling as bad as before."

"Well, let's not head back there too soon. You don't have to try and be strong all the time, you know. Your body needs rest!"

I say nothing more, and continue to work on my portion, absorbing its warmth and flavor.

"Thank you, Kitso. It's wonderful," Krys tells him.

"I appreciate it, Krys. I think we'll try some of those berries that you picked after we left our little home. If they're still good, that is."

She gives him a sideways look. "Actually, I was thinking of using them for something."

"Oh? For what?" I ask her.

"I was inspired to make a drink from them like the sumacade we had in Timbervale. It was really good, and I want to make my own kind."

Kitso grins. "Hey, that sounds like a pretty swell idea to me. Let's finish this broth, then you can make it."

"What'll we sweeten it with?"

"Hmm. I'll look around to see if any bees are hibernating. Then we'll have our own Sumacadra."

"Please be careful, Kitso," I groan.

"I'll light a torch to smoke them out, if I must."

So it was, that we finished Kitso's cooking, while he went out for some honey. Krys cleaned the cooking pot, melted some snow, and worked the berries into a base for her sumacade.

Thankfully, it hadn't rained as much as I expected it to. A small drizzle was all the sky had to offer—not more than a few minutes at a time.

Kitso returns, bearing a waterskin full of what I presume to be honey. He's holding his arm in hand.

I sit up. "I see you've found us honey. And what of your arm?"

"Yes, more than I could manage. And nothing, aside from a stubborn bee trying to take my honey back."

I laugh as he sits beside me. "Did you forget to tell the bees that you were coming for your honey?"

"Ha-ha, funny. It isn't my fault they had no idea I was coming. Don't they know who I am?"

"Krys has been at work since you left. I think she's boiling down what she can."

She glances at us. "We had enough berries for three good portions. May I have the honey?"

"You may," Kitso says as he hands Krys the skin.

She goes right back to making it without so much as a word, completely focused on the task.

"She really is something," Kitso remarks aimlessly.

I nod to myself, wondering how far Adleborough is. It's odd—perhaps selfish, even—but I find myself also hoping we don't come across it for some time.

"There, it's done."

Krys pours some into each of the goblets, and fills the cup Kitso had made with most of the rest.

"Sorry for the stained cloth, Kitso. I needed to filter it somehow."

"No worries. Doesn't it look amazing, Pansa?"

"It does. Let's find some quiet, now."

We all sit with drink in hand, giving our own regard for nature and each other, and enjoy the peace.

All three of us sit by a warm fire, dancing flames casting lively shadows about us. Aside from the gentle crackling, it is almost entirely silent. No wind bothers us tonight, and our mantles rest by the warmth.

Kitso is carving a new figure for me. I am handling the bag containing my collection, admiring each one he made in addition to the one I had found. I hope that I can look upon them all again some day, happily gazing over a shelf within our home, wherever that may end up being.

I still find myself at a loss for thinking of our time with Krys before we arrive at her destination. I know that she has her heart set on this, and that it will be nothing but good for her, but I also know that I will miss her greatly when that time comes.

"I wonder if we can find some information about my village soon," Krys wonders aloud.

"We might. Who knows?" I reply.

"Well, I just hope, that's all."

Kitso speaks to me intermittently while he's carving. "It's no question… just a matter of time… wherever we end up next… we are sure to find something." He blows the figure clean of dust, looks it over, and continues to work at it.

"But what if we don't find anything about her village, Kitso? I am only thinking of the possibility that there is little or no information to be had."

Krys breathes heavily, settling under Kitso's mantle while he's occupied. He doesn't notice until he realizes Krys has stopped talking.

He sets his craft down, and comes over to me. Leaning over, he whispers. "Look, I know that we haven't found anything yet. I also know you aren't feeling your best, and that you are probably upset at the thought of when Krys must depart from us, but you really ought to try and keep that part to yourself."

Kitso wanders back over to his sleeping area, and lies down facing the rock.

His words sting a fair bit, but he makes a point. There's no use in making bad of our situation. I know everything works out for better—I just don't know how.

* * *

Morning dawns on us, and before I know it, I'm looking at the sunrise. A soft, blustery sun peers abroad.

Kitso and Krys are sleeping soundly. I wander off to relieve myself and wake up to the day.

The snow has solidified quite a bit from the light rain yesterday. It crunches from the impact of my steps, resounding with silenced echoes within the groups of trees around me.

I return, and take up my bow with arrows, a few of the waterskins, and go over to Krys. I crouch down to her, watching her sleep. I don't want to disturb her, but I am determined to make this day one to remember.

Gently, I caress her shoulder, and murmur her name. "Wha...? Oh, it's Pansa."

Krys opens and closes her eyes to rouse herself awake, and stretches with a long yawn. She sits up, eyes closed, and I wonder if she really is awake at all.

"Come on, Krys. It's time to wake so we can hunt."

My mention of hunting seems to do the trick.

We spend a short time sitting about while she comes to fully. I wouldn't want her to go out hunting half-asleep, as it would likely cause more problems than it would be worth. I want her to enjoy this outing as much as she possibly can.

When she finally gains awareness of the day, we pack what we need and set out, bows in hand.

"What do you think we'll find today, Pansa?" Krys asks, breaking the silent morning.

"I'm not sure, but whatever is out there, it's sure to be a surprise."

"I am excited to see what!"

We take our time traipsing through the woods, employing all that Kitso has shown us along the way. Not more than thirty minutes or so of walking and short breaks to gauge the land do we find some tracks.

"Oh, look, prints!" exclaims Krys.

"Yes, I see! Be sure to not scare away whatever they belong to."

She takes note of that, and hushes herself, following the direction of the prints.

I look at them closely. "They don't appear to be spaced out much, so whatever it is, it couldn't have gone far. What do you suppose it is?"

"Hm, maybe a raccoon, or a really fat squirrel."

I chuckle. "I am betting on the squirrel."

Soon, we cross paths with our prize-to-be. It is indeed a raccoon.

Krys whispers closely. "I wonder what it's doing out here in the morning."

"It probably got hungry. Do you wish to have the first shot?"

I could feel exuberance emanating from her at the suggestion, and so I fall behind a bit, letting her lead.

She follows along at a turtle's pace, taking care not to startle her prey. When she believes she is within range, she nocks her arrow, and takes aim. I watch as she readies her shot.

A sudden moment later, I hear the prick of arrow against the raccoon's body. It slumps, dead in its tracks.

Krys jumps and throws a hand through the air. "I got it! Did you see that, Pansa?"

I applaud her. "Yes! Way to go!"

We wander over to her kill, and I string it on my shoulder. "What'll we find next?" I ask rhetorically.

Krys answers anyway. "A great, big buck!"

"Now, don't get ahead of yourself…"

She looks up to me, and I frown internally at how my statement sounded. I proceed to raise her upon my shoulder, and jog through the trees. "… Because I am coming with you!"

"Ha-ha, yeah!" she cries, raising her bow overhead victoriously.

* * *

My eyes open, and I find rock staring back at me. Recalling the prior night, I sigh and hope to find the others resting behind me. I roll over, and notice that they're gone.

I slowly shift to prop an arm beneath me, and rub at my eyes. I feel remarkably rested despite my choice of bed.

When I finally feel ready to get up, I sit against the wall, and leer at the sun, squinting. "Okay, you better stay put for at least ten seconds."

The sun refuses to move faster than it normally does. I breathe out. "Now that I am certain I'm not dreaming, I think I'll help myself to the remaining sumacade."

I speak to myself occasionally. It helps me to ease into my day when no one else is about. Perhaps it helps me to gather my thoughts, or keeps me occupied while I relax. I've not given this habit a whole lot of thought.

Whatever the case may be, it's helpful as usual.

As I find myself sitting peacefully with drink, I hear an odd crunching of sorts. It sounds as though an injured beast is dragging its hindquarters, desperate for solace.

I set my drink down, and get up to investigate. I round the far end of the overhang, and to my surprise, I see two figures dragging what appears to be a rather heavy load.

Grinning at the display, I run over to them. "What're you both carrying, a tree?"

Apparently, they've managed a buck so big that it took the both of them to bring it back to the site. I see a long trail, ground into the snow behind them.

"Just help us, Kitso," demands Pansa.

We drag their game into the site, and sit for a break. "You two take a spell to recoup, and I'll begin working on him. He's quite the prize!"

Pansa hands me a raccoon. "Krys is the one who found them both. She got this little guy, and I got the buck."

"Astounding! At this rate, I can retire completely."

"Will you really?" Krys inquires.

"Not in the least. Hunting's too much fun."

Pansa helps me to prepare a nice lunch for us. I cut up what I can for her to roast, and have Krys help me to remove its hide, which we set aside for tanning later. We begin to preserve what meat we can, until I realize that we've run out of salt.

"I suppose we'll have to freeze the rest in the meantime," I express at the realization.

"I could make us more," Krys says in a carefree manner.

"Well aren't you just the source of endless utility. My tribe would be proud to meet you, if you weren't already set on your own path."

"I just need to go out and gather some hickory roots."

"That sounds like a good plan. Pansa, will you take Krys to find what she needs after cooking the meat?"

She looks at me with frustration. "Can't you? My feet hurt, and are cold."

"Alright, I'll take you along Krys, after we eat."

It was a very good meal, and I find myself quite satisfied. Krys and Pansa agreed that it was one of the most amazing meals they've had since we left our home.

As promised, I bring Krys to where she wants to go. She tells me where she found several hickory trees with mostly clear ground. I bring my knife and hatchet along. Krys brings with her a shard of rock she found that seems it'd be great to dig with.

She and I find the small gathering of trees, and we begin to work at their roots.

''How much do you think we'll need, Krys?"

"Probably several large hands full. I only worked with them once before, and remember it taking many roots to get a small amount of salt."

I nod, and cut away at some we manage to expose.

When we finish filling a bag with roots from one tree, we move on to the next. I tell her that we probably shouldn't get too many from a single tree, so that it can continue to grow strong.

About midway into the afternoon, we rest a while.

"This sure is difficult," Krys tells me.

"Yeah, but at least it's a pleasant day."

As I finish my sentence, I notice snow crunching behind us. "Have you come to join us, Pansa?"

I turn, and am met with a blow to the side of my head. I hit the snow in a daze, barely retaining consciousness.

"Kitso!" shrieks Krys. I notice the shadow of a figure grab her by the arm.

"There you are!" exclaims a gruff voice. "We've been searching for weeks!"

I rack my mind for that familiar accent, and remember hearing it from the guards sent by Telios.

"Release her!" I gasp, coughing as I try to get up. I feel a heavy boot try to shove me back down, and I roll over to grab at his leg.

"Hey, get off me!"

Krys manages to free herself, and runs a few yards away.

The guard tries to go after her, dragging me a short distance through the snow, the cold biting at my face.

"That does it." He kicks his leg from my grasp, and steadies himself, unsheathing a sword. Lunging at me, I draw up my hatchet, barely parrying his blade in time.

I right myself, and take a defensive stance. We stare at each other for what seemed to be several minutes.

"It's scum like you that keeps me from getting a raise!"

"What an interesting coincidence. It is scum like yourself that occupies me with keeping young women from getting man-handled."

He charges me in a rage, and I swiftly dodge, glancing his side. Wincing at the blow, he swings around, catching me off-guard. I suffer a cut into my right shoulder, and stagger backward. A tree keeps me from falling completely.

I reach for my knife, and find that it's gone missing. I wait for him to drop his own guard, and swiftly loose my hatchet at him. To my dismay, I miss by an inch, and wish that just once I were ambidextrous.

Accepting my fate as it rushes toward me, I close my eyes. Suddenly, the guard bumps straight into me, a blunt pain striking my sternum, unlike the sharp stab I had initially expected. I throw my eyes open at the shock, and see him standing almost still, eyes frozen with fear, my knife's hilt protruding from his neck.

He falls over, and I maintain my gaze into the distance, unsure of how to react. As my heart slows, I look over to Krys, and now understand how my knife went missing.

"For sooth, if it isn't a cracked rib, then it's a near fatal cut! I swear you're trying to kill yourself!"

Pansa wrings the cloth, resoaks it in the hot water, and presses it once again to my arm.

"Gah, that hurts!"

"Keep complaining, and I'll make it hurt more!"

I brace myself as she cleans it. Krys is poking at the fire, legs against herself as always when she is in deep thought. She must still be recovering from such an encounter with—

"Ow! Watch it!" I almost flail my arm.

"Sorry! That wasn't supposed to hurt."

If I hadn't known any better, I would laugh at my own misfortune. It seems I cannot even let my mind wander.

"Hey Krys, are you okay?"

Krys almost startles at my question, and she nods before returning to herself.

"So Telios found you two while you were digging?"

"Yes, the guard ambushed us—ah—and wound up paying with his life. If it weren't for Krys and her quick action, I'd not have made it back."

"I am proud, Krys," Pansa remarks. "That was very brave of you."

"I didn't know she could throw a knife. It must have been all that practice with the bow."

"Well, with that guard from Telios finding you two, maybe we should head to another town right away."

"No, we can't," I mutter.

"What? Why not?"

"If there was one guard, there is bound to be many about these parts. It won't take more than a day at most for them to find the one we killed. Once that happens, they'll all be on our tracks with madness. If we post in a settlement even only for a few hours, it'll be that much easier to find us."

"Then what are we supposed to do?"

"Our—ow—best bet is to endure in the wilderness, as far from here as we can get, and as quickly as we can manage. We'll have to take any path we can find free of snow until we locate an inconspicuous area to rest."

Krys interjects. "When must we leave?"

I ponder the situation. "I am going to go hide the guard's body. That should furnish us several more hours."

"Let me do it, Kitso," Pansa pleads with me. "You are far too injured."

"It is because I'm injured that you must protect Krys."

Pansa wraps my shoulder with reluctance, and I take off.

Chapter 21

All three of us left our site behind, feeling the urgency of the tension that arose from the situation. I had given us an hour.

We had packed what we could in such a short time, storing some food on each of us with the rest of our belongings. What we could not take with us had been buried in deeper snow. The shelter was dismantled, and scattered as naturally as could be. Only the most trained eye could recognize any disturbance in the area.

I had consented to carrying the hide, as I was not going to forget my promise to Krys about her new mantle. If we were going to be wandering for a time, she was going to need it.

Pansa was dragging a branch every which way behind us as we traversed the intermittent trees, covering what she could of our tracks. When she tired, Krys took over, breaking any patterns in our movement by the difference in her stride. Perhaps I was overly cautious, but it was better this way.

There were several clear spots where we suddenly altered our direction. We wanted to make our path as dynamic as possible to confuse anyone that comes our way.

For hours, we continued to press on, until we felt we could no longer walk. Every minute that passed by counted toward our survival.

Panting, we begin to slow tremendously. Krys drops the branch, and sets herself against a nearby boulder. Pansa joins her, and looks to me. "Is this far enough, Kitso?"

I drop to the ground. "Yeah... that's good."

With very little light left in the sky, we drop our bags, and I work on a fire from some tinder I brought. "My plan is to use the branch we dragged for the firewood. It won't be much of a fire, but it will help. We won't be able to make one tomorrow night. Thankfully, that little pond will refresh our waterskins, and allow you to prepare this hide."

Pansa helps me get the fire started, and we all huddle as close as we can.

"Pansa, I need you to set this hide for treating right away in the morning. I am going to work on it throughout the day."

Krys shakes her head. "You don't have to do that, Kitso. I will be okay."

"I still remember how we found you that cold night. It'll only get colder, and that will only make it harder to travel."

She seems to acknowledge my point.

"As for tonight, I am going to find us a little more food to replace what we'll be eating tonight to recover for tomorrow's long trek. Will you two make something nice?"

"Yes, Kitso. Krys and I will make a fantastic dinner."

"Thanks." I set my bow, and head into the late evening.

* * *

"He really works himself a lot, doesn't he?" Krys says.

"That's one of the reasons I love him so. He never seems to sit still for long, unless it's snowing," I reply with a laugh. "I do hope he takes care of that shoulder. It looks pretty bad."

Krys and I portion out some meat from the parts we were unable to salt. I get to cooking it, while she tenderizes the roots into a workable form.

When I finished cooking, Krys had begun making the salt. It was a peculiar process, but effective.

"That's incredible. I had no idea roots were so useful."

"I didn't believe it myself when I was told about it."

While waiting for Kitso to return, we keep the meat warm by the fire, and bag the salt.

"I hope those guards don't find us. I don't ever want to return to Telios."

"Kitso and I will do our best to make sure that doesn't happen."

The last of the sun's presence fades behind the horizon. For what this area lacks in trees, it seems to make up for with shrubs. Although it is less shaded, we're a lot more exposed.

I keep thinking about what was said regarding Telios trailing us, and suddenly feel very concerned for Krys' safety. I hug her close to my side, and she leans into me.

"Are you frightened, Pansa?"

"Yes, a little."

"I used to think that when you grow older, there is less to fear. Now that I've seen more, I know better."

"There is never a time in your life where you won't be afraid of something."

"But are there ever times when you don't have to be afraid for your life?"

"Well, yeah, what I meant was that there is always something to be afraid of, but you needn't always give in to it. You can find peace occasionally."

Krys resettles to wrap part of my mantle around herself. "When I ran away from my uncle, I always felt like someone was following me all the time, waiting to grab me and bring me back. I couldn't even sleep sometimes because I was so scared. When I found you two, I felt like someone else was watching over me, protecting me from any kind of harm. Do you think that is unusual at all?"

I nuzzle her. "Not at all. I know that there are forces out there that we can't rationalize. I have experienced them in some ways."

We see Kitso make his way back, both hands full.

"I am back, you two. I found us a possum, and a pheasant. They should carry us half a day."

He hands them to me, and I set them aside. "The fire is going out, Kitso. Should we feed it, too?"

"No, let it burn out. We should huddle together to keep any warmth and energy we have left."

After we eat, we settle for the night. Overlapping our mantles, Kitso and I wrap ourselves against Krys. It's a bit unsettling, but given the situation, I know better than to say anything at all. I just have to trust him.

As soon as I wake, I release myself from Krys and Kitso, and tuck the mantles under to keep them warm.

The weather is fair, which makes it difficult to ascertain the time of the next snow.

I take the hide and skins over to the pond, and notice that ice has begun to form around the perimeter of the water.

"Ah, the last thing we need is for the water to freeze while I'm treating this thing. I'd better check on it often."

I leave the hide to do its work, and return with the waterskins filled. I sit down next to the giant mass of sleeping fur, waiting for them to awaken.

You two get as much sleep as you can. Today is going to be a difficult one.

Are you so sure about that? It seems decent enough.

They're drawing nearer as you sit here...

I find myself restless, and get up again, whispering to myself. "Why am I so nervous?"

Pacing about, I finally give in to my nerves.

"Kitso? Krys? It's time to get up."

Krys shuffles beneath the mantles. "Pansa?"

"Yes, it's me."

She pokes her head out. "What is it?"

"It's time to wake. We've got to stay alert."

I help her up from under the covering, and Kitso wakes. "What's going on?"

"Pansa says we have to be alert."

He pulls the mantles tighter over his head, muffling his voice almost inaudibly. "I want to sleep some more."

With a sigh, I go to check on the hide. "He's the one that said we must keep moving."

The sun disappears behind thick clouds, and I sit down to help myself to a parupeteng flower.

You did the right thing, Pansa. They are coming, and will find you if you tarry for long.

I feel bad for us all.

They must feel bad for you, too.

You're just pitiful.

I drop my head into my knees, sighing again. I can't even discern my own thoughts anymore.

Footsteps come toward me, and I raise my head to see Krys approaching.

"Please, Krys. I just want to be alone right now."

"I only wanted to make sure you were okay. What's that in your hand?"

"It's… no good for you. Never mind."

She doesn't say anything else, but instead just sits where she is, a few feet from me.

I draw a hand to my face, wanting to disappear.

It's no use. She must know something about it.

Will you tell her?

Maybe it isn't a good idea.

"It's parupeteng. It is dangerous and almost impossible to get away from," I tell her.

"Can I help at all?"

"No. It isn't by choice."

"Okay, I understand."

No, you don't… nobody does.

We both sit in silence for a short while, and Krys goes back.

I feel both relieved and lonely.

I don't care if it kills me. I will not remain bound to this forever!

That is good to know. That will make things easier.

I cannot recognize these voices anymore, and am not sure if the last one was positive or negative.

Chapter 22

"Here we are! That should just about do it."

I fit the mantle around Krys' shoulder, sizing it up against her. It hangs a tad loose, but otherwise looks great.

"It looks really good," comments Pansa, admiring the mantle's form.

"How does it feel?"

Krys looks it over. "Pretty warm. Thank you so much."

She hugs me. "You're welcome. Just don't trip on it. You'll be thankful for the extra length come bedtime."

We had spent most of the day traveling, taking a small break here and there. I used every free moment I had since Pansa brought it back. I'm not sure what took her so long, but Krys told me she needed some alone time.

Pansa needs that a lot.

I wanted for us to gain as much ground today as we could while we had light. Now that it's getting dark again, I hope our guise remains hidden from anyone else in the area.

"We should keep going," I say, knowing to expect disdain.

"Kitso, we spent all day walking. I hardly got to rest my legs from last night's trek."

"We're doing this for Krys. Not for me."

Krys walks away from us, and begins to glance around, despite the lack of light.

"I feel like I've been here before."

Pansa questions her. "What do you mean? When could you have been?"

"I don't know. It just feels familiar." A small wind picks up. She stops walking, resting a hand on a tree. "Do you hear that?"

I slow my breathing. "Yeah, I do. Is that a hollow of some sort resounding?"

Krys nods. "It sounds like a cave."

"I don't know if I'm up for a cave at this point. Don't bears stay in caves throughout the cold?"

I cross my arms. "I am sure a bear won't mind if we room with him for a night or two. Probably less dangerous than a band of guards brandishing swords."

"Okay, so I can't disagree with you on that. Where do you think it is, Krys?"

"Down this way."

Pansa and I follow her. A couple minutes later, we find it.

I walk inside, and return promptly. "There's no bear. It's a lot smaller than I anticipated, but it should suffice. If we conceal the entrance with snow and brush, we'll be fine."

"It's a risk, but it's better than walking," says Pansa.

As the night grows darker and colder, we pile snow in the opening, and gather all the loose brush we can find, drawing it against the snowbank, enclosing ourselves within.

The cave is dark as pitch, and we resort to feeling around.

"Pansa, do you have the rations?"

"Yes, I do. Here."

"Is that the fish?"

"Yes."

"Where's the buck meat?"

"Krys has it."

"I thought Kitso did."

I sigh. "Fish is fine."

"Don't take them all!"

"Sorry, I thought that was just one."

"I'm going to lay down to try and sleep. Move over."

"That's not me."

"Sorry, Pansa."

"It's okay, Krys. You didn't know."

"Oh, sure, Take it easy on her."

"She's smaller than you are, Kitso."

"And I'm hungrier. Go to sleep."

I hear Pansa grumble.

Soon, Pansa is snoring, and I toss the fish bones aside, content enough for the night.

"Kitso? Are you asleep?" whispers Krys.

"No, that's Pansa. Are you sleeping?"

She chuckles. "No, silly, or I wouldn't be talking."

"Well, with any luck, we should be able to take our time tomorrow. I don't want us to have to keep walking all day."

"Neither do I. Hey, Kitso, what is parupeteng?"

My chest tenses a bit. "It's a terrible thing. A type of flower that one uses to cope with all sorts of things, as I hear. But it's also awfully addictive, and I believe it shortens life."

"Why does Pansa eat them then?"

"She says they help with pain, and she seems to calm down after having one. When she does have them though, I feel like I am not really talking to her."

"What does that mean?"

I fiddle with one of the bones. "It's hard to explain. Pansa has a certain way of expressing herself, and she usually does so in a brash manner. When she consumes a flower, it's as though she loses her ability to be blunt about her feelings. Not that it's necessarily a bad thing. She's just... different. I am used to her being straight-forward."

"I can kind of see what you mean. Pansa sounded a little different when I went to talk to her this morning."

"Yeah, that's how it goes before she has one."

I hear a deep yawn. "I'm going to sleep now, too. Thank you again for making my mantle."

Krys hugs me unexpectedly, and I reciprocate. "You're most welcome."

She proceeds to kiss me on the cheek, and lays down. "Good night, Kitso."

"Good night. Sleep well."

I suppose there isn't much to do in here but sleep.

I place my head against Pansa, and try not to kick Krys as I attempt to stretch out. When I feel solid stone, I concede to curl up, and wrap myself in my mantle.

The cave becomes quite warm as we lay still, insulated by snow and brush, and drift off in the peaceful dark.

"What have you found?"

I suddenly come to from a stifled voice.

"Find out where they've gone, and report back!"

I feel a sudden lurch at my feet, as Krys wakes. She almost yells as I find her mouth with my hand. "Shh. It's coming from outside," I whisper.

She nods slowly, as we listen. Inaudible banter. Furious crunching sounds above us. "No, I don't care! Whoever is responsible for this *will* be killed! If you have nothing to tell me by the end of the day... it will be yours."

A set of feet begins to run off, and then I hear walking. "Yeah, and when they are, I'll take care of you, you worthless excuse for..."

The voice trails off with the footsteps, and I can only hazard a guess at what was said. I hope to myself that Krys couldn't hear it.

"Do you think they're gone?" she whispers to me.

"I am sure they are. Don't worry about it. Just try to sleep." Settling back down, Krys starts to sob. I sigh, and lay down next to her, embracing her in my arms. "I promised you before, and I'll do so again: we will protect you, little sister."

After finally finding sleep, I open my eyes to the darkness, and notice pinholes of light peering betwixt the branches of our cave's opening. I am still tired, but that's to be expected after the last two days.

Both Pansa and Krys are still asleep, and I am thankful for that.

I don't recall dreaming, and wish that one would come the next night. It is incredibly rare that I don't dream at all, but lately it seems to be the norm. I dread the thought, and close my eyes again.

I still have Krys in my arms, and feel sorry that she must endure all this with us. I know she will do anything to find her home, if not, Adleborough, and we will do our best to see that happen. Though, to ask all of this from a fifteen-year-old is just too much sometimes.

Pansa had her own share of hardship throughout her life. It is no wonder that she became increasingly stressed from recent events. I count my blessings with her perseverance.

I think of my tribe, and miss home very much. With each passing day, I imagine all the excitement from everyone as I relay highlights of my adventure, and how much it has deviated from the expected path. Not one story I've heard from amongst my kin and friends has been so colorful. I imagine Vulpena would be quite proud.

Pansa, even if I cannot see us through to the end, I promise that when you return to me, there will be a grand celebration for us. Your own family could not deny all of the great things you've helped me with.

A smile broadens my face as I imagine my return.

"Kitso? Krys?"

My mind reverts back to reality. "I am here."

"And Krys?"

"She's asleep. I have her here in my arms."

I feel Pansa sit up and lay down with me. "You're too cute sometimes. You're like the perfect brother to her."

"You think so? I am not so sure with all the danger I bring to her, what with Telios."

She rests a reassuring hand on my shoulder. "These things happen. Given the circumstance, you're just doing what any responsible brother would do. You didn't ask for her to run away, nor did you beckon for guards to follow, yet you place all you have in her wake to protect her in her travels."

"You're also a part of this."

"That is true, but I still look up to you when it comes to making decisions on where to go and what to do. I know that I'm not the most stable one to be with, and you still deal with both of us every day."

Despite her reassurance, I still feel uneasy. "You think that I am doing all the right things?"

"Kitso, I know that you are. Nobody can question that, not even Vulpena."

"I cannot wait until you meet her and everyone else, Pansa. You will love them."

She hugs Krys and I, nuzzling my neck. "I cannot wait."

Pansa pushes the brush aside, filling the cave with daylight. I cover my eyes, trying to adjust.

"Do you think it's safe to go out?" Krys wonders.

"I'll go and see," Pansa replies.

She leaves the cave slowly, looking all around for any sign of company. Turning back to us, she smiles. "It's all clear."

I crawl out, Krys following behind me. "Somehow, with the light, that cave seems even smaller. I am surprised I didn't bump my head. Being tall has its disadvantages, you know."

Krys chuckles. "I guess I'm thankful for being short."

When we all make it out, I look around, and realize that it snowed in the night. "Huh, well fancy that. No wonder any sign of our trail wasn't found. I am actually thankful for the snow this time."

Pansa glances at me with bemusement. "You? Thankful for snow? That's one for the books!"

Krys gasps. "Oh my gosh!"

I almost panic. "What is it?"

"I know why this place seemed familiar now. I passed through this area when I left Telios. I have no idea how I crossed your shelter from here, but clearly I took a different route than the one we did."

Pansa sounds hesitant. "Then... we must be near the city. Which way did you go when you left?"

"Um... that way." Krys points off to the south, then to the west. "And that's the direction I went."

I cross my arms. "We got here from the north, so I suppose our only option is east. That means our destination also lies out there. Let's just hope that the Telios guard is heading elsewise."

We all take off with haste, anxious to get away from Krys' nightmare. It doesn't take us long to be met with another forest, and apparently, this one has been shorn of trees.

Two hours pass by on foot and in rest. The deeper we go, the greenery becomes interestingly thinner. Many moss-covered stumps array the lands, as though it were a woodsman's paradise.

I slow to a walk. "Either this forest is popular with the axe, or there are hungry beavers afoot."

"It's both amazing and depressing," Pansa mentions.

Krys joins quietly. "Timbervale would be sad."

Going forward, we begin to see small huts crafted from stone, with shafts of lumber adorning their tops. Strips of bark decorate the sides, acting as shutters for both window and door. Smoke curls upward from most of them.

"Another village?" I say, curious at the sight.

With a nod, Pansa observes the area. "I'd say so. Despite the felled trees, the builders were obviously more interested in using stone. Firewood, perhaps?"

We near the collection of humble hovels, and see a sign posted into the ground. "Tinderburg," Krys reads. "It's Timbervale's most popular trading spot, next to Telios."

"If I recall the meeting correctly, they will be stopping by today," I comment. "I wonder who is to be part of their excursion."

I lead us to the larger of the huts, which sits in the center. It lacks windows, but features an intricate door. I knock, and hear a familiar voice respond. "Who's there?"

"We're travelers, recently from Timbervale. We've come to seek direction, if not, temporary shelter."

The voice speaks again. "If you've come from Timbervale, then who do you know from there?"

"Well let's see, there was Byron, who greeted us upon arrival, Gwen who saw the inn, Sybol that records the town's information—"

"That's enough." Footsteps sound, and the door opens.

"And you're the one that concluded the council meeting."

Another voice interjects. "Julian? Who is it?"

"They were guests of ours for a time."

"Well, see them in!"

Julian steps back inside, and we enter. Upon entry, I see Katara and Byron sitting near a bright fire, accompanied by an elder individual which the other voice must belong to.

"Friends!" Byron cries. "I am convinced that it's no coincidence you decided to come here during our excursion. How are you all?"

"We've been better. Actually, we were more or less forced here," expresses Pansa.

Katara cocks her head. "How do you mean?"

The stranger speaks up. "For heaven's sake, let them sit first!" He gets up, and brings a couple extra stools by the fire. "I apologize, you three. You happened to catch us during an intense conversation."

"Come now, Dalton. Discussing our trade and future plans is hardly intense!" Julian retorts.

"I expect no less coming from the top of the council head." Dalton mutters. "We'll pick up from where we left momentarily. Now, you all are obviously expended. What brings you all the way out here?"

* * *

After a lengthy divulgence, Dalton sits back, sighing heavily. "Well it's no wonder. Telios has been known for its brash actions, which is why we refuse to engage with them."

"That is just from the time we met Krys," Pansa tells him. "Kitso and I have been through a bit ourselves."

"And you are certain that their guard remains on hunt?"

"Yes. Kitso and Krys were attacked only a couple days ago. This morning, we overheard them from our hiding spot."

Byron stands up. "If they're circling back around Telios, then they are most certainly headed this way, regardless of your trail."

"Please sit, Byron," says Julian. "The council of Telios is adamantly ruthless about seeing its business to the end. I fear that you're all in quite the danger."

"The only reason we retain trade with them is because of our lack of travelers like yourselves," Katara adds. "We hope that your findings on our behalf cause otherwise, though."

Dalton continues. "The representatives of Timbervale here tell me of your kindness, and their friends are ours. Tell me what we can do for you, and we'll see to it personally."

A sudden rap on the door surprises everyone. "Who's out there?" asks Dalton as he jumps up, tosses aside a rug I hadn't noticed, and throws open a hatch in the floor. He beckons us, and we make haste for the opening.

No sooner than it shuts over us, the front door slams open. "The guard of Telios, sir. We apologize for the rude entry, but we've come to inform you of an outlaw in the area."

"Outlaws? In these parts? Never in ten years!"

"We assure you, they're within your bounds. One of our guards was found dead less than nine hours ago."

"Tell me, what does this outlaw look like?"

"We're not entirely sure, but we have reason to believe that they are well-armed and very dangerous. If you find any strangers to come by, you must inform us immediately, do you understand?"

"Yes, we'll do so."

Heavy steps thud across the floor. "Your rug is apparently disturbed. What is that hatch for?"

"I was cleaning before my friends here arrived. It is where we dispose of our waste. Would you like to see for yourselves? There are bound to be a few dangerous rats."

"N-no... thank you." The floor creaks as feet pace above. "You *will* inform us of any suspicious individuals."

"Absolutely. You've my word as confidant to the province, and as you well know, I *always* keep my word."

"Good. Let's move out, men."

After the last of the guard tromps out, the hatch lifts slowly. "Are you alright down there?"

"Yeah, we're okay." I say, as we climb back up.

"Will you really tell of us?" Krys whimpers.

"Hm, now let's see. You all are neither suspicious, nor strangers as far as I'm concerned. What have I to tell?"

As we settle back down, I inquire of Dalton. "You mentioned that you can help us?"

"Well, as far as shelter goes, it may be a tight fit, but something tells me that you three make do."

"That would be very appreciated. We seek information mostly of the landscape, as far as we can travel on foot."

"Ah, that may be a bit of a stretch. We do have a couple of maps, but only of the direct surroundings, mostly for the sake of referencing others like yourself to local steads. Of course, that would be of no help to you, as you've practically traipsed all they could show."

"We won't burden you then," comments Pansa.

"Hold on, I'm not quite finished on that point. You see, we lack cartography efforts ourselves, but have attained copies of these maps from a traveling caravan that deals in all sorts of things. If you can catch up to them, they may just possess what you seek."

"Which way were they headed?" I ask.

"Eastward. If anything, it'll only take you further away from Telios. The caravan is known for wandering from place to place on a very deliberate route, so following in their stead shouldn't pose a problem. They stop moving at sundown, so if you leave tomorrow, and travel at a decent pace into much of the night, you should find them by the next morning. Alternatively, you could wait for their return trip, as they'll be passing through in four days."

"What do you think, Kitso? Should we go, or wait?"

I look to Krys, and then back to Pansa. "We will pursue them east. We need to maintain our travel."

"Then it is settled. You can stay in here tonight if you'd like. The Telios guard will be keeping an eye around here."

"Is anyone in the mood for tea?" Katara asks aimlessly.

"I'll fetch the water," replies Byron.

"I think a spot of tea will do nicely. What say you, Julian?"
"Yes please, Dalton. Tea sounds wonderful."

With nothing but the sound of light sipping and few idle words, we rest in solace of good company. It reminds me of nights where our tribe would gather around a fire to reminisce about past events, such as stories of our travels and sights we've seen, or even highlights of the hunts.

It is strange to me, as I have never been granted the opportunity, but I miss my family quite a bit. Yet, as I think of them and our tribe, I don't feel out of place when I see Pansa and the friends I have made along the way.

I look down into my tea, and push a small leaf around.

"Kitso, are you alright?" Pansa rests a hand on my lap.

"Huh? Yeah, I am fine."

"You look sad."

The others continue speaking to one another, but I notice their attentiveness in the air.

"I am just... thinking of my tribe again."

"Well remember, I said that if it came to be far enough along, I'd—"

"I know, and I really am thankful for that, but I am determined to see this through."

She smiles, and returns to her tea.

I glance over to Krys, and see that she is having a great time. *May you never know any more troubles from here on out, Krys.*

Chapter 23

We consent to retiring down below, on the chance that Telios should return in our sleep. Dalton has taken the liberty of informing other villagers. Byron, Katara, and Julian decide to spend the night for our sake. I feel blessed having such good friends around me.

Kitso, Krys and I are sitting in the dark with a lamp. The air down here is warm, which is unusual for the season. The structure must trap some heat overhead.

There isn't much to do but wait for sleep to come, and for tomorrow to follow.

"I'm excited to see what we find," Krys says, grinning.

"We are sure to find answers," I tell her.

"I wonder where the tea was from," ponders Kitso.

"Krys asked Dalton. He said that it's been imported from a coastal town quite a way from here. A trip of a couple days on ship, we were told."

"I really was out of it, wasn't I?"

"You look like you haven't slept in a while."

He places his head into his hands. "That's just it. I know I've been sleeping, but I don't feel rested."

"Maybe it's because of all that we're going through," adds Krys. "I am sleeping, but I often have dreams that are no fun."

"At least you've been dreaming. I can't recall any, or if I even have dreams, and I almost never lack them."

I hug him, and Krys joins. "Kitso, I love you, and no matter how hard this gets, I am here for you, as is Krys."

"Thank you. I love you both."

I feel his tears run down my arm, and I hum softly.

He sniffs. "I'm supposed to do that for you."

"Well, let me return the favor for once."

For the first time, Kitso is asleep before me. I admit that it concerns me, but I know he must need the rest. I watch him as he breaths steadily, and softly pet his tail.

Krys looks just as much at peace in her sleep, and I pray that they are enjoying wonderful dreams.

I consider how things will fare for us. I don't know what we will find from this caravan, but it seems to be our only hope for now. We just need one more day, and then maybe only a few more after that.

What if this place doesn't even exist, though? Would we end up in a blind chase for nothing?

No, I can't think of that. There has to be something out there. Adleborough just has to be there, somewhere.

I am thankful that Kitso has decided to be here every step of the way. I don't think I could do this without him. It looks to be of no concern to him that his family awaits his return, even if only for a short time. I'm sure they are wondering about him, too.

I wonder how my own family is. I've not given them much thought since I left. My purpose of getting away was for their sake, but with every day that passes me by, I feel as though I have just a little less intent to return at all. Why I feel this, I don't know, but I refuse to abandon them entirely. No matter what happens, I must return some day.

I lay down on my side, and gaze into the lamp. The little flame burns steadily unless I breathe out. It seems to be perfectly content to be encased within, until it's disturbed—it dances around, looking for a way out of the movement around it, until it resettles once more.

Every time we find some point of relaxation, we must move again. When will our seemingly endless travels travels come to a rest?

Frustrated, I blow out the light, and darkness closes in. Sometimes, I find it easier to calm myself when I can't see at all. Out of sight, out of mind, I guess.

I close my eyes, and listen to everyone above sleeping. They are louder than I imagined they'd be. Then, silence.

I open my eyes back up, and notice that although it's still totally black, I can sense the outlines of the room around me, as well as Krys and Kitso. I sit up to rub my eyes, and also see the hazy outline of smoke rising.

Are you asleep, Pansa?

Does it matter?

Of course it does.

Confused about the individual thoughts, I try to clear my mind, and realize that there's no distinguishing them.

Oh, it is so fun to confuse you.

Why do you confuse me?

I just told you.

Then you have no other purpose?

It isn't I who is without purpose. You lack any specific direction for yourself, engaging in an entirely pointless journey for a goal you aren't even sure about.

That's not true. I am helping Krys to find her cousin's refuge, and maybe even her old home.

You're helping no one. If anything, you'll be leading everyone right into a trap.

How would you know this?

My dear, I am orchestrating this. Haven't you figured that out yet?

My heart drops, and I lay back down.

You can't ignore me. I am a part of you.

I shut my eyes tightly, straining to close everything out from my mind.

I will never go away.

The dirt below my face becomes wet.

So long as you draw breath, I live.

I press my palms into my eyes to the point it causes intense pain.

Why won't I wake up? Please, wake up!

Hahaha! You can rest as long as you like here.

Please!

"Please!"

Light. I stare off into space.

"Why won't she wake up?"

Water hits my face, getting into my eyes, and I almost slash out with my nails.

"Pansa, I'm sorry! You looked terrified!"

I finally find breath, and put my hands over my face again. "It's okay, Kitso."

"No, it isn't. You weren't breathing at all!"

"I'll be *fine!* Just... let me be."

I hear him climb up through the hatch, and hear unsteady breathing coming from Krys. "Sorry for what happened, Krys. You don't deserve to see me like this."

She doesn't say anything, also heading up.

Well, you got what you wanted again, Pansa.

I sit still for a little while, and then go up myself.

Dalton and Krys are sitting by the fire. They glance over to me, and Dalton beckons me to sit with them.

"Kitso went outside for some fresh air. He didn't say much of anything."

Maybe I should go outside, too.

"He did, however, look irritated. Is everything okay?"

Then again, maybe not.

"Perhaps you should go check on him."

I huff out a sigh. "Yeah, I'll go out in a moment."

When I step outside, I can feel my hands tense, wanting to withdraw a parupeteng flower. Kitso is chopping at some wood, and he doesn't appear to notice me. Each time he swings down, I flinch.

Well, what will you do then?

I begin to circle around the back of the hut, and stop. I go to turn back, and stop again.

Come on, Pansa, what's more important? This isn't that hard.

I edge toward Kitso, hoping that he will notice me approach, but he retains total focus on the task.

Another swing, and another log falls apart.

I clear my throat.

He sets a log. "... Yeah?" Down comes the axe.

His response surprises me, even though I expected it, and find myself at a loss for words.

"I don't imagine this to be exciting to watch." He splits another log.

Sitting upon a stump, I rest my chin on my hands, looking at the chopping block, waiting to see him chop.

Instead of putting a log up, he swings down, setting the blade into the block. "Would you like a turn?"

Without even thinking, I stand up, and go over to resume his work. He places a log, and sits where I was just a moment ago. I pull up the axe, and let it back down, slicing the air. The log flies apart, and I replace it.

"You know," he begins, "chopping wood is one of those mundane jobs I actually find quite a bit of fun in. It releases so much energy, and feels great to do."

Once again, I hew a log.

"It is one thing that Vulpena did not teach me. I saw one of our tribe members engaged in chopping, and after watching for a little while, he offered to let me try. It didn't take long to get used to, and I eventually picked it up for everyone."

Set. Swing. Split.

"The residents here came upon the land in this condition. That's why their huts are mostly made from stone. You were right about them using wood for fires. That is why they trade for it from Timbervale."

I embed the axe and sit on the stump, faced away from him.

"Are we ready to go, then?"

"I don't know, Kitso. I feel like every time we make a move, trouble happens. Are you sure you don't want to wait here?"

"Trouble happens whether we go anywhere or not. We may as well make progress."

"We're not actually making any progress, though! We haven't found a single clue anywhere."

"Just because we don't find anything, that doesn't mean we aren't progressing. Every attempt is one less thing to try, and the less we have to try, the greater the odds of finding something."

I laugh outrageously, startling him.

"What?"

"You make it incredibly difficult to argue with you sometimes. Your logic is dizzying."

I hear him smirk through a huff. "It's my specialty."

He hugs me from behind, and I cross my arms, holding his hands. "What other specialties do you possess?"

"Well, I can make very good food. I also eat a lot, so I guess those cancel each other out. I know I am a great comfort to be around, though."

I lean my head against his. "Mm, I like that one. No matter how you upset me, you always make it right. I know that Krys also finds comfort in you."

He sighs. "I hope she hasn't gotten used to us too much. It would be all the more difficult for her to leave."

"I imagine she is pretty much set on leaving."

"I meant difficult for us."

I chuckle. "Oh. I can understand that one."

After lounging for a while, we both go back inside to pack up. Dalton embraces each of us, and holds Krys at her shoulders. "You take good care of yourself, now. Your friends sacrifice a great deal for your sake."

"Yes, sir." She grabs her mantle and bag.

Dalton hands me a small pouch. "Some of the tea leaves we had last night. It is quite expensive."

"Thank you very much."

He hugs me again, and whispers into my ear. "I hope it helps you in your times of stress."

Opening the doors for us, he sees us out. "I pray that you all find what you're looking for. Be well out there!"

We set out for the day, the snow pressing under our steps with soft crunches. It appears to have warmed a little, despite the cold breeze.

I shiver. "The wind is a bit much today."

"It is," Kitso agrees. "It makes me want to wrap my face into my mantle."

Krys draws her mantle up around her head, face protruding. "Mine is long enough to do that!"

He pats her head. "Lucky you!"

She giggles, and pretends to lead the way, spacing out her steps—presumably for our stride.

"She's so cute when she does things like that," I say.

"I guess that's her primary specialty—being cute."

"What's mine?"

He rubs at his chin. "I think yours is being stubborn."

I give him a stern look.

"I mean that in a good way! No matter how hard your opposition shows itself, you never back down."

"I don't like to give up."

"Giving up never does anyone good. Unless it's giving up something bad, of course."

I look down toward the snow.

"Oh, wow, look at that!"

Glancing up, I see Krys running off, Kitso following after. I jog to catch up.

We stop at a waterfall, its top half mostly frozen over.

"That's amazing!" shouts Krys.

"It certainly is," expresses Kitso. "It seems to have begun forming ice overnight."

"It looks like it bears a diadem of crystal," I add.

The waterfall continues to cascade around the ice, presenting its watery veil for us to admire.

Kitso turns to me, and looks back at the waterfall. "Maybe I'll get you one."

"Don't be ridiculous. You can't get me a waterfall."

"No, I meant a tiara."

I blush. "Oh… you don't have to do that."

"I know, but I want to."

All of us wander away from the beautiful sight to continue. *I wonder if he means to include a veil.*

The forest starts to thicken with trees as we see fewer stumps around the path we take. The sky begins to darken, clouds blotting out the sun, but we press on.

What began as a gentle breeze has picked up to a brisk wind. Blowing around loose snow, it bites at my face, making it hard to keep my eyes open. I notice the others having the same problem.

"It's hard to see much through this wind," mentions Kitso. "We might have to stop for a short time."

He wanders off the path to a large tree, and we join him, bracing against the wind with heads concealed.

A muffled voice comes from Krys. "The wind is so cold. My hands are freezing."

I tuck her hands beneath my mantle and into my tunic. "You'll be alright. Let's just sit until it settles down."

A shallow knock sounds directly above my head. Too startled to move even a little, we purvey our surroundings cautiously.

"It's an arrow!" Kitso exclaims.

I shelter Krys instinctively, as Kitso draws his bow, looking to where the arrow came from. He shoots, and we hear a shout in the distance.

"You're done for, now!"

The guard starts after us, another two joining him.

"Pansa, take Krys out of here!"

"I am *not* abandoning you, Kitso!"

"Do it!"

"No!" I take out my own bow, as does Krys. We take aim and loose, but to no avail.

The guards run for us, raising an arm overhead.

"Run into the wind!" Kitso yells. "They're at just as much of a disadvantage trying to hit us."

We make way through the trees, weaving about. Another arrow flies by, missing me by mere inches.

Huddled down by a tree, I nock an arrow. I try again, and hit one of them, only to hear a sharp clank. *Of course they're wearing metal armor...*

I sit back down to rest, and hear a heavy thud against the tree. I look back around, and see a throwing axe sticking out. Grabbing it, I yell to alert Kitso and Krys. "They've got throwing axes!"

"Oh, great," Kitso complains. "So much for wind."

I hear Krys scream, and find her being grappled by one of the guards. She bites him, and he bellows, striking her very hard with his gauntlet. She hits the ground, unmoving. "I'll deal with you later, missy!"

Before I know it, I am flying through the air, claws outstretched. I slam into him, and he crumples under my momentum. He punches my chest, but I feel nothing as I rip at his face. He tries to struggle from out of under me, but fails to do so. Time and again, I strike at him, my pulse distorting my vision. After a minute, I stop slashing, realizing that he has ceased altogether.

I retract bloodied nails, panting, the heat of a deadly vengeance escaping through my breath.

I escape with Krys, grabbing her up into my arms as I run. I don't know which direction I am headed, but I keep running until my own legs give out.

* * *

I wait patiently behind a tree, bow in hand. I have run out of arrows, as I've given Pansa and Krys a share of them.

Steadying my breath to conceal my presence, and to stop taking in the icy chill, I sit totally still.

The guards wander for a little while. "Where'd they go?"

"I think they ran off. Did you see where the girl went?"

"Which one?"

"The little one, you idiot! I'm not interested in killers."

"No, I didn't. And stop calling me an idiot!"

"Then stop acting like one!"

I hear them argue, and then a thud, followed by a slump. "Idiot." A heavy clang sounds.

Trumping through the snow, the guard wanders closer.

That's it, just keep coming this way...

He stops. "I know you're out there! Stop hiding, and face me like a man!"

A classic trick. Shouting as though you know someone is near—I won't fall for it.

A few more steps approach, and I lash my bow around the tree, whipping him in the face.

"Agh!" He brings his hands up.

I draw the bow over his head and circle him, twisting and pulling it against his neck.

"No you don't!" He yanks it forward, taking me with it.

I strike against his back, the blow to my front devastating me. I gasp for air, the cold wind freezing my chest.

He snaps my bow from his neck, sending splinters out, and pulls his sword from its sheath. He cuts at me, missing my head by an inch, and I drop back to roll out of the way as he comes down, slicing the snow.

"You must be the murderer!"

I would have said something, but my lungs burn with ice, and I cough harshly.

He cuts at me again, catching my mantle, tearing it as I pull away. "You won't get lucky for much longer!"

I withdraw my knife in time to parry another strike, and he comes at me again. I stop his sword against the hilt of my blade, the force of his swing shooting a painful shock through my arms.

He kicks me, sending me into a tree, and I hit my head. Focus lost, I struggle to breathe, and feel a grip at my throat, the ground floating away from me as he raises an arm.

I feel his breath against my face. "You die here."

* * *

I drop to the ground, Krys still in my arms. My muscles burn, both from the pain of exertion and the cold air.

I begin to weep, rocking back and forth. "It's okay. We're safe now. I only hope that Kitso is, too."

She doesn't appear to breathe. I set her in front of me. "Don't you leave me, Krys! Don't you dare!"

I shroud us both with my mantle, holding her face in my hands. "I can't lose the both of you."

My tears drop endlessly. *No! You're not taking the both of them away from me!* I press my face against hers. *Kitso, you told me to take her from danger, and I did! Now look what's happened!*

Cradling myself, I continue to hover over Krys, tears stinging my eyes. *Please... don't leave me...*

I feel her chest surge, scaring me. I halt my breath.

She coughs. "Salty."

Crying, I can't help but to laugh slightly, making a strange sound.

"... Pansa?"

"Yes, I'm here." I drop down, wrapping my arms around her.

"Where's Kitso?"

"I... I don't know." I whisper, starting to cry again. "I just got us away like he told me to."

"He has to be okay, because he's strong like you."

I hold her, saying nothing.

She falls into a whisper. "He just has to be..."

The wind is gone, and Krys and I are kneeling by a pile of kindling, trying to start a fire. The sun is setting, and Kitso has not been found.

We get the fire going, and I open a waterskin. Pouring a bit of water into my hand, I wipe Krys' face.

"Am I bleeding?"

"Yes, you are. Don't speak."

Krys is bruised badly. One of her eyes is bloodshot, and she bleeds from her cheek.

"Are the guards gone?"

"No one is around anymore. Please, hold still."

I take her jaw into my hand, and clean what I can. She flinches from pain in her mouth, and I release her.

"Your jaw is damaged, but nothing too serious."

She goes to say something, but thinks the better of it.

"I know you want to know if everything is okay, but you need to try and rest. I don't know where Kitso has gone, and I don't know if any more guards are after us. I don't even know where the trail is, but I do know one thing—we *are* going to make it."

Krys nods slowly, and looks down. Blinking tears from her eyes, she lays down, and I cover her up in both her mantle and my own.

I stare into the fire, strength escaped from my being.

I don't know when I fell asleep. The last memory I retained was watching the fire when Krys had laid down.

I awake to find the sun had not started its day, and to see Krys still asleep. The air was completely still, as though time itself had frozen with the season. Only our breathing occupied my ears.

Kitso was out there, alone and cold and undoubtedly hurt. Silently, I prayed to myself. Thoughtless emotion filled my mind, a shroud against reality.

"Krys, we must go."

My voice stirs her. "Hm? Where are we going?"

"We're going to find the trail, and go from there."

"Shouldn't we wait for Kitso?"

"No. Let's go." I help her up, and although she feels hesitant, she concedes with apparent reluctance.

My heart burns with malevolence at my own action, and my mind sinks at hopelessness. Sitting in the freezing cold will bring nothing but our own demise. Somehow, I know that he will not be arriving as we remain still.

Krys holds my hand as we wander about. She points out my tracks from last night, and we retrace them as best we can. I had no idea I went so far, nor how long we sat out here afterward. Everything happened so fast after we fought, yet it went on for hours.

Walking through the early morning, the trees cast a haunting array of shadows. They reach out to keep us where we stand, as if they refuse to permit anyone before the sun. I stand strong against them, vigor pulsing throughout my body. Mentally and physically exhausted, my muscles strain and my thoughts cloud. Whether we walked ten minutes or ten dozen, I could not be sure.

I can feel Krys straining to keep up as we walk, and I almost feel as if I am dragging a bound creature. She must want to rest, but I can't allow that with us being so near to our goal.

Finally, we cross the path, and see the tracks of wagon wheels set into the snow. The caravan!

"It couldn't be far off! We must hurry!"

I begin to run, and Krys' hand slips from my grasp. She almost falls forward, but catches herself. She is panting heavily.

"I can't... breathe."

"We are so close, Krys. You need to keep up!"

She kneels into the slush, an arm pressed to her face.

I want to scream. To scream at her for holding us up. To scream at myself for being so harsh.

But I don't. I stare at her, total contempt for myself, and kneel down right in front of her. With solemn embrace, I stroke her head, and tenderly rock to and fro. "Don't ever stand for inexorable treatment. You do not deserve any less regard than anyone else. You may be young, but you are significant, and your feelings are just as important."

Krys begins to wail uncontrollably. "I miss him! I just want him to be okay!"

I cannot help but to release my own emotions, and also cry. "I know. I do, too."

"I want to be where I don't have to worry anymore."

There'll always be worries, Krys... but I want you to retain that innocent outlook forever.

My legs become stiff and aggravated, but I don't budge. I don't care if we never catch up to that caravan. If it meant that I would sit here with Krys, then so be it.

She cries on, until her breath casts nothing more than silent, pitiful sobs. Not even my own breathing makes a sound, and we abide in taciturn.

Clack!

My ears perk. *Finally, a sound to break the silence.*

Creak.

Wait... sound?

I open my eyes, and stare over Krys' shoulder. We both cease our breath simultaneously, our hearts beating defiantly.

Beyond the decline of the road, I see a strange shape peer abroad. As it rises with a gentle clatter, I realize what it is I see.

"Ho! Steady, girl. That's it, bring it up slowly." A strong, but gentle feminine voice goads.

Krys looses me from her grasp, and turns to look.

"Marcus, watch the back—she'll make it over. Prairie here isn't one to give up."

As a cart breaches the curve, I see the head of a horse rise and fall, pulling to keep itself and its load moving.

"Aye, watch it!" Another female speaks up. "Prairie might not, but this set of wheels has seen better days."

Closer, they edge. Neither Krys, nor I, move.

The caravan makes it up and over, and with the horse's movement carried, it almost runs us over.

"Whoa!"

Hooves trump two feet from us, and only then do we stand up.

"Have ya lost it?! What are you doing down there?"

"I'm sorry. We were just—"

"Lookin' for a quick death, it seems. Sorry we didn't oblige you."

"Abigail, who's up there with ya?"

That must have been Marcus.

"Just a couple o' strays. Are you two lost, or just beggin' about?"

"Yes, we're lost." I say, at a loss for much else.

A head pokes out from the cart. "Abby, don't be a boor—oh." She stops herself. "What a sweet child."

Abigail interjects. "Mind yer own, Ingrid."

"Her name is Krys. Mine is Pansa."

"Pansa, Krys. A pleasure." Abigail clears her throat with a cough. "Tell us, what brings you all the way out 'ere in the woods?"

"We were actually looking for you. We'd heard that you headed from Tinderburg last—"

"Ah, Tinderburg. A mostly humble, but occasionally profitable village." She winks.

"Yes, Tinderburg. Anyway, we were going to catch up with you, but it appears we somehow fell ahead."

"Sorry about upsettin' your plans. Ingrid 'ere accidentally left something behind, so we had to turn about for it."

"It was my mother's armlet! It means a lot more to me than anything you hold!"

"After we retrieved her *precious* armlet, we 'appened upon a spot of trouble. Some poor, defenceless sod was being picked on, beaten half-dead."

I drop my head. "We've seen more than our fair share of trouble the last week alone."

"We know 'ow it is. I thought it was a fox at—"

"A fox!" I feel like a dolt for my seemingly obtuse statement.

"Yes… as I was sayin', some brute had 'im near death at his feet. It was only natural we'd paid our respects." She draws a knife from her side, running a finger along its edge.

I stare at her, afraid to ask. "… What happened?"

She sighs. "Well, when he paid us no mind, I dismounted, and walked over to 'im. I asked real nice like to let the poor thing go. He shunned me in a most foul manner, so I let 'im have it. Apparently, one wasn't enough—we were all on 'im at that point."

Ingrid pokes her head out again. "I wanted to bury the poor little foxie, but he was still breathin'…"

Marcus hops out of the back. "We decided to pick him up to take along. Maybe there's a reward awaitin'."

Abigail stares at them. "Forgive my companions. It's obvious that he would have a mind of 'is own, though he's still unconscious. Would you like to see 'im?"

My legs feel as lead, but I force myself to walk around the back, Krys tailing behind me. Marcus opens the flap, and I look inside.

Under the dim light of a hanging lantern lies Kitso.

I almost shout, catching my voice half-spoken. "Kitso!"

Marcus cocks his head. "That's an unusual name."

I hear Abigail call out. "I take it ya know 'im?"

"She knows 'im. I know that look in her eyes anywhere," Ingrid says, pouting.

It appears that Kitso has lost his mantle and garb in the midst of battle, as he lays there unclad.

I feel Krys press into my side, and set a hand upon her shoulder. "Yes, he's alright."

The trio of traveling merchants invites Krys and I aboard for a short ride to their next stop, being a small town near the mountains.

I expressed our intention to find some information on our whereabouts and Krys' memories. Marcus explained that business is bad to deal with on the road, and that they'd happily talk more upon arrival. He left the cart to help guide Prairie in the snow.

So we go with them. Krys wanted to ride up front with Abigail, as I cuddled with Kitso in the back.

Ingrid leans over some crates from the front. "We found him laying cold in the snow like that. His clothes were torn to shreds." She peers around the cart. "He's awfully warm to cuddle up to, though."

I clear my throat. "Thank you, Ingrid, for taking good care of him."

"My pleasure!"

I brush his face with my hand. "Could I maybe have a couple moments with him, please?"

"Oh, sure." She goes back to sorting through goods.

Peering down, I see wounds all over. "I know you can't hear me, Kitso, but I'm just so glad that you're alright. I really missed you..." A tear slides down my cheek as I soothe him. "Krys missed you, too."

Chapter 24

Early afternoon pours in with a gentle, warm breeze. As the snow on the trail begins to melt, the sloshing of Prairie's steps becomes more audible, as though it shifts aside with increased grandeur, welcoming us into a new territory.

I had read that the outskirts of the province we had left felt mysterious to any normal passer-by. It's as if the lands hold a fresh air of relief from the troubles, and I welcome it openly. If there was one thing I was pleased with, it was that we were not going to return any time soon.

The caravan slows down, the bumping of gravel settling beneath, and comes to a halt.

A bold voice confronts Abigail. "Hold it. How many aboard?"

"There's six of us."

"Foreign riders?"

"Three."

"Last points of trade?"

"Timbervale, the Lupino tribe, and Tinderburg."

"Alright, see yourselves through. You know where to stop upon entry."

"Yes. Thank you."

The caravan moves again, only to stop once more after a few yards. Ingrid hands a sheet of parchment upfront.

Abigail recites a response to an inaudible utterance, the exhaustion of routine in her voice. "Seven bags, three crates, four scroll tubes, five map cases, three jewelry boxes, nine baskets, two weapons, three purses—"

"And a foxie who's been bore free!" Ingrid says with a titter through the front, before withdrawing.

"She's not joking," Abigail states with a sigh. "As for our own belongings, nothing beyond the usual for self-defence and trade."

Marcus opens the flap. "Alright, you'll have to get out here and take Krys to the office. Since Kitso is incapacitated, he'll go with us to see the doctor."

I give Kitso a quick kiss, and hop down. Taking Krys' hand, we follow a stranger to the town's office.

The door is opened for us, and we step in.

"Welcome, you two. Please, sit down, and we'll have you checked in here."

A larger woman sitting at a desk looks at each of us. "Hello. What have you come through for?"

"Hi, my name is Pansa, and this is Krys. We're here because we got a ride from the caravan."

"Go on."

"We wanted to trade with them in hopes of finding some useful information, and then we'll be out of here with our friend who is currently unconscious."

The woman stares at me in skepticism. "You have the strangest business being here. If you say so."

She scrawls something in a book, and hands it to us, asking for our names. We sign it, and give it back, which she places in a bin.

"Well, I suppose there's nothing more to discuss. Enjoy your short stay here in Clastodon."

I take Krys out the door. "That was strange."

Krys looks up at me, and then around the town. "Everybody sounds bored."

"Perhaps they just have a routine way of doing things around here."

"I wouldn't want to be royalty and have to do things the same way all the time."

I smile at her. "I'm glad you welcome a dynamic lifestyle. It'll serve you well in Adleborough, I'm sure."

Some time later, we find Abigail, Ingrid and Marcus toward one end of Clastodon, setting up their goods with other merchants. Each party has their own stall to surround with whatever they have, some being larger than others. Theirs is pretty big.

"This reminds me of times my father took me into the market," Krys said, admiring the varied displays.

Marcus notices us, and beckons to join him and the others. We go over to meet up.

"Glad ya made it through the process alive!"

I shrug. "Thanks, Marcus. I was certain we'd die of boredom had we stayed another five minutes."

"Well, now the fun begins!"

Krys and I watch as they finish setting everything.

Ingrid starts to count at her purse, and Abigail tends another individual.

"So, what is it ya two are looking for, anyway? New garb, possibly? Or maybe a book? I bet I'm close."

"We're looking for maps."

"Maps! Give me a moment." He turns to open a crate, revealing tubes of leather in assorted lengths. "Y'know, I like to think of a map as a type of book. Is that strange to ya?"

"Not at all. What we need is something to show us as much land in detail as possible, preferably on the outskirts of our province."

"Ah, I've got quite the atlas for that. I'll lend a quick peek so ya know what you're gettin'."

Marcus slips the map from its holder, and unrolls it along the crates for us to see. "It's the only one of its kind. We traded a fair bit for it, and intend to make a decent return."

I scan it over, and notice the incredible details.

"I think that's exactly what we're looking for!"

"Great! So, what have ya to exchange? I'd say anything valued around a few ounces of gold is a good starting price."

My heart skips a beat. "I'm not sure we have anything near to that."

Rolling the map back up, he sighs. "I'm sorry, Pansa. We all might be friends, but merchants have to make a bit of living, ya understand."

"Yeah, I do," my voice cracks.

As he slides it back into the case to put away, I see Krys fingering at her neck. I gasp and shake my head, but she gazes at me, a sadness glazing her eyes.

"Will this do, Marcus?"

He turns to her, and she hands him her locket.

Turning the jewelry about, he examines it closely. "A remarkable piece. Sure ya want to pay with this?"

Krys nods, wiping at her eyes.

"Well I'll be… I'd say it's worth the map alright, and the case to boot." Marcus hands the case to her. "A pleasure, milady!" He slides the locket into a silk bag, and carefully tucks it into another box.

Krys walks away from the stall, bearing the case in both arms. I walk over to her, and she looks up to me, a mixed look of sorrow and joy. "We're going to find my home, aren't we?"

"Yes, Krys. We sure are!"

We walk around for a bit, looking to see what others have available, and see someone vending in clothing.

I approach him. "How much for that piece there?"

"What have you got?"

"Do you dabble in herbs and plants?"

"Nah, not interested."

"Well, how about meats?"

"No perishables!"

I turn my mouth, and slide my mantle off. "Fine. Garb for garb, then."

"That, madame, will do! I'll even wrap it for you."

Browsing finished, Krys and I requested direction to the town's doctor. We find the place, and enter.

"Hello. Is this where we can find a doctor?"

"Yes it is, but he's busy right now. Are you ill?"

"No, I'm looking for a patient who came here today."

"Oh, who might that be?"

"Kitso?"

"Ah, the fox. You can find him in that room there."

"Thank you," I say, as we go in.

Lying down on a mostly barren bed is Kitso, tucked comfortably beneath a thick blanket. He lies still, his chest slowly rising and falling.

Krys goes to the bedside, and sets the map case down. She peers at him, tilting her head from side to side, as though she is trying to figure something out.

She finally speaks. "He's breathing."

I giggle, joining her. "That's always a good sign."

"When will he wake?"

"I'm not sure. Hopefully by dusk. If not, we may have to stay somewhere for the night."

* * *

I ease my eyes open, and find Pansa leaning against my chest, sleeping. I tilt my head to the side, and see Krys on a chair with a tube in her arms, also asleep.

There's a package on my lap. I slowly adjust to sit up, trying to not disturb Pansa, and look the parcel over.

"Hm, a gift perhaps? Probably to welcome me back."

I tear at it, finding it to be more of a chore than it should. I must have taken a serious beating, but I am glad to be alive. Before I manage to open it all the way, I wonder to myself how we wound up here. *Where even is here? And where the heck are my clothes?*

Sighing at questions that will inevitably find answer, I finish opening the gift. Inside is a beautifully crafted tunic, obviously made with expensive materials. "Oh, wow!"

Pansa jerks upward, blinking. "Kitso, you're awake!"

Krys shifts with a stretch, and glances over to me with a smile. "Hi, Kitso. I'm happy that you're okay."

"Me too, Krys. What have you both been up to while I was out of it?"

"I took Krys away from danger, like you asked me to. We barely escaped."

"I'd forgotten about that."

Recounting the details of their escapade, Pansa fills me in on how we all got to where we are, and what they did in the meantime.

"I would like to thank them personally for all of this."

"They're vending their goods right now. We got a map from them, of which I think will help us find Krys' home."

Krys gets up, and hands me the tube. I remove the map inside, and draw it open to examine.

"This is incredible. What did you trade with?"

"Krys... exchanged her locket."

I breathe out. "You made quite a sacrifice, Krys."

"I see you opened your present. What do you think?"

"I love it! And I suppose it doesn't take smarts to figure out what you traded away."

"Please don't be mad..."

"Pansa, how could I? Sure, I made it for you, but this means a great deal to me, really it does."

She hugs me.

"Ow..."

"Sorry."

As we're looking over the map, the doctor comes in.

"Kitso, was it? I can see that your friends have found you in good condition. You are free to leave when ready."

"Thank you very much, doc."

"You're welcome. Just do us both a favor, and try to take it easy for a few days."

Pansa grins. "I'll make sure of that."

He leaves, and I narrow my eyes. "Will you now?"

"Kitso, don't be a fool. The most you'll be doing for now is walking and eating."

I look back at the map. "Well isn't that a cute little place," I say, pointing at a village by a river.

"Hm, Kindrall," Pansa remarks.

Krys jumps up, scaring me. "Kindrall? Oh my gosh, that's my home!"

"I thought you said you couldn't remember," I say.

"I couldn't, but hearing it, I know that must be it!"

We exchange glances. "Kindrall it is, then!"

Pansa and Krys bear our things, much to my reluctance, and we make our way out. At least I can wear my new garb without pain. It's very comfortable, and a perfect fit.

"I like the color. A fair bit darker than my old one, but appealing nonetheless."

Passing through the market, someone comes up to us.

"Hey Kitso, glad to see ya! I'm Abigail, and that's Marcus and Ingrid."

"Oh, you must be the ones who found me. You all have my utmost of gratitude."

"Aye, don't mention it. We fight for our lives nigh every day, so it was nothin', really."

"They were Telios guards that ambushed us."

"Eh, guard, bandit, makes no difference to us. When you take advantage of someone like that, you're plain asking for it."

Ingrid hugs me, causing me to flinch. "You take good care of these girls now. They're mighty special."

"We wish ya three the best!" says Marcus.

With a final farewell, we head out of town, and start to make our way back onto the trail.

"So apparently, the river Kindrall extends from the waterfall we saw," remarks Pansa, looking at the map.

"May I carry it? Surely it doesn't weigh much."

"I'll let you carry it when we get there."

"Do you mean at the waterfall?"

"No, Kindrall. You can rest your arms for now."

I groan. "How are you then, Krys?"

"I'm pretty good. How are you?"

"My arms and legs hurt, but otherwise I think I'll be swell."

I take note of a cut healing on her cheek. Hopefully those guards haven't done too much damage. Telios will hear from me personally if Krys or Pansa suffer anything more.

When the evening comes to a close, we set up camp a distance from the trail. Pansa seems to know the area.

"This is the area that Krys and I came through when we escaped..."

"It seems to be safe enough. Lots of trees here."

"I want to make the fire!"

"Okay Krys, you can make it. Just let Kitso tend it after."

"Oh, you're actually going to let me do something?"

"You'll do it whether I let you or not."

I chuckle. "You know me so well."

When Krys finishes, she reclines against a boulder. Not long afterward, she falls asleep.

Pansa sits against me, and I poke at the fire, dousing the stick in the dirt whenever it catches flame.

"If you're not careful, you might burn your foot, Kitso."

"Hey, let me have some fun."

She leans back to kiss me. "I am happy that you're back."

"I'm happy to be back."

"From the looks of it, we should see Kindrall by tomorrow evening. With a few minutes here and there, of course."

"So it finally comes to a close, eh?"

"There's no guarantee that we will find out where Adleborough's location is just by walking into Kindrall."

"I'm just considering the possibilities."

"I know," she tells me, before heaving a sigh. "I want to enjoy our last day with her, alright? Even if only for seven or eight hours."

I stroke her arms. "I love you. We'll make it special."

"I love you, too."

* * *

Morning dawns upon us, and I wake to see Kitso and Krys still sleeping. I remake the fire, and cook us the remaining fish, while I enjoy a cup of the tea given to me by Dalton.

Krys comes to, and she takes one of the fish.

"Thank you for breakfast, Pansa."

"You're welcome. Are you excited for today?"

"Yeah! Even if we can't find Adleborough, I'm sure my village will help me."

"We can stay to help you find it if you want us to."

She takes a bite. "But you've already done so much, and I know that you and Kitso really want to start traveling together."

I smirk. "For a kid, you're pretty darn insightful."

"I learned from the best," she says with a smile.

Kitso joins us after a small while, and helps himself to the other three fish.

"Kitso! Don't be a pig!"

"Hey, I'm hungry! I haven't eaten since I had my butt handed to me." He shoves half a fish into his mouth.

Krys laughs. "You two are funny."

"I'm glad you seem to think that. So Kitso, what should we do today, it being our last together?"

"You won't let me use my arms, so hunting and fishing are out of the question. And building a shelter of any sort will be pointless."

I look over to Krys. "Sorry, Krys. I really wanted to make this last day special for you."

"What do you mean? Every day with you two is special!" She hugs me, and my eyes begin to water. "I will always remember all our fun times together, big sis."

Contented from our meal, we leave behind the last site, admiring the beauty of the day before us.

It seems that much of the snow has receded for now, making room for the next storm. For Kitso's sake, I hope it doesn't get any worse than the last.

"I'm so glad the snow is going away," Kitso says. "I don't want to see any more crazy storms."

"I was just thinking about that. Are you a mind reader or something?"

"Now there's a novel idea. Who could really say?" He smiles. "What do you think, Krys?"

"Nah, I think you're just really smart."

"Hmph, what does that make me then?"

"Smarter!" Krys bursts with laughter.

I stick out my tongue at Kitso. He sneers in return, and decides to laugh.

I have always appreciated Kitso's ability to laugh at himself, especially when a situation seems dire. It's his light-hearted nature that fills my days with joy when I am feeling sad.

Each day has been painted with such color since Krys stepped in unexpectedly, and now that she is leaving us, I can't imagine what life will be like without her around. I know that Kitso will be with me beyond that, but she feels almost integral to our adventure.

Even now, the hours are passing me by without notice, as though the day itself has business to tend in the midst of ours.

"Will you at the very least let me hold your hand?"

"Oh, alright." I grab Kitso's hand, stealing a kiss.

"Hey, that was mine! Give it back!"

"Get it back yourself."

He leans in to kiss me with embrace.

"Hey, that's more than a hand!"

Despite my objection, he knows I am not serious, and maintains his posture for quite some time.

"Come on, you two. We have to go."

I wink at Kitso. "I think she's jealous."

Kitso releases me, and grabs at Krys, kissing her cheek with an audible smooch.

"Eeeww!" Krys says, giggling out of control as she rubs her face.

"There, now you're both equal. And you're just rubbing it in deeper, Krys."

"You both are adorable," I say.

Before I know it, we near a large bend in the river. Giant, rectangular rocks are lining an edge.

I look at the map carefully. "This… must be it."

We all stand still, looking at an array of hide tents.

"This is my home?" Krys peers around. "I can't believe I'm actually here."

"Who's that over there?" Kitso points out someone stacking boxes and sacks. "He looks like he's taking inventory or something."

The individual notices us at that moment, and wanders over. "Who are you all?" When he nears, he stops suddenly, staring at Krys. "Krys? Is that you?"

"Um, hi. Do you know me?"

"W—wait here." He runs off.

Kitso scratches at his neck. "That was odd. Do you know him?"

"No. I don't think I do."

The stranger returns a moment later with a woman. "Look, it's her!"

The woman gasps, drawing both hands to her mouth. "It really is! Sweetie, you probably have no memory of who we are, but we're your godparents."

Krys appears cautious. "Why was I sent away?"

Her kin look at each other. "We were told that your uncle in Telios had a great deal of resource held for your benefit," states the woman.

"A famine had struck us at the time. When your parents had fallen ill, they had us swear to have you safely transported. They only wanted the best for you."

Krys stamps a foot. "I hate him! He demanded so much from me, and was mean all the time. He even tried to force me into marrying a cousin of mine. I'm never going back!"

She drops to the ground, sobbing. Her godparents kneel down to console her.

"Had we known he was that way, we would never have sent you there. He promised us that you would be cherished. We're so sorry."

"We care about you very much, and we're happy to know that you're alright. Whoever you two are, we appreciate you from the bottom of our hearts."

An elder figure comes toward us, bearing a walking stick. "Who's there with you?"

Krys' godparents face him. "Your granddaughter."

"Little Krys? That's impossible. She is in Telios."

"No, these two brought her back by her accord."

He looks us over, and glances down at Krys. "Stand up, girl."

She does so, sniffling.

"Where's your locket gone?"

"I traded it away so I could find my way home."

"Turn around."

When she turns, he reaches out for her neck, and gently lowers the collar of her garb. "That mark... so it really is you."

"When I ran away from my uncle, I crossed upon Kitso and Pansa. They took care of me, and promised to help me find Adleborough when I asked them to."

"Adleborough, hm? Now there is a place that I've not forgotten. Your cousin is doing just fine with her mission."

"I really want to live with her and help her."

Her grandfather takes a step toward us. "I have no words for what you've done. You have an old man's gratitude for life. However… you both must leave before I can honor the wishes of my granddaughter."

"Why can't they come see Adleborough with me?"

He sighs, thumbing at his walking stick. "Since your cousin began her mission, we decided to hold it a secret from anyone outside of our village. It was almost discovered, and lives were nearly lost for its sake. I will not get into the details. You must understand this."

I nod. "We do. Kitso and I are more than content knowing that Krys is home."

"We won't intrude, sir. You have my word as a representative of the Vulpani tribe."

"Then I take your words to the ends of the world. Farewell, you two."

Krys runs up to us, almost knocking Kitso over with a hug. "I love you both so much!"

He reciprocates. "We love you, little sister. You go now, and be with your kin. By mountain or sea, you will hear from us again some day."

Chapter 25

Pansa and I walk in silence. Neither of us have said anything since we left. No matter how many times I mull it over in my mind, I cannot find anything helpful to say.

With atlas in tow, I mumble to myself, making mental notes of Kindrall's surroundings.

"Give it up, Kitso. Even if we found the location, I want us to respect his wishes."

I put the map away without a word.

Pansa continues. "I just don't understand what the big deal is. We risked everything to get her home safely, and we can't even be trusted."

Looking at her, I can't help but to feel her frustration.

"I mean, it isn't like we aren't able to keep a secret. Why would we go jeopardizing everyone after what we did?"

I nod absentmindedly.

"Will you say something, please?!"

"What do you want me to say?!" I stop to gather myself. "Look, I'm sorry that they don't trust us, but we got her back safely, and that's what matters the most."

Pansa closes her eyes. "I know... I should be grateful to have gotten to know her. I just miss her so much already. I'm not supposed to!"

"Pansa, you *are* supposed to miss her. That just proves how much your care. That's never going to go away. Yes, it will dwindle over time, but that, well, takes time."

"She was my little sister, Kitso..."

"I am absolutely certain she will always think of you as a sister. She will never forget all we've done. And when we can manage, we'll find a way to get in touch with her."

"Promise?"

"I promise with my life."

Pansa decides to help herself to a parupeteng flower. I am put off, but I know that she is not realistically in the mindset to refrain.

I hold her. "You know, out of all the days we spent together, the one I am most fond of involves the time when we took Krys for some hunting practice for the first time."

"I enjoyed the time we all went spearfishing together."

"Krys really got to learn many valuable skills during her time spent with us. I hope she gets to put them into practice throughout her time in Adleborough."

"I imagine her cousin will appreciate what we've taught."

Crossing back into the deep forest, night befalls us, and we settle into the old cave. I mark the map.

"Do you plan on coming back here some time?"

I put the map away again. "You never know when a hidden location might come in handy."

"I suppose so. Do you think it's safe to build a fire?"

"If Telios is still around, I don't want to risk it."

"Yeah, you're right. I think I'll just cuddle up to you, then."

Pansa hugs me, slowly pushing me to the ground.

"I imagine with your mantle, we'll be warm—"

She presses her lips against mine, sliding her tongue betwixt. Entangling her fingers with my own, she sighs.

I can feel the warmth emanate from her face during her embrace. Her heart begins to hasten, and I cannot help but to reciprocate her passion as I reach around to gently massage her back.

"That feels wonderful, Kitso."

She slides her mouth over to my ear, subtly grazing her teeth against it.

I giggle. "Heh, that tickles."

After a while, Pansa gives me a squeeze of a hug, and rests her head upon my chest. My body is still sore from the other day, but I don't complain.

"I love you so much, Kitso."

"As do I you, Pansa."

I hear a sigh. "Kitso?"

"Hm?"

"Does it upset you that we may never bear our own?"

I consider her comment. "Not really, no. To become wed and spend my life with you is more than enough for me. Whatever we ponder for a family, I will be happy."

"I'm glad."

We awaken to a new dawn, and Pansa heads out for a little while, encouraging me to sleep more, to which I oblige.

I come to for the day, only to feel her snoring against me.

Silly Pansa. She's fallen back asleep after her morning.

The daylight conceals itself occasionally with passing clouds, and I lay still, hoping there is no snow to be had.

I think of my tribe, and how they may be faring. Undoubtedly well, what with my mother heading another hunt in the midst of the season, as Vulpena tends to young and old alike, her gentle nature bringing an additional light of its own to everyone's day.

It is still quite early for my trial to commence, having been only a month, but I am certain everyone will be thrilled with my return home and all that has become of my time away.

Though, despite how short it has been, it feels as though I've been away for over a year. Each day in itself seems to have gone quicker than the last, presumably due to more being done with the time we were given as it passed. Yet, I would not trade a single event out, for they've provided me many opportunities to learn and to grow, and have matured me well as a wine.

Helping ourselves to what little is left of our rations—being mostly herbs and mushrooms—Pansa and I walk hand-in-hand through the woods.

We pass through Tinderburg, and see Dalton enjoying the fresh air in front of his place.

"Afternoon, you two! Out and about for the day?"

I wave to him. "We return from Krys' home."

"Oh, so you've found her back then? Good to hear! Have you had any of that tea yet?"

"I did. It was absolutely wonderful."

He walks over to us, and hands Pansa another bag. "I picked up a little extra just for you, on the chance you stopped by again."

She hugs him. "Thank you so much, Dalton."

"You two be well, now!"

A couple hours later, we wander by the territory of Timbervale and notice Byron is out, chopping at a tree.

"Hey! Kitso, Pansa, how have you been?"

I shake his hand. "We're swell. How about yourself?"

"Eh, another day, another tree, but seeing you both makes my day truly great. Did you happen to find what you were looking for?"

"Yes, that caravan helped us in more than one way finding what Krys sought."

"That's good. Will you two return with me to say hi?"

Pansa shakes her head. "Sorry, we're going home."

"So soon? Well, suit yourselves then, and take care!" He resumes his work, as we take our leave.

Taking the scenic route to ensure we steer clear of trouble, we admire the surroundings of a fair afternoon. Clouds begin to gather, and I shout at them for threatening to ruin our day. Pansa laughs at my entertaining display.

The sun starts to slide further beyond its apex, and I spot our old cabin. Smoke eases from the fireplace's vent.

I knock on the door, and it opens, revealing a young female rat. "May I help you two?"

"Hey, you'll probably think me strange, but my mate and I built this place, and we wanted to see how it fares."

"How can I trust you?"

I go to great lengths to describe every detail, and she allows us to enter, if only to stop me from talking extensively. She invites us to sit for a little while, and we talk about our times we spent in this part of the forest.

"You put a lot of work into this place. It's quite comfy."

"We're just happy that it is in good care," says Pansa.

"Are you out here by yourself?" I ask.

"Yes, I am traveling the land to admire it all."

I nod. "That sounds wonderful. We ourselves are travelers, and have seen lots of interesting things, but our favorite place was a town called Timbervale."

"I've heard of that place. Maybe I should see it."

"Definitely. Tell Byron that we sent you. Oh, and be sure to steer clear of Telios—only trouble to be had there."

"I will, thank you."

We set off again. The sun decides to resume its descent, as we make our way back to my tribe.

My heart picks up pace as we near, and I stop briefly.

"Kitso, is everything alright?"

"Yeah... I'm alright."

"You really have missed home, huh?"

"Much so. I imagine Krys felt the same way."

I take Pansa into our village. She is fascinated with what she sees.

"So this is home for you? It looks warm and safe in the midst of the cold."

"I appreciate that. The Vulpani have always harbored a pride for comfort, family and close friends."

“Where is everyone?”

“Out on a hunt, it seems. Lots of game to be had before the next snow storm. Let me show you where I live.”

As we near my home, we are spotted by a tribe mate.

“Kitso, you’re back! Good to see you!” He hugs me. “Who might this be?”

“This is Pansa. She is my mate.”

“Swell. I am pleased to acquaint you, ma’am.”

Pansa chuckles. “Please don’t call me that.” She offers a hug in return.

“Is my mother on the hunt?”

“Yes, they left two hours ago. You both seem tired, so I’ll let you be.”

Upon entering my home, I work on a fire, as Pansa helps herself to making tea.

“How long does a hunt last?”

“Usually three hours at most. I imagine we have a bit of time to spare.”

Evening is approaching, and I hear voices nearing the village. That must be them.

“Kitso, do you hear that?”

“I do. Everyone is returning!”

Someone comes barreling through my home. “Kitso! Kitso, it’s really you!” My mother grabs me into an embrace. “I have missed you so much! And it’s only been a month. What are you doing back so soon?”

“Mother, I feel that I’ve learned all I can from my trial.”

My mother sounds excited. “Oh, is that so? You must tell everyone tonight by the fire.” She glances to Pansa. “Hello there, young lady. Are you a friend of my son?”

"She is my mate, mother."

Pansa appears abashed. "My name is Pansa."

"Oh, well then." She examines Pansa closely. "I pray that you and my son are very happy together."

"Thank you, Vixona."

"Mother, where has Vulpena gone to? I want her to meet Pansa!"

She stares at me.

"... Mother?"

"Kitso... Vulpena passed away."

I am unable to find words.

"I'm so sorry..."

Pansa and my mother left me alone. I cry silently upon the floor. "Vulpena... I can't believe it... everything I have come to know in life for my survival. My trial was successful, but without you here... I just feel empty.

"I've taken up a mate, Vulpena... she really is wonderful, and I wish you could've met her... she'd have loved you. I'm unsure what the future holds for us... we've consented to traveling... to make the most of life, and hopefully a family of my own."

I pound my fists into the earth, my tears soaking into the dirt. *I swear to you, I will fulfill a legacy on your behalf!*

My mother comes back in. She sits on the floor to rest a hand on my back.

"Mother, I miss Vulpena..." I say through strained voice.

"I know, sweetie. It was only last week, but it feels like a year has gone by. She passed in her sleep."

"I am glad that she is at peace."

"Pansa and I will be getting the fire ready for tonight. You take all the time you need for yourself."

When she leaves, I sit up and gather myself. "I swear it... you have bore a legacy in me."

Later that evening, I recount all our ventures to everyone as we dine near the fire. I reserved the honor to suggest our meal tonight, and had chosen for us to have simple roasts with some sumacade. Pansa helped with the drink, as no one had heard of it.

It was a pleasurable experience to be with my tribe again. We ate and talked, and enjoyed a few songs. I noticed Pansa getting along with everyone, as her sociability tends to allow. It makes me very happy to see her like this.

No matter what troubles come our way, we always seem to find bliss amidst our sorrows. It is with this notion that I know we'll be alright in the end.

Night settles, and most of my tribe has gone to sleep. Aside from Pansa, myself and my mother, there are only two others awake, tending to the leftover food and the fire.

"When will you two depart for your travels? I hope that you'll stay for a while."

"We'll be staying for a little while, mother. As you heard, Pansa and I have been through a lot together."

"I am proud of you, Kitso. So very, very proud."

* * *

Kitso & Pansa

The next day comes, and Kitso takes me with him to go fishing. We use normal rods this time, as we sit by the pond. It is a bright and decent day.

There are few fish about, but we don't mind. The peace of a tranquil afternoon is just what we need.

"Thank you, Kitso."

"For what?"

"For everything! Becoming my friend, building our first shelter, helping to fulfill a little girl's dream. Just … everything."

"I am pleased that we could help Krys."

"I was actually talking about myself, but yes, Krys also." I lean into him as we watch the day before us go on.

"Kitso."

"Yeah?"

"I've been wondering about something. When I went through your satchel that day I was helping Krys with her bow, I noticed a book. When I asked you about it, you didn't really say anything. May I know what it is?"

He smiles. "If you really need to know, it's a journal highlighting our adventures. I was saving it for when I had more to write about."

Kitso pulls his satchel near, digs around inside, and withdraws it to let me look.

It's titled "Kitso & Pansa".

~EPILOGUE~

We stay with my tribe through the rest of the cold season, and into the hot. Pansa and I were wed after that time—it was a very warm afternoon. Much of my tribe was there, as well as Byron and his mother, Sybol, Gwen, Abigail and Marcus. Our friends bore gifts and the best hopes in our travels.

* * *

Julian sent us a letter some time later:

Congratulations you two. I am very pleased to hear that you've made things work out.

We have seen a few merchants this season. They mention that you recommend Timbervale for trade, and as predicted, they've brought an abundance of spices. Through many negotiations, we have arranged a regular supply, and are working on a new storehouse for it all.

Please give Krys my regard when possible!

* * *

Krys had also sent a letter to us:

I am having a wonderful time helping my cousin here in Adleborough! She says hi, and thank you for taking such good care of me.

We heard that Telios has called off the search after they saw what happened to some of their guards. I'm glad that I don't have to worry anymore.

Pansa, thank you for being my big sister, and for talking to me about many things in life. I'm able to express my feelings better.

Kitso, all the skills you taught me have been very helpful in caring for those who need us. I want you to take good care of my big sis, okay?

* * *

We received another letter, this time from Ingrid to me:

Hello Pansa, it's Ingrid. The band is doing well in trade, especially when Marcus found a good home for the locket Krys traded to us. Apparently, it was an heirloom traded to her family. Who'd've thought?!

I heard about your being wedded and all. I'm so happy for ya! You've got a really sweet foxie, so you'd best make him happy, or he'll be mine!

* * *

"Well, I suppose it's time to head out then," I remark.

"Yeah, I guess so."

My mother is standing at the edge of the village with us, tears in her eyes.

"I know that you two will make for a grand life together. I had better hear from you now and then, young man!"

I laugh. "You will, mother. You can bet that Pansa will see to it personally." I begin to walk away.

Pansa swats at me. "Write your mother!"

"Yes, ma'am."

"I told you, don't call me that!"

I hear my mother giggle under her breath. "You are so sweet together."

Abigail: /'a-bi-gāl/ The leader of traveling merchants

Adleborough: /'adl-bə-rō/ A hidden refuge, overseen by a cousin of Krys

Byron: /'bī-rən/ Ambassador of Timbervale

Clastodon: /'class-to-dän/ A town bordering the eastern mountains

Dalton: /'dal-tən/ Chief of Tinderburg

Gwen: /gwen/ Caretaker of Timbervale's inn

Ingrid: /'iNG-rid/ One of the traveling merchants

Julian: /'jü-lēən/ Head councilman of Timbervale

Katara: /ka-'tar-ə/ Representative of Timbervale

Kindrall: /'kin-drəl/ Krys' village of origination

Kitso: /'kit-so/ Member of Vulpani tribe. Main character

Krys: /kris/ An orphaned snow leopard. Secondary main character

Lupino: /lu-'pē-no/ A tribe briefly mentioned in name by Abigail

Marcus: /'mar-kəs/ One of the traveling merchants

Pansa: /'pan-sə/ Member of Panteo clan. Main character

Panteo: /pan-'tā-o/ Clan that Pansa comes from. Primarily consists of panther-like creatures

Parupeteng: /pä-rü-pə-'teNG/ Plant that Pansa consumes. A white and purple flower with barbed stalks

Renado: /re-'nä-dō/ Kitso's father

Sumacadra: /sü-mə-'ca-dra/ A ritual of thankfulness that's performed in Timbervale with sumacade

Sybol: /'si-bəl/ Archivist and historian of Timbervale

Telios: /'tè-lē-ōs/ City known for brash methodology. Home of Krys' uncle

Timbervale: /'tim-bər-vāl/ A village proud in its usage of wood

Tinderburg: /'tin-dər-bərg/ A hamlet on the road between Timbervale and Clastodon

Vixona: /vix-'ō-nə/ Kitso's mother. Lead huntress of the Vulpani

Vulpani: /vul-'pä-nē/ Tribe that Kitso comes from. Inhabits mainly fox-like creatures

Vulpena: /vul-'pæ-nə/ Mentor of many Vulpani inhabitants